ON THE EDGE

Nicola Garrard

Copyright © Nicola Garrard, 2025

All rights reserved.

No part of this book may be reproduced or transmitted in any form or by any means, electronic, or mechanical, including photocopying, recording or by any information storage and retrieval system, without prior permission in writing from the publisher.

Old Barn Books Ltd
Warren Barn, Fittleworth, West Sussex, RH20 1JW
Email: info@oldbarnbooks.com
Web: www.oldbarnbooks.com
Follow us on Facebook, Twitter/X or Instagram:
@oldbarnbooks

Teaching resources for our books are available
to download from our website

ISBN: 978 1 910646 75 5
eBook ISBN: 978 1 910646 55 7

Distributed in the UK by Bounce Sales & Marketing Ltd
www.bouncemarketing.co.uk

Editor: Emma Roberts
Cover design by Michelle Brackenborough
Typeset by Christian Francis

Printed and bound in the UK by CPI Group (UK) Ltd, Croydon, CR0 4YY

Old Barn Books' authorised representative in the EU for product safety:
Easy Access System Europe Oü, 16879218
Mustamäe tee 50, Tallinn, Estonia
Contact: gspr.requests@easproject.com
tel: +372 56 968 939

1 3 5 7 9 8 6 4 2

Praise for *On the Edge*

'Tender and angry, salty and sweet... a heartfelt novel shaped by powerful undercurrents'
Michael Morpurgo

'The prose, rich with salty metaphor, often sings an alluring siren song... a beautiful book'
Anthony McGowan, winner of the CILIP Carnegie Medal for *Lark*

'An important and powerful story of family, community and love'
Matt Goodfellow, author of *The Final Year*

'This book is magnificent'
Katriona O'Sullivan, author of *Poor*

'A beautiful, immersive read which crackles with tension, heartbreakingly provocative... weaves powerful themes of family and belonging. A brilliant read'
J.P. Rose, author of *Birdie*

'This book stole my heart, I loved the boys so much'
Independent Book Reviews

'It just gripped me and held me in its grasp... Just buy it!'
Book Monitor

'Atmospheric and thought-provoking, packs an emotional punch'
Jake Hope, literacy consultant

'I was captivated from the very first page... a timely and nuanced exploration of financial hardship, masculinity and adolescence.'
Just Imagine

'Nicola Garrard evokes fiercely and with skill young male lives unfolding in coastal shadows, battling outside forces with scant regard for their existence.'
John McCullough, author of *Reckless Paper Birds*

'Raw and lyrical... dives into brotherhood, belonging, and a boy's fight to hold on.'
Matthew Tobin, lecturer in Children's Literature

'This stunning novel is a modern tragedy, a love story and a warning, both political and deeply personal'
Astra Bloom, *Common People: An Anthology of Working Class Writers*

'Angry, poetic, funny, and empathetic, and it demands that we see, and that we care'
Sarah Brooks, author of *The Cautious Traveller's Guide to the Wastelands*

'A novel of rare power, dazzlingly original and full of heart. Prepare to be swept away!'
Juliet West, author of *Before the Fall*

'Immersive, haunting, atmospheric'
Sarah Harman, author of *All the Other Mothers Hate Me*

'Has the reader surfing atop a wave of hope and familial love. Just beautiful!'
Cauvery Madhavan, author of *The Inheritance*

'A raw, tender story... with heart, humour and defiance.'
Prof. Sheelah Argawal, Centre for Coastal Communities, U. of Plymouth

To Miriam

GLOSSARY

Devonian words used in the novel

backalong – in the past
dimpsey – the light at dawn and dusk
grockle – tourist
grommet – very young surfer
gurt – big
proper job – expression of agreement or approval
tidy – great, brilliant
tor – a granite outcrop
yarn – a tall tale

Note to Reader

Please be aware that *On the Edge* contains content that may be upsetting, including depictions of grief, suicidal feelings and substance abuse. If you are affected by these issues, please turn to the back of the book, where there are helplines and other sources of support.

'A man is nobody underneath a big wave'

Alice Oswald, *Nobody*

PART ONE

The Pride of Lythcombe Bay

ONE

Former local hero, Rhys Fisher, had featured on the cover of the *South Devon Express & Echo* when he was seventeen. His wetsuit was peeled down to his hips and he held a gold surfing medal between his teeth. Hard to believe that was only last August. On either side of him were his little brothers Dav and Owen, and there, half-cropped out, was their dad, Phil Fisher, holding the prize-winning surfboard deck-side to the camera, so that the brands of potential sponsors might be seen. The paper's digital edition had six likes and one comment:

> *Go on Rhys lad! Up their arses with a weever fish mate. You can go all the way.*

Who were the Fisher brothers?
Salt boys. Rock boys. Motherless boys.
Reckless boys.

People think it was being untended by a woman's hand that had made Rhys reckless. Even as a squirt, he had little fear of height or consequence. He would do backflips off the harbour wall at low tide into a metre of watery silt, not caring for the rusted can or scallop shell's cut. High places drew him; he could not go near Lythcombe's cliffs without lying on his belly and letting a gob of spit fall over the drop. And last year, when Owen let go of his new kite by the lighthouse cliffs – the Fishers always had their birthday picnics there – Rhys did not shrink from climbing down to rescue it.

'Stay here with Dav,' he had told the snivelling Owen because Dav was a teenager and sensible-like. 'I'll get it for you, mate.'

Sad to say, Rhys never did find the kite, even after scratching through gorse, slithering down a wet gully, and scaling rocks at the foot, only to arrive perpendicularly below where the three brothers had been, far up at the top.

Where had the kite gone? Taken in the teeth of an albatross, was seven-year-old Owen's theory.

Reckless he might be, but inside Rhys was soft. When he was ten, he used to worry about the sheep grazing the cliffs – how they sometimes spook and run the wrong way.

It comes with the territory: soggy turf, sharp edges, no room for error. After a storm, the first anglers of the day find them lying on the rocks. Tides come and go, sloshing the bodies till they are eaten by gulls or otherwise moved.

A few years ago, a young man fell off the old cliff path. According to the coroner, ketamine was both cause and small mercy, since, like a sedated pony, the victim would not have felt much. If he'd had a wingsuit, like the ones Rhys has seen on the internet, that man would have swooped in the air like a bird or a kite. And when the time was right, he could have deployed his parachute.

If I threw myself off, Rhys sometimes thinks when he is at the lowest ebb of his tide, *there'd be a moment when I, too, would fly.*

But Rhys does not own a suit, and without one of the winged variety, a man falls at fifty-three metres per second. The tallest of Lythcombe's cliffs being eighty metres, it would take two seconds to meet the rocks below.

He would be well and truly shattered.

Like an egg. Like glass. Like a wave.

Despite hankering after surf winnings and sponsorship deals, Rhys never planned to be famous. Now, at seventeen, all he wants is to be happy and to have a proper home, and maybe marry a nice girl one day and have kids who are happy at home with their mum. And he wants to work hard and do no harm and for the men in town to see him and say, 'There's Rhys, he's a good man who takes care of his kids. He doesn't take jobs on the continent when he should be at home.'

And when you need a man to turn up ready with the tools to do a job, Rhys will be that man. And when you want someone to talk to and tell your fears, he will be there for you. And if you are short of money, or need a place to stay, as long as there is a few quid to spare and room on the sofa, he will help you out. And if you are thirsty, he will be at the bar ordering two pints, one that has your name on it. And when you need someone brave, Rhys Fisher will be your man.

A good man in bad times will do the right thing. Like when someone's little girl is stolen by a rip current from the beach and swept fast into the distance, he will be the first there, reckless of his own endangerment, swimming out to drag her back and haul her gasping onto the sand, and pump the water out of her lungs till she comes to life again. He will do all the right things at the right times in the right order. No mistakes made or opportunities missed or future lessons to be recorded by the coroner.

'Missus,' says this kind of man (who is Rhys) to the mum as he carries her baby girl, light as air in his arms, 'your kid's going to be okay.'

But there is no more space between bravery and recklessness than there is between a shearwater and the sea. That same summer of his great win, later that August, when clouds were darkening, Rhys waded into the surf, thinking, *Seeing a lightning storm from shore is all well and good, granted, but in the waves, it will be another thing altogether.*

So he waded in, waited for the snap, crackle and fork-flash, and counted the seconds till the thunder came. Then he said a small prayer for ships in international waters.

The first flash smote offshore but Rhys could feel

it tickle his insides like a jellyfish sting. The water lit, then followed a smell like burning bladderwrack. The air turned electric, like being in a junction box, all soldered parts, hot metal and salt. The rain thickened and the beach huts on the prom disappeared. He was alone in the Atlantic, though his feet touched the sand.

The next flash was hot. His hair stood on end and Rhys thought, *I don't like this any more,* and then he told himself, *Don't be soft.*

He turned seaward. Soon, there was no counting between flash and bang; they came both together. And he would have stayed, were it not for his dad, Phil Fisher, come running in the water yelling, 'Son, get out of there right now!' over the crash of wave and thunder.

'Don't stop my fun,' said Rhys.

'I'd sooner stop your fun than lightning stop your heart,' said Phil Fisher, who locked his fist round Rhys's wrist like the monstrous-muscled hand of a giant squid and dragged him to the number 7 bus stop.

'What were you thinking?' said Phil Fisher, perched on the thin sloping bench, a measure against junkies sleeping in the bus shelter. 'Have you so soon forgotten your lifeguard training? You could've been killed. I'm going to Santander tomorrow. How can I bloody earn a living if I can't leave you safe?'

Now that the storm was safe behind the plastic glass of the bus shelter, Phil Fisher switched to his soft voice for all the whys of it: the recklessness, the danger to fish and boat, the burns and scorches and hearts stopping at once like a flicked switch. Then he put his arm round his son and said no more, for there was nothing more to say, only that, sometimes, you can get caught up in things like lightning storms that seem like a good idea at the time.

Rhys did not speak, but, later, he wanted to ask his dad, 'How can you tell if you're being brave or just being a dick?'

※

Rhys's so-called challenging behaviour as an older teenager came as a surprise to everyone. His primary school teachers called him quiet, not speaking except when spoken to, not moving unless told, doing his work to the best of his ability; that is, not too well but with a hope of improvement. But when secondary school bored into his soul like the mighty pile-drivers he would later learn about in NVQ Level 1 Construction, something inside him was let loose. He was like a net-snagged cormorant set free and ready to fly.

The signs had been there. Ask anyone in Lythcombe and they will tell you of Rhys's great leap, back when he was in Year Ten. Holding your eyes with an honest look, they will swear a bare-faced guarantee that Rhys did drop, via an open classroom window, three storeys down to the flat roof of the PE changing rooms below – an allegation containing one part falsehood to two parts truth.

Rhys had been first at the classroom door, home-time on the day of his brother Owen's seventh birthday, when the teacher stopped him before he could leave.

'You will stay,' she said, 'for non-completion of tasks and your generally stinking attitude.'

'Will I?' said Rhys, polite as you like. 'I don't think so.'

The teacher stood guard, body against the doorframe, ballet pumps flat for maximum grip, jammed between carpet and door, knees bent in the brace position, white knuckles on the handle. The other boys watched, not daring to say a word.

'You will.'

'Can't make me,' said Rhys, smiling. He made one last try for the handle – one short, ugly tug during which he learned that if he was to cross that threshold, he would also be overleaping a line crossed by few and those among them banished by permanent exclusion. Though he was stronger than his teacher by several orders of magnitude, he did not want to add assault to his list of misdemeanours nor lay his gentlemanly hands on a female member of staff. He turned his back.

'You will stay,' said the teacher again, through gritted teeth, 'until your detention is done.'

'I don't think so,' said Rhys, again.

He went to the window, appearing calm for all the pounding on his ribs by heart and blood, spreading adrenaline into the parts that give surfers courage. Outside, there was no view of sea or beach, school being at the arse-end of town in a dip below the horizon made by the Jubilee housing estate where he lived.

But he could smell the waves, and that was enough.

The safety catch was set too narrow for a body to

pass, so when Rhys opened the window, there was only enough room for the salt-tang air to stream through. Once upon a time, these classroom windows had opened wide, before risk assessments judged them too dangerous for kids prone to bouts of rage, self-injury and despair. Now, they only opened a fraction, not just for the protection of those inside the building, but also in case some idiot might want to break back in.

There was the drop: a full three floors, dizzying to all, though a mere hop and skip for wagtails and corvids.

And there: the changing rooms roof where a great white gull, the biggest of its kind, hunched on the edge. It stretched out its wings as if to jump, then changed its mind.

And here: the iron downpipe to freedom.

The catch was hard to break, but Rhys was not deterred by safety mechanisms cack-handedly attached as an afterthought by the caretaker and bent with age and misuse.

If I cannot walk through the door, I will fly through the window, Rhys decided in his head, where he was more dangerous and daring than in real life. He gave the window a sharp push in a direction wrong for the catch but right for his dark purpose.

'What the hell are you doing?' asked the teacher, who had scant understanding of the tensile qualities of aluminium and of stainless steel screws ill-suited to high-load applications – something Rhys knew a bit about from studying construction.

As soon as the catch pinged off, Rhys threw his leg over the ledge, as he had done on the harbour wall many a time. Reaching round, he grasped the drainpipe, rust-scabs of ceramic paint not lending themselves to confidence, then abseiled, monkey-hand over monkey-fist, before settling like a nesting tern onto the flat roof of the changing rooms.

Startled, the fat gull scrambled to the air and swooped down. Rhys followed, leaping, to his mates' cheers, to freedom. He looked up and grinned at his class, Jakey, Adam and Declan crowded at the window.

'You will stay!' said a shrimp-pink face above. Teachers do not know what to do with a boy like Rhys.

'Will I?' Rhys said back. 'I don't think so.'

Witnesses who saw all this cannot tell the next part of this story.

Rhys proceeded at pace over the perimeter fence and across the Jubilee estate, along the main road through Lythcombe, past the shops and harbour, the fish market, processing plant and promenade, and past the Shepherd's Nook cabin, where retreating writers write and painters paint the same thing time and again – you would think they would weary of it. He was as light as any boy not weighed down by his school bag and he did not stop till he reached the dunes at the far end of the bay. There, the tide out, he got to cover and laughed at what he had done, and not long after, he cried, sand sticking to the tears rolling down his face.

He was crying for his mum, gone that same day seven years before. Owen's birthday.

Unbeknown to his teachers, Rhys – half-man, half-boy, half-hero, half-villain, half-good, half-bad, half-this, half-that and half-of-the-other – added up to more than any measly whole. The classroom ceiling bounded not the sum of him, for he was greater, even if school tests measured him short. The answers were always there in Rhys's head, tucked down somewhere with the words, like sleeping crabs packed in an ice box. They just never showed themselves when required. Rhys was not nil, nor was he the square root of nothing. He was underestimated, is all, more than anyone could have calculated.

More than Lythcombe could ever know.

TWO

Living in a seaside town where grockles come on holiday is what you might call a game of two halves. In the summer half, the place is mobbed. Cars back up the hill with no regard for parking restrictions. Girls show off their bellies in crop tops while boys wear their board shorts low, thinking they're in Hawaii, though it may be raining and the vandal winds have spilled the bins over the prom again. The fish and chip shop queue goes round the block, herring gulls supervising from the sky.

Every year brings the same kind of grockle. There's a deck-shoe man and he goes like this: 'Darling! They're saying a forty- to fifty-minute wait. Okay? Or shall we try the pub? I don't mind waiting. Be nice to take food back. The Airbnb is so…'

Now comes the things grockles say about Lythcombe, like, 'Quiet', 'Restful', 'Tranquil'.

'Picturesque,' says the man.

'That last one means pretty,' Rhys tells Owen as they stand in line for Angie's chips. 'It's a hard word to say, but you've got to try. You catch a hold of all the words you can, squirt.'

Since meeting Rupert Cavendish – or Dodo, as he is better known to his friends in Exeter, where he plans the revolution – Rhys has warmed to words and their meanings. Dodo, as in extinct. Tidy nickname, if you ask Rhys. He fancies something like that for himself.

Not many grockles find their way down to the cove past the lighthouse, hidden as it is by a wall of gorse and broom. Most set up towels on Lythcombe beach, slap-bang between the lifeguard flags. They rent foam learner surfboards or come with their own vintage fibreglass, cracked epoxy, ex-retirement, ready-stacked on the roof rack. Not to worry – the first wave soon dusts off garage cobwebs.

They wear jelly shoes, too. Sheep shit and rock edges put them off. They have a preference for flat surfaces, campsite grass, safety barriers. They like to know where they are.

But once they have called their grockle-sprogs in and gone back to their B&Bs, holiday cottages, tents, caravans, and then to their homes in landlocked places, the brothers get Lythcombe returned to them – though that comes with its own trouble.

In October, everything shuts: the car park ticket shed where Rhys works in summer, ice cream parlour, penny arcade, crazy golf, café, board shop, surf school, souvenir shop and the deckchair hire. The pub goes drinks-only – no servers or glass-collectors needed, so go home and twiddle your thumbs till May.

Town dogs are the only ones that don't mind when the council batten down the public conveniences. They run where they please from October to April, cocking their legs on washed-up kelp, rolling in rotting jellyfish like clover.

Of course, Mr Vadic's SPAR and the off-licence stay open in winter. The betting shop too, because you never know when you will be a winner. It could be you. In fact, it bloody well should be you. The fish processing factory and the box wash, where fishing boats get their catch tubs cleaned, carry on as usual. And school. School's bloody endless. Rhys would rather not be walking Owen to the primary school, checking he is wearing socks of the permitted size and colour so that Mrs Hill, the Year Four teacher, does not phone their flat like she did at the start of September, when Owen was new to her class, asking, 'How are you?'

Rhys wanted to say, 'How the hell do you think we are?' while weighing up some honest options in his head: that he and his brothers were salty, sandy, hungry, chilly and abandoned, in no particular order. Instead, he told her, 'Fine. We're fine. I'll tell Dad to give you a call as soon as he gets in from work... Yes, later today.' He put the phone down.

At that, Owen jumped off the sofa, sending lumps of its insides into the electric fire. 'You never said Dad's coming home today!'

'No, Owen,' said Rhys, getting the foam out from the bars so that their flat won't burn down next time they turn the fire on. 'Not today. Today's Wednesday. Dad goes Mondays and he comes back Fridays. There's a pattern to it, mate.'

'But you just said—'

'I know what I said, but the truth is, sometimes I have to make stuff up to protect us. You want us to be split up, two hundred miles away?'

'No.'

'Me neither. So smile in class, do your homework, and if anyone asks, on the phone or at school or whatever, say, "Dad is coming home today".'

'And is he?'

'No!'

*

Their dad, Phil Fisher, says, 'If you live in a city, there is very little you can get for nothing.'

In Plymouth, for example, you have a sea of shops but everything costs money and money does not grow on trees. It is different in Lythcombe Bay. There is a lot of free stuff if you have the time to look. Between July and October, Rhys often comes back from his wanderings with his pockets full of spuds, red as the soil from which they were pulled. They taste better than instant mash, even if their dad does say, 'This is what the Marines eat!' when he boils the kettle to mix the powder.

There are also: blackberries and damsons, and when the weather gets colder, hedge sloes, if you dare eat one knowing your tongue will shrivel and dry; wild raspberries in the woods and whortleberries on the moor; sweet rock-pool winkles all year, tasty if you don't think about the contents of their digestive tract as you pop them in your mouth. Shrimp are easy enough to catch, just hold still and wait for them to walk into your hand; spider crabs, less so, but Phil Fisher has shown Rhys how to dive to the seabed for their long legs of meat. And not forgetting cockles at low tide – look for squiggling worms of sand, which is where the cockles will be, and dig fast because they can dig faster. Boil them in a baked-bean can on your beach fire and they will open. Lovely, as long you're not allergic.

'We eat like kings,' says Phil Fisher. 'Who's like us? None but us!'

And who needs to pay for bait where there are lugworms at low tide? Granted, a lug is a horrible creature with two mouths and inside-pincers, like something from a nightmare, but they are for fishing, not eating. Wintertime is best. Some days, lugs will get you a million mackerel for your tea, throwing themselves onto your hooks as if they are begging to be caught. Other days, nothing. Where do fish go? Are they like flocks of birds?

What is more, if Rhys wants to talks to a girl there is plenty to keep Owen occupied: smooth sea glass, rope, man-made bricks moulded into pebbles by the waves to match the rest – they are also red and crumble, so are good for drawing. A yellow welly, just the one; someone is hopping mad somewhere. Sharks' eggs called 'mermaids' purses', sponges, buckets, fish trays, nets, floats, plastic bags. Bottles with no messages, though you have to check.

Kelp makes a roof for baby crabs. Do not cry if you

see their dinky bodies because they did not die. They just shake off their too-small shells and grow new ones.

Grockles buy their shells from Lythcombe Natural Healing & Souvenirs so they can hear the sea back in Slough or London, but Rhys tells any girl he likes that shells only perform magic if they are found by your true love. Once you have been given yours, keep it safe.

Owen picked up a nice oyster for Rhys's birthday. 'This is better than pearls,' Rhys said. 'It is the *mother* of pearl.' He sanded down the edges and it went on a string round his neck, where it stays. Dav found a dog whelk for Owen that goes wherever he goes, even the bath.

Owen whispers in its ear before sleep, 'Daddy cares more about lettuce than us,' because Phil Fisher is often pulling two tonnes of it in his trailer along the autopista from Murcia to Santander.

'Yeah, but how else is he going to get that rod you want for your birthday?' says Dav.

'Who even likes salad?' the little boy sulks. 'Make him come home.'

At the start of term, in early September, Rhys opened the letter about Dav's Year Ten mentoring scheme and discovered that the authorities meant to level his brother up. Phil Fisher would have opened it himself, but he was driving across Spain – away five days at a time, coming home for two days and then off again. But the gist of the letter was that certain clever coastal kids had been identified as underprivileged and opportunity-starved, like crablets picked off by gulls on the high-tide line. Exeter University had offered to take some of them under its long wing.

Rhys thought the letter was right about that, but also wrong, because a lot of people from elsewhere-places, like grockles, are in their own way starved of opportunity. For example, how often do they get to see Lythcombe's bioluminescent algae visitors, which is like having the aurora borealis itself sparkling between your toes, or play mile-long football any day they please on a sandy pitch, or swim with gentle basking sharks and come out of the water with their lives switched back to day one, like a baby born to start again?

Sitting in their city traffic jams, they don't get to cycle up to the tor, where you are as high as a circling buzzard. Nor do they get the ocean swell, pushed around the planet by current, wave and wind, delivered right to their little sock-free toes and all that comes with it.

If that is not privilege, Rhys doesn't know what is.

No need for Children's Services to get their knickers in a twist, he thinks. *We brothers have plenty.*

By plenty, he means a sofa long enough for their dad to kip on but not Rhys by a head; bunk beds for Dav and Owen; for Rhys, a blow-up mattress on the floor. Once deflated, it fits in the kitchen cupboard, should nosy parkers from school or the council turn up out of the blue. There's a loose floorboard under the front doormat for hiding Rhys's skunk and their emergency cash, and three grey mushrooms growing in the hall, watered by cracks in the taped-up window of their one-bed ground-floor flat on the Jubilee estate. 'Don't touch,' says Rhys. He means to get them tested. They might be magic.

'Are magic mushrooms like magic beans?' says Owen.

'Maybe,' says Rhys. 'So don't touch.'

There are also pallets in the yard – not so much a yard as a shared bit of concrete, bordered on one side by allotment sheds and on the other two sides by the council garages, some of which are sublet to grockles so they don't have to go to the bother of dragging their dinghies down from London, and where a man with cancer had lived the last year of his life on account of the rent being reasonable.

As well as having enough parking for Phil's Iveco lorry cab, this yard is where Rhys keeps his business venture: building rabbit hutches out of pine pallets for breeding lop-ears. 'Going to make a total packet!' says Rhys. He just needs some chicken wire, and also a pocket saw to finish his other job: Owen's 'palace', a clever construction of delivery pallets started four years ago when school shut for Covid. Like a treehouse without a tree, it has a room only Owen can fit in, and a ladder to a platform as high as the kitchen window of Mrs Morris, their neighbour in the flat above.

She has a silver-furred cat called Thing, who climbs down the pallet palace into the Fishers' flat each morning and paws Owen's ears on the bottom bunk for breakfast. The brothers all like Mrs Morris, and she them, though she likes a bottle of vodka more.

In the yard is also where they keep Rhys's Kawasaki dirt bike and the bicycles. At the moment, Dav's bike has a flat back wheel and also needs a new brake cable. 'You'll have to use your legs for now,' says Rhys. 'It's on the list, but don't use my racer or you will regret it.'

Rhys used to have a nice surfboard that Phil Fisher had bought him out of their NHS negligence and error compensation money. When that broke on the harbour spit in June, his thoughts turned to buying a car, because with a car you can get work, and with work you can get money, and with money you can get the best Gerry Lopez board hanging in Mr Barker's surf shop.

Soon as he got his provisional driving licence, he bought a Micra for £100 and took it out in Lythcombe. Phil Fisher had warned him that the gap between getting a car and keeping it was wide. Though Rhys had worked all July and half of August to fill it, he found that his dad was right. Most times it didn't start and then it didn't stop, aquaplaning on the prom after a heavy tide had left a slick of silt.

A week later, at low tide, he drove it down the slipway onto the sand to see what it could do. 'Hard as concrete,' he said when Dav worried they'd get stuck. The vehicle bottomed out on the cockles and sank right up to the exhaust box. Mrs Grundy fished it out with her tractor's boat tow before the tide came in, but the brake shoes were salt-screwed. 'I'll never afford new ones,' said Rhys. 'Not this side of getting a job.'

To get shot of it, he had planned to push it over the

cliffs by the lighthouse car park. No fence – stick it in neutral and edge it over, sheep being the only witnesses and they don't talk. But the lighthouse was his mum's special place where sea pinks grow, so instead he torched it in a lay-by and stood awhile, mesmerised by the pillar of flames, the burning tyres.

'I'd like to report a robbery,' he said the next day to the insurance people. 'My car was parked outside when I went to bed and when I woke up it was gone.'

He only got sixty quid off of them; that's what they said a Micra was worth. It was criminal, but at least that fire and theft money covered getting a dirt bike of some age and oxidation, its radiator now dismantled in the yard.

Gaps dog Rhys, no matter how hard he works.

THREE

It was in late September, in the working-Kawasaki days, that Rhys first met Dodo. Rhys and Jakey were headed to Plymouth for a night on the town.

'We'd best get off and walk,' Rhys said, heavy-ballasted by Jakey at his back and a rucksack clinking with bottles. They were halfway up a steep incline above Kingston and the overheating engine was melting his best tracksuit. 'You can have a turn on my helmet at the top.'

'No thanks,' said Jakey. 'I've done my hair.'

As they free-wheeled the last hill, engine off to save fuel, a lovely sunset deepened over Devonport Royal Docks turning the sky dimpsey. They had planned this, 10 p.m. being the more common opening times of big-city places of dancing and entertainment. Though they were always welcome in the King's Arms in Lythcombe, there were never any girls to talk to, only men with fish scales caught in their beards who'd come off the sea wanting a cider to take away that flat feeling land gave them under their feet.

'They've got about a million clubs in Plymouth,' said Rhys, having heard it said. 'On account of Marines having their night off. They don't ask for ID.' Of this last fact, Rhys was less sure. 'But if they do, say we're on a nuclear sub. Submariners have got to be eighteen, see?'

'Wouldn't catch me in a sub,' said Jakey. 'I'm a surface kind of mariner.'

'Ay,' said Rhys, thinking of the sound rain makes on waves and the feather-storm of herring gulls telling where the shoals are. You'd miss that if you were sunk in a tin tub below the catch. All you'd hear would be nothing, or maybe whales singing and fish grinding their teeth. But probably nothing but electrics and fission and the sound of your own banging thoughts echoing against the hull.

On Union Street, they smoked a joint and, seeing their first Royal Navy boys, they joined a queue for the Blue Lagoon feeling undergrown behind the cream of Tyneside and Clydebank; a wall of shoulders bench-pressed on the shell-racks of HMS *Raleigh*.

'Who put manure in their wellies?' said Jakey. 'You sure they'll let us in?'

Up close, Rhys did feel something like a sprat in the net, but he was not yet for bailing. He picked a fancy bottle with a red ribbon and wax seal from the rucksack and took a swig.

'Bloody hell,' he said.

Though 'cider 'pon beer is good cheer,' as Phil liked to say, it remained to be seen how cider would act upon the fancy liqueurs Jakey's sister had lifted from the big house she cleaned in Dartmouth, lifted in turn by Jakey from under her bed.

'Amaretto, Frangelico, Grand Marnier?' Rhys said, looking more closely at the bottles. 'Where'd you find these?'

'One of Liz's houses was sold in a hurry by its London owners. They left a cheque – settling her hours-like – and told her to bubble-wrap the bottles in their cocktail bar for the DPD man. She might have forgotten a few.'

As they inched to the door in the shadow of the sailors, a girl slipped between their ranks. She was not much more than sixteen, her make-up architectural.

'All right?' she said to the big fellows. From her accent, Rhys guessed she was from over the river in Cornwall and likely lived somewhere like Jubilee, out of sight of the pastel-painted waterfront cottages with the BMWs parked outside. 'Who's buying us a drink?'

At this, she caught Rhys's eye and looked away because in that second, she must have seen he knew everything about her, from the pudding bowl under the drip in the ceiling to her rinsed-out socks in the bath.

A sailor slipped his hand round her waist. 'That'll be me,' he said in a Scottish accent, flushing at his mates' laughs.

Inside, the club glowed green, shot through by lances of light, like looking up from the seabed at the surface on a sunny day. Rhys felt a tightness in his chest, a need to come up for air. 'We could sit on the harbour awhile,' he said. 'Watch the boats.'

'You bottling it?'

'No.'

Ahead in the queue, the sailor bent over to kiss the girl. The door opened and in they marched, no questions asked.

Rhys and Jakey shuffled forwards.

'Sorry, boys,' said the doorman. 'Come back when you're eighteen.'

'We're submariners,' said Rhys, standing tall but swaying from the swing of the drink. 'King and country. Nuclear, like.'

His words may have been slurred, for the doorman was having none of it. 'Go home and sober up before your mums find out. Your hair's too long for the Navy, any rate.'

Behind that doorman was a world of light and movement, like kelp dancing when Rhys opens his eyes underwater and finds his vision clear as a dolphin or seal's. Who needs a mask?

'I was only messing,' said Rhys. 'But honest to God, my mate here's a trawlerman. We risk our lives at sea.'

'Day fishing,' added Jakey, chest swelling. 'Crab. Macks. Hand-lining, mostly, and the odd pilchard purse. We put fishies on your dishies!'

The last thing Rhys saw, as the man shut the door, was the Cornish girl, a fry flitting between big fish, swiping an unattended glass of wine. She looked at Rhys, shrugged, then darted away.

Given its reputation for fights and pricey drinks laced with Tamar water, it was fortunate that they were not admitted to the Blue Lagoon, but for Rhys and Jakey, it was a blow in the broadside.

Had they had come thus far, thirty miles, for this?

'That's that, then,' said Jakey. 'Better go home.'

He was mistaken; there was more to see and do in Plymouth. First, they headed to the quay where the sea played halyard music on aluminium masts, then climbed around a pontoon's spiked gates, swinging out over the water, and walked down the jetty to see yachts and leisure cruisers nodding at their berths, great gulls asleep on the wheelhouses. Jakey took out the permanent marker he'd found abandoned on a teacher's desk and they lay on their bellies to illustrate the port-side waterlines of hulls with the top halves of boobs and willies, drawings that would be completed at sunrise by the mirror of a glassy sea.

After a security guard chased them off the marina, they stopped at a tackle store where fishing rods gleamed behind glass like something out of Owen's wildest birthday dreams.

'See that Daiwa Sandstorm? Twelve-foot six.'

'£129.99. Sweet.'

A brick would do it but Rhys was too scared.

They headed back to the bars where they found a pub with no bouncers, and benches outside. A band inside played Springsteen with a tambourine instead of a drum kit, rattling away where the bass should have been. But with Jakey by his side and a lax attitude on the part of the publican to pot-smoking on his pavement, Rhys was now as happy as Owen sticking his finger in a tide-pool anemone to save a crab from disaster.

While Jakey went in for the drinks, Rhys observed the city way of things. More boys than girls, it was true, but not insurmountable, he thought, seeing a pretty girl on her own on a picnic table made for six.

'Mind if I sit here?' Rhys said to the girl. She nodded, not looking up from her phone. 'Want a drink?' This last he mumbled, hoping she'd say no. They only had enough money for two each, but they could offer the Frangelico neither of them liked. Rhys could not believe what rich people drink in their spare time.

'No, thanks,' she said in a posh voice. 'Are you here for the meeting?'

Rhys thought. She had long blonde hair. Her tie-dye top was very pretty. Altogether, she was extremely beautiful despite her icy tone.

'Yes,' he said and waved at Jakey, coming out of the bar. 'Over here now, mate! This here's the meeting.'

'Meeting?'

'Ay. Meeting.'

Jakey fumbled the ciders on the gaps between planks, splashing the girl's purple DMs. 'Right-o.'

'Are you active?' asked the girl, mid-text.

'Mostly,' Jakey said and thumped his friend's back. 'Rhys here, more than most.'

She looked at Rhys for the first time and a faint light of admiration fell on his handsome face. 'What sort of things?'

'This and that,' said Rhys, not wanting to mention

being his recent Not in Education, Employment or Training status. 'You know. Whatever it takes to get the job done. I keep myself busy, like. What else can you do?'

The band inside the pub took up Guns N' Roses and the girl smiled. 'I'm Milly. Dodo'll be here soon. You know Dodo?'

Rhys nodded in a non-incriminatory fashion, neither wanting to confirm nor deny his ignorance. 'We've heard his name.'

'On socials?'

'That'll be it. He's your boyfriend, then?'

She took a long draw from a thin joint and exhaled the smoke into his face. 'We don't live by bourgeois classifications.'

'Granted,' said Rhys and raised his eyebrows at Jakey, who smiled.

Sometimes, walking the foreshore at low tide, Rhys has noted how tiny streams in the sand divide and branch off in deltas, a thousand routes to the sea. That's what Plymouth felt like to Rhys: a place of action where things happen, if you have the money – the pub spitting distance from the marina, the Santander ferry terminal, a launching-off point for the world. Yes, there was also left-over crabbers' bait, like Lythcombe, rotting on the wharf and the familiar smell of river brack and salt sea, but there, over the water, was the chandlery, a wonder of cleats, creel rope, net-locks and brass barometers.

A tall man slipped alongside Milly and their kiss

was lingering. Four others, university students by the cut of their dungarees, joined them, and an old woman in a potter's smock splattered with paint.

The man took twenty or so rolls of black sacks from a canvas army surplus bag and stacked them on the table in a pyramid, patting the edges so that they were true. He would've made a good fish-packer, but Rhys deduced from his soft hands that he did not have a trade, let alone a sea trade. Rhys appraised him further – creamy skin, long oil-slick hair. Did he, too, have trouble with hot water? Also, he wore a roll-neck Arran sweater, the same that yachting grockles liked to wear on their boats, not seeming to have discovered the light and quick-drying qualities of polyester.

The man leaned back to survey his friends, as if waiting for them to applaud him for a witty turn of phrase.

'What's this, Dodo?' one of the students asked.

The streetlights flickered and the guitarist limped through the rest of 'Paradise City' before Dodo spoke, his voice low, his eyes shining. 'Try as we might,' he said, 'we will never consign capitalism to the dustbin of history from our laptops and phones. Without action there can be no reaction.'

The old woman in the smock began to dab at her eyes with a tissue. Dodo opened her hand gently and placed in it a black roll, like a priest tool ready to stop an eel.

'I understand,' he said with an earnest look. 'The heat of capitalism burns us. Like drowning.'

Jakey snorted into his cider. Rhys elbowed him and indicated Milly with his eyes. She was gazing at Dodo like she was watching a film star. No one else was laughing.

Dodo rolled the rest of the bin bags to the others. He stopped at Rhys and Jakey.

'It's okay,' said Milly. 'They're active.'

'Where?'

'Lythcombe, born and bred,' said Rhys, looking at Milly for the light to come back on.

'Tub men,' Jakey added in a phlegmy cough, having just drawn a toke of her joint.

'By tub he means his boat,' said Rhys. 'Pocket trawler, that is. Mackerel and crab.'

Dodo held Rhys's gaze with watery blue eyes reddened around the lids. The shadow of a smile twitched at the corners of his full, soft lips. 'Fascinating,' he said. '"Bait the hook well, this fish will bite."'

'Right enough.'

'Pseudonyms?' Dodo asked. Rhys looked to Jakey for help. 'Your names?'

'I get you. This here's Jakey and I'm Rhys.'

Dodo sighed. 'Well, to work.'

Dodo's idea of work dragged on with a fair few words of many syllables sending Jakey for a slash and more cider.

'We're halfway there,' said Dodo in his educated accent, holding his finger in the air like they were stargazing – a futile occupation in a city. Then he unwrapped a pack of lighters, the kind you find cracked on the beach, their flint mechanisms rusted by sea. 'We have laid the groundwork. Now comes the hard graft. Are you ready to get your hands dirty? Your faces hot?'

'Always.' Rhys nodded, thinking groundwork a thing better done in summer when rain doesn't clag up the red soil making it heavier on the shovel than it need be. 'But let me fetch Jakey back first. We come as a pair, like, when it comes to a job of work.'

He found Jakey helping the old woman load a tray with drinks at the bar. 'She's buying,' Jakey said, as she left with the trayful. 'Proper nice people, these. One more, eh? Then we'll go dancing?'

He turned to leave but Rhys held his arm. 'Hold fire. Dodo has a job for us.'

Jakey's eyes lit up. 'How much?'

'They're talking terms now.'

Jakey frowned. 'That's a bad sign. He should state his rate up front.'

'They're negotiating-like. Come and see.'

'Well, don't trust him unless you see his money,' said Jakey, following Rhys out. 'He looks like he should take a turn on deck, if you get my meaning.'

'He can't help being smart.' Until five minutes ago, Rhys hadn't heard of the West Country potato famine or the Swing Riots turning threshing machines to ashes, but he understood a little of how it feels when work is scarce and prices high. 'Some people just know a lot of stuff. He's giving out free lighters, too. Something about "kindling flames for the future". It's a metaphor.'

'All right. What does a metaphor pay?'

As they took their places at the table, Dodo stopped what he was saying to ask Rhys if had any Welsh ancestry because of his name. 'I'm a quarter Welsh,' said Rhys, glad someone had noticed. 'Named after my mum's dad from Carmarthen. I never met him but Dav and Owen, that's my brothers, they also have Welsh names from Mum's side of the family.'

Dodo seemed happy with that. He clapped Rhys on the back and said they needed a Welsh warrior like him because the Welsh knew what to do about rich incomers pricing out local people. They'd had an organisation by the name of Meibion Glyndŵr – Sons of Glyndŵr – that targeted holiday cottages.

'What did they do?' Rhys asked.

'Fire-setting,' said Dodo.

Rhys rolled the flint of his new lighter under the table and held it lit till it stung his thumb and singed the wood as he waited for his new friends to go back to the subject of paying work.

But all eyes and ears were trained on the flowery words rolling across Dodo's tongue and each sentence spun further from groundwork towards something that struck Rhys like a spade in the bedrock of his belly, a history he had never heard spoken of at school or from his dad.

According to Dodo, Meibion Glyndŵr were the great-great-grandsons of Owain Glyndŵr, who many centuries past had run the English out of Wales with his broadsword and his men kilt-clad like Scots and daubed in paint.

Rhys liked the sound of that.

The upshot was that they had seen the things that were wrong in Wales and took, as Dodo put it, 'direct and irreversible action'. This all kicked off in the seventies after Maggie Thatcher (she that was Prime Minister at the time) had stolen everything – pit jobs and souls – and the offspring of working men were made to eat charitable baked beans and tinned sketty hoops every day for the length and breadth of their childhood, and no milk given at school.

Rhys wondered if she'd shut hospitals, also, but was too shy to ask. Dodo was on a broad reach, his gennaker full-filled, eyes glinting with noble purpose.

Had Rhys not known that his family had been 'screwed into the gutter' with a twist of Maggie's heel and spat at with 'tax breaks for high net-worth individuals'?

He had not.

'What happened next?' Rhys asked, and was duly answered.

Outsiders flooded over the Severn Bridge and across the border into Wales from London, and with said tax breaks and poll tax savings, they bought up fishermen's cottages and Black Mountain smallholdings and whole hamlets of pretty Pembrokeshire granite for their leisure and profit.

Much like Lythcombe's own grockles they came – weekends, if they could, if the weather was fair and they could be arsed. And they did not spend their money on milk and bread at the SPAR, nor did they buy stamps for their letters in the post office, or send their kids to the primary. These places were closed down and boarded up, and not just in summer, as in South Devon, but all year round.

Often, these outsiders did not come at all, waiting instead for their property portfolios to accrue in value from rampant inflation beyond the wildest dreams of today's reckless bond-trading scumbags like 'Father', as Dodo called his dad.

Granted, this happened a long time before Rhys was born, in the Modern History Dodo learned about in Oxford – a town he mentioned more than once – but Rhys soon saw that history has a history of repeating itself and patterns of reoffending may be observed, as with today's rulers and their fondness for landlords.

Jakey kicked Rhys under the table. 'What about the job?'

'Shut up.'

It was a lot to take in. And Dodo was only warming his engine, telling how the Sons of Glyndŵr had marched, not with broadswords this time, but with Zippo lighters, bottles of spirit and dishcloths cut into strips as a wick. These items they lit and hurled through cottage windows, their English owners fast asleep in Islington beds, dreaming of money and how they would make more.

In other words, thought Rhys, *those Welsh boys stuck a middle finger up to the Volvo army coming along the M4 and put the fear of fire in their lily-livered hearts.*

'Wasn't that illegal?' asked Jakey.

'One man's terrorist is another man's freedom fighter,' answered Dodo, melting a bit of Afghan resin for crumbling. 'Arson was a modern response to late-era imperialism and, important to say, not a soul was hurt.'

'Well, what else can you do?' Rhys said, forgetting his shyness. 'When you run out of food and the Londis has gone bust and the nearest Tesco is a two-hour trip and petrol prices are highway bloody robbery? Can't live off whelks.'

'Indubitably,' said Dodo at last, having smiled at Milly first in a manner Rhys was not entirely comfortable with. One thing Rhys cannot abide is being laughed at, but any bad feeling was soon smothered over when Dodo passed his bong in Rhys's direction.

'Essentially...' Dodo reached over to help relight the buds. 'Meibion Glyndŵr would not render unto Caesar what was Caesar's. And neither should we.'

The embers reddened as Rhys sucked and Dodo's voice dropped to the details of more immediate action: a bin-bag campaign, political poetry and graffiti with artistic merit. Also, an ancient woodland, up at Lee Moor, was threatened by the aggregate plant and needed warriors to defend it from corporate Japanese investment.

'I hate aggregate,' said Rhys, quite fancying himself a warrior and knowing from his Construction NVQ what concrete-dust does to lungs.

The old woman had already started on the graffiti – an Arts Council-funded mural in a village hall –

Dodo was writing a few poetic words and the student-men signed up for the woodland gig. Lee Moor being beyond the range of his tank, Rhys asked if they had something closer to shore.

'Lythcombe, you say?' said Dodo. He turned to Milly. 'Where's Lythcombe again? Is it on our list?'

Milly consulted her phone. 'Attractive fishing port. West of Salcombe.'

She met Rhys's eye for less than a second, in which he felt his heart catch. She was, he realised, far more beautiful than he'd first thought. And she knew Lythcombe.

The bin bags, it so happened, were to be hung from the letterboxes of holiday cottages and second homes between midnight and dawn, to expose the number of unoccupied properties blighting coastal communities. In some of the more desirable towns and villages, indeed, four in ten will be marked by black.

'By morning,' said Dodo, 'there will be a media frenzy. Our name will be heard: Mebyon Dewnans. Sons of Devon.'

'When do we start?' said Rhys.

'In a few weeks. Await my signal.'

'Will that be by text?' asked Jakey. 'Or semaphore?' He looked to Rhys, perhaps for confirmation that this was a whole heap of bollocks, but none was forthcoming.

Rhys's heart had sprinted ahead of him.

He knew exactly which houses Dodo meant – whole streets of them the closer you get to the prom:

shuttered-up, blinds down, undecorated at Christmas, no trees in the window, no Santa sleighs in the front garden. The lights-off places you don't bother trying at Halloween because no sweets will be coming. In summer, a different car on the drive every Saturday for the changing of the guard. The million-pound rebuilds on the hill only used for regatta week.

Rhys felt the cold slice of a filleting knife run through his life, teasing out the gubbins from the white flesh. There were listing things that wanted righting: iniquity, greed and the theft of native soil.

Why had no one thought of this before?

At that moment, Rhys understood that he was not alone. Lythcombe was not alone. There was a whole battalion at his back whose boots he had never heard. And he and Dodo held something important in common, if not in strength or advanced schooling, then in a general willingness to venture their lives for others; in Rhys's case, up till now, against the sea's violence that wages war on bathers with dark and fast waters, and in Dodo's, against the undercurrents of greed that drive house prices up and locals out, leaving behind whole streets of silver key-safe boxes Rawlplugged to the masonry.

'Goes on a bit, don't he?' whispered Jakey. 'I'm not saying no exactly. We just don't have enough time to get round all of them. Maybe just do Jubilee, eh?'

'Mate, you don't get second-home owners in Jubilee. It's falling to pieces.'

'Ron's got a caravan.'

'Don't count.'

'And there's his berth on *Sweet Irene II*.'

'You can't rent out a berth on a day-boat,' said Rhys. 'Not if you don't clean out your pots. This is about London folk, anyway. Can't you see? Like Liz's place in Dartmouth.'

'Well, she's sore she lost that one now. They paid eight quid an hour and the vacuum cleaner was one of those lightweight battery ones. Dyson. Could've done with borrowing it for the galley—'

Seeing that everyone was looking their way, they stopped talking and folded their hands in their laps, meek as children before the headmaster.

'The masses will rise against capital,' concluded Dodo, sliding a lighter Jakey's way, along with a small bag of sweet-smelling green buds.

'Cheers, mate,' said Jakey. 'Count us in.'

There were no cardinal buoys flashing in Rhys's mind as he Bluetoothed himself into Dodo's phone.

'I've got your number,' said Dodo with a doglike smile, adding Rhys to his WhatsApp group. 'Join us. We will fall upon our foes like eagles.'

At this juncture, Rhys did not know that Dodo was a proper poet, and thus accustomed to over-egging his pudding, but he knew right enough about the way a kestrel hangs in the air like a photo till it falls, then perches on a hairy-lichened granite post, tugging at a poor kit. One-two and it's back on the wing, a curl of fluff caught in its empty claws.

Life is always worse for something else, Rhys thought

then. Imagine living like a rabbit, always afeared, always running, till judgement day when a talon comes from nowhere, straight through your ribs to your Skittle-red heart.

Next he thought of Jubilee – his home, his warren. Owen will turn nine this year – just six weeks hence – and soon he will be as big as his brothers. Phil Fisher asked the council for a two-bed place and was told he was lucky he had a roof at all. The waiting list runs out of the county.

Being a rabbit was one thing. Better by far to be an eagle.

'Nice fellow,' said Jakey, flicking his lighter as they tacked through the cobbled Barbican streets where laughter could be heard issuing from the full lungs of posh students and Naval boys.

What Dodo said is true, Rhys thought. *We're in love with our abusers. So long as there's a decent queue at the chippy and the ice cream parlour, who cares about being slowly crapped on by grockles and foreign money?*

They went to the lido, built on a promontory of land jutting out into the Sound. The place was quiet, being shut for the night. The fence was not too hard to climb and soon they were down to their boxers, swimming to the fountain in the middle.

'Why do folk pay for swimming' asked Jakey, 'when they've got all that?' He nodded his head to the sparkling sea all around them and took a gulp of midnight-blue pool, jetting it out in Rhys's face.

'Don't drink the water,' said Rhys, feeling sober and wise. 'Babies piss in it all day.'

They sat on the rails watching Mount Edgecombe and Drake's Island like they were on the bridge of a galleon. Jakey rolled some of Dodo's buds into a long, fat joint and sparked it up with the free lighter. It tasted sweet – a superior varietal.

But the pleasure was short-lived. Draining the last of the Amaretto, Rhys was overcome by a memory of peeling marzipan off his mum's Easter cake. His eyes watered from the chlorine, or else smoke from the fine skunk.

'Screw this place,' he said, because the dark granite coast and those ship lights flickering on the horizon had brought up the possibility of leaving. He'd thought about that before, but where to? His mum was nearby, under a plaque in Plymouth crematorium.

He threw the empty bottle onto the concrete floor of the changing room where it skidded and shattered.

'Mate, what'd you do that for?' said Jakey. 'The caretaker'll have a job in the morning.'

'Screw the caretaker, and Amaretto, and grockles.' Rhys thought of the Blue Lagoon. 'And the Navy, too. Screw everyone.'

Jakey's face dropped. 'Not me, though?'

'Not you.' He patted his friend's arm. 'I just don't want to be here any more.'

'The lido?'

Rhys did not answer. The moon painted a white

whale-road all the way to Biscay. His dad had left on the ferry to Santander that morning and would still be out there tomorrow; twenty hours at sea, then ten hours of driving to Murcia and ten hours back to Santander, then another twenty hours at sea coming home.

Jakey looked east along the silhouetted coast. 'I dream of going away, too,' he said. 'But when it comes to it, I don't want to go.'

They smoked till a haze-glow illuminated the sky over Dartmoor. Then Rhys had a thought suddenly come to him. 'Tomorrow,' he said. 'I'm going to do something big.' Jakey laughed through his nose. 'No, really. I am.'

'What's that, then?' asked Jakey. But the thought had slipped Rhys's net as soon as he'd caught it. 'Full of shit, you are.'

Rhys flicked his lighter and remembered again: a Welsh fire lit in his mind.

But revolution would have to wait; there was breakfast to be made and school bags packed. If they left Plymouth now, he'd be home by six – before Dav's alarm but long after the fishermen had left to pull up their pots.

Watching the fuel gauge very closely for the last miles, they stopped just short of Lythcombe. Rhys's dirt bike had a small tank, not meant for adventuring beyond.

Rhys chose a car outside one of those houses with the big windows looking out over the bay.

'How do you know it's not diesel?' asked Jakey.

'Classic cars don't run on diesel,' said Rhys, getting out his siphon. 'And they don't have fuel-cap locks.'

He sucked upon the hose till the fumes tickled his tongue, before whipping it into his own tank. The flow was good, thanks to the steepness of the hill and his bike being downstream of the car.

'This here is an Austin Healey. Fifty grand secondhand.' Rhys patted the bonnet three times, leaving fifteen incriminating fingerprints, then used his T-shirt to smear them to a high polish. 'You look her up.'

Drips of petrol expanded around their feet, catching every star in the sky, including the boys' faces in a swirl of colour, before contracting to nothing. It made Rhys think of Milly's tie-dye top and the kiss Dodo had taken from her, and a cuttlefish just before it is killed.

Having got the fuel, Rhys left a bin bag in the letterbox – by way of revolution, though he didn't think the owners would mind. Bin bags always come in handy and you never have one when you need it most, like getting Owen's duvet to the launderette after he has pissed his jimjams in the night.

They had trouble starting the bike. Rhys found out later the radiator was screwed, but Lythcombe being at sea level and they on the hill, they were able to coast the last mile. Engine off, it was a quiet ride.

Back in town, he dropped Jakey, then free-wheeled the last hundred metres to the yard, leaving his Kawasaki next to the pushbikes by the pallet palace. Inside the flat, Dav was still sleeping and Owen was up drawing sail boats; a good little artist, he was – they had rivets and shrouds and a zip-up bag on the prow where the spinnaker was stowed.

'Where were you?' asked Owen, not looking up.

'Went out for a spin. It's a nice morning. Go and jump on Dav's face for me, will you? It's time to shine.'

FOUR

'Fire's got a lot going for it,' Rhys told his brothers as they sat on the beach, the week after hearing Dodo speak of its cleansing properties in Plymouth. 'The point is, sometimes it's better to burn stuff down. You have to get rid of it and start again from scratch.'

Lighting fires, though, is harder than it looks. Rhys has been practising since he was a small boy. 'God help us,' said the neighbours. 'Hide the matches. Lock up the lighters.'

Yet when they want to cook mackerel on the beach, Rhys sometimes can't get a fire started.

Humidity matters, rain matters, and whether the wind is on- or off-shore; the sea state matters, whether the waves are high and spraying; whether the last tide touched the dunes and how long bleached driftwood has been in the sun; and whether Phil Fisher has brought them pine pallets home, still hot from the depot in Spain, to take along ready-chopped as kindling.

On good nights, when conditions are right, there's a row of fires, laughter crackling along the beach – like landing lights.

Rhys remembers how, back in May and June, he often got six macks on one rod-line from the beach. Fish need gutting if they're fatter than a finger; straight nick from bum to chin, quick scrape and rinse in the waves. Blackhead gulls will tidy up their insides. But small fry, like whitebait, do not need filleting. They go down in one, their sweet charcoal-black skins crispy, dipped in bean juice or squashed in a hotdog roll.

Though beach fishing makes their food budget stretch, Rhys also works hard for the family, seeing as how he is often mother and father to his brothers, with their mum gone and dad driving. In summer, the car park pays all right for sitting in a shed clicking a clicker and taking tenners all morning, fivers after lunch. He'll put in a good word for Dav when his brother turns sixteen, bump him up the list, his natural heir and successor. Dav has said he needs to save for university because he has been told it is not cheap. When Phil Fisher heard that he said, 'Don't worry your head, Dav; I'll do double hitches to make sure you go, if university is what you want.'

Double hitches? thought Rhys. *When he should be at home, looking after his sons?*

But not long after Rhys met Dodo, the car park shut for the winter season and Rhys came to the conclusion he hated the owner for making a fortune – upwards of £800 a day, unless it rained. For his part, Rhys took home £44.80 for a seven-hour shift, rain or shine, and now nothing at all. How can that be fair?

'Better than fair,' said Dav. 'Glass collecting's five

quid an hour. And I can't do my homework working in the pub when it's raining, not like you can in the car park shed. Do you know how much revision I could get done on a wet day if I had your job?'

'You don't get it, do you?'

'Get what?'

'You wait and see!' said Rhys. 'The masses will rise against capital.'

'Numpty.'

'Collaborator. You're no better than Dad.'

Rhys was not always angry. In summertime, there is enough natural light and heat to make a tenner last a week in the electricity meter, even allowing for the daily standing charge. Before the Rip Curl Championship, he still had his Saturday job at Mr Barker's Sunrise Surf School where he taught grommets, finishing early enough for a game of football or an evening surf.

Who thinks of revolution when there are waves to surf and balls to kick and grockles owed a drubbing?

It was last summer season that the locals had their finest victory. On Lythcombe sands, mile-long football matches have no corners or sidelines. Not even the ocean counts as a throw-in, so it took a while for the Away team (grockle boys) to understand the rules. Grockles are used to solid things like indoor sports halls, paint-line pitches, astroturf and concrete playgrounds. They stay on their feet, fearful of a dive tackle in the surf.

Unfair advantage to Lythcombe, you might say, since a week or two in a caravan or Airbnb is not enough to teach visitors the way wind-wave action plays along. It only takes one muppet to miskick and a gust, playing for the opposition, will snatch the ball skywards, making a neat cross into the surf. On Atlantic days, even a light offshore makes for a long swim, as happened on that last game of the season when conditions were Light, occasionally Moderate, according to the Douglas sea scale.

Rhys grabbed Owen by his hood. 'Leave it to the big boys,' he said when his brother was ready to dive in after the ball. He stripped off his top and chucked it on the goal pile. First he jump-skip-flew over the little breakers, then front-crawl-dived under the rollers. In the side of his salt-stung eye he spied two grockle-sprogs high-stepping, hitching up their Rip Curl O'Neill boardshorts, hot on his tail. Since there are no corner flags here, fetchers have the kick; Lythcombe was one-nil down, so it was worth the swim.

Rhys tucked in his chin and pulled his arms hard, jeans tightening round his legs. The sea went from chopped-up white to grey to green to black. One grockle boy backed off to the shallows, thinking he was safe, right in a lightning-fork of the stream bed. Not a smart place to stand, where freshwater mixes with salt. He did not know about the weevers waiting for the underside of his soft foot.

Through kindness rather than strategic sense, Dav called that grockle away from the stream bed, though a quality left-wing defender with a stinging foot in a bucket of piss would have been a better outcome for the Lythcombe boys.

Meanwhile, Rhys ploughed on; the water saw him coming and split between his paddle hands. He trod water, caught his breath for the span of two waves, blew out his ears and snared a slippery line of snot on a bit of bladderwrack.

A long grey body slid under him.

Turn back. Turn.

His heart crashed against his ribs and the second grockle-boy, who was closer to the ball than Rhys, saw the shape, turned and sprint-crawled to shore, where he cried those bitter-salt tears that boys reserve for times of fear, failure or shame, which mercifully cannot be distinguished from sea on a wet face.

Rhys's brothers on the sand, the cliffs, dunes, town and the bracken tor behind looked very small. Rhys was small too, alone in the ocean and far from home. He could not help feeling that more wrong days were coming.

There were shouts from the beach, phones held like shields against the sunset.

Grockle 1: Shark! Shark!
Owen: Shark!
Dav: No, you twit. See the fluke?
Grockle 2 [jumping]: There's more!
Owen: Dolphins!
Grockles: Dolphins!
Dav: No. See their noses?
Owen: Whales!
Grockles: Baby whales!
Dav (arms folded): Porpoises, you mugs.

The ball whipped Rhys's way, a neat arc into his hands, perfect top-spin from a tail kick, deflected by a nose-punt. Who would have thought porpoises liked football? Holding the ball under his chest, Rhys belly-surfed in on a gurt wave, though that's not what he told the others when it was 3-2 to Lythcombe and darkness blew the final whistle.

It so happened that this night on the beach with Dav and Owen, the week after meeting Dodo, was a fair one with conditions just right, so Rhys's fire lit well. While the macks sizzled, he dried the front of his jeans, then turned to get his back done. From the prom, the steam must have made him look as if he was on fire.

'Can't say we don't eat like kings,' he said, squinting at the sunset, copying his dad.

After tea, Rhys buried his cider empties and spliff ends in the sand with the bean tins, like jagged-edged weever dorsals waiting for an unwary foot.

'Better recycle,' said Dav, digging them out to take home.

'All right, Greta,' said Rhys, helping him.

On the horizon, ships blinked hellos over nautical miles. The brothers counted navigation buoy flashes, knowing their language and how they told the deepness of things.

'Time for bed,' said Rhys to his brothers. 'I promised Dad we wouldn't live on the beach like stray dogs.'

'He won't know if you don't tell,' said Owen, meaning he won't guess if they stop here under the stars by the fire with the waves shushing them to sleep, a long time washing in from America, flopping down on Devonian sand at the last. That is why grockles come here. It is a proven fact of physics that energy cannot be created or destroyed, so when outsiders sit on Lythcombe beach, they catch a bit of that energy and take it home with them.

'But I'll know,' said Rhys. 'And I'm in charge.'

Later, on the phone, Owen told their dad, 'Rhys rode on the back of a shark today.'

'A cetacean, not a shark,' said Rhys, towelling off Owen's sandy salt-mop hair before bed. 'Don't exaggerate.'

If Children's Services had their way, there would be no barefoot football or big waves. When Phil Fisher is driving in Spain, Rhys is in charge and must remind his brothers to say nothing of their dad's whereabouts because he worries Children's Services will mistake them for orphans.

They have come for Rhys, Dav and Owen before, when they thought Phil Fisher could not cope being mother and father both whilst driving here and there in his Iveco. First, they sent Owen to a couple in Torquay who specialised in babies. At this, Phil Fisher dented a social worker's car so they came back for Rhys and Dav, who went to a lady in Plymouth where they shared a bedroom but she had no room for Rhys's rabbits, Mrs Kevin and Ginger. Being small, Rhys could no longer meet his lop-ears' needs, and so they were given to someone who could. They will be old bunnies by now, bless their cotton socks and scuts. Rhys hopes they're having a good life.

Anyhow, the Plymouth lady did not have space for Phil Fisher either, which is daft because the Fishers do not have that much room now, but they fit. 'We'll Tetris it,' says their dad when life gets squashed – two big men, one nearly big and one dinky squirt still growing. And they were all so much smaller then, even Phil Fisher. But it made no difference to Children's Services. Phil Fisher, his sons and their bunnies were split apart like a dying star, a black hole, matter exploding to the far reaches of the galaxy.

It is a good thing Owen can't remember those days.

On the last Wednesday of the half term, three days before the October holiday, Rhys dropped Owen off at school. 'Whatever you do,' he warned his little brother, 'don't mention lettuce to Mrs Hill. She'll be casual-like, but that's a trap, saying, "Oh, I love a bit of baby-leaf," but they can stay the hell out of our business.'

'What'll happen if I forget?' said Owen, who often discloses sensitive information without thinking, finding it hard to remember what he should and should not say.

'Children's Services, mate. They'll do a risk assessment. They'll look in the cupboards. They'll check the fridge and shake their heads. They'll send child psychiatrists and social workers round and call Dad reckless and ask him what he's doing on a foreign ringtone.'

'Good,' said Owen. 'That'll bring him home.'

'No, Owen. They'll move me to a different school,' said Dav, 'and that means I won't get a university mentor.'

'Good,' said Rhys. 'You don't want to be going to university anyway.'

'I do,' said Dav.

'Any rate, squirt,' said Rhys. 'They'll take your palace away. They'll call it a fire hazard.'

That shut Owen up.

Of course, there was a time before Children's Services when the brothers weren't poked and prodded at like shrimp in a rock pool, when their mother was alive. You would think Rhys's memory of that time would be unreliable, the way wind rubs out footprints in the dunes or tides wash the sand flat. But no, his memories are clear as a millpond-sea on a blue-sky day.

When Rhys was very small, he used to play hide and seek with his dad, in those white valleys where sand scorches your feet and you have to run quick, *pat pat*, down to the wet sand to cool them. His mum had been there too then, feeding Dav her boobs, but not Owen, who was not yet in her belly but on her to-do list.

On one occasion, Phil Fisher, chuckling to himself, thought, *I've got a good trick*, because he sneaked off to the water and dipped himself in it, head to foot, then rolled down a dune, sticking sand all over himself. Only his eyes were left, a horrible thing to behold: a menace from the deep.

Not finding his dad, Rhys sat down with his mum

till Phil Fisher turned up and charged down the dune to where Rhys was playing and his mum was rocking Dav; you could hear the milk sloshing in his fat little belly.

'Roar!' said Phil Fisher. 'I am the Sandman!'

Rhys looked at his mum and brother whose eyelids had been dropping, a smile on his baby face like nothing bad could ever happen and they were safe for ever. And then Rhys eyed the monster coming for them.

'Normal-wise, a toddler would squeal and cry,' is the way Phil Fisher tells it in the King's Arms, 'but not our Rhys.'

Rhys balled his fists and sunk his milk teeth in that grainy shin till the Sandman howled on his knees and wiped his face and said, 'My love, my love, it's me, your daddy.'

Even at seventeen years of age, Rhys may be heard shouting in his dreams. If Phil Fisher is home, he whispers, 'I'm here, my love, it's me,' and hugs Rhys back to sleep while Dav pretends not to have seen. When Phil Fisher is away, Dav gets down the ladder from the top bunk, kneels down by the blow-up bed and takes a turn to be the one to say, 'I'm here,' instead. But Rhys is often only half-awake and soon falls asleep, the tide lapping in, sand clean, but very sweaty, his hair wet. Dav smooths it back and if Owen wakes, he lies atop Rhys's chest, puts his arms around him and stays to keep bad dreams away, like a puppy or a kit rabbit in a furry knot of warmth.

Rhys was mostly all right about having Owen in his bed, but not since he met Dodo and the grockles left and Rhys was back to being skint.

'Sleep in your own bed,' he said to Owen, knowing he could never bring a girl like Milly home. 'Binty stinks, get it off me!'

Owen put his rag to his nose. 'Rhys doesn't mean it, you don't stink.'

'Where's my kecks?' said Rhys, kicking the dirty laundry bag. 'This place is a bloody muckheap. Dav, you little toad, you've got mud on my trackies. I was going to wear them today. What if I had a date?'

All day at school, Owen thought about how to make Rhys happy. He settled for drawing a picture of his family on the beach, yellow dots for the sand and a red bonfire at their feet. He gave Phil Fisher and Rhys criss-cross lines where the Spider-Man muscles go, and drew his mum for Phil and a pretty girlfriend for Rhys. In Rhys's other hand he put a Pyzel swallow tail shortboard, the kind Rhys read about in his surfing magazines. For Dav, he drew a handsome boyfriend with a scientific calculator (criss-cross lines where the sums go) and himself in the middle with a new rod, covered in yellow sandy dots. He drew all this, probably thinking, in the way squirts do, that if you draw enough smiles and mums and calculators and Marvel musculature, your better dreams will come true, not your nightmares.

When he got home, Rhys was calmer. 'Nice bonfire picture, squirt,' he said, and Dav said, 'Pointillist now, are we?' because by the time Owen had dotted in the beach, the Fishers were very hard to see.

*

Rhys does not blame Phil Fisher for the driving he does, but there have been times when Rhys would rather his dad quit his job, like on his seventeenth birthday when they were supposed to be going out on Jakey's boat and Phil had promised Rhys a half of cider in the evening.

Rhys is not stupid. He knows they have bills to pay. He knows that private flats in their parts do not come without sky-high rental deposits, it being an area of outstanding natural beauty. There are currently eighty-six two-bedroomed houses listed on Airbnb and three advertised at the local estate agents, of which two are limited to a six-month tenancy. Their council flat, though small, is their only hope of staying where they belong, within sniffing distance of the ocean.

He also knows that his dad has but one wage, whereas many families have two. And it's true that a man has to work and look after his kids. But here's the rub: when his dad's freight logistics boss called him in, Rhys's birthday presents were half-open and half-not, and the Fishers were in pyjamas all, bacon frying in the pan and the whole day ahead of them, not even school to spoil it.

No one made Phil tug his forelock and say, 'Yes, sir, no, sir, three bags full, sir.'

No one made him say, 'Sorry, son,' and fetch his Iveco keys.

Rhys was angry then. Not any more. He has since learned that his dad is also a good man. The problem is, things don't often go well for good men like them – Dodo explained the serried forces of capital greed against them, but Rhys already knew the places on the trawlers are numbered, their catches weighed and found wanting. The college course he started in September did not work out and he tries not to dwell on the fact that he was once called a 'promising young talent' for his surfing performance in a six-foot swell against grown men of muscles, including one from Cornwall, one from Monterey and another from Hawaii where they invented the sport in the first place.

His picture was nearly printed in *Carve* magazine.

But his luck was like his fins – always and evermore snapping in high seas.

FIVE

The main difference between Rhys and Dav is girls. Rhys falls in love with girls every day, and every day his heart gets broken. In summer, he stares at their boobs in bikinis when they are not looking, and if they spot him, he turns lobster and looks away. He thinks about them all the time – how their hair flies in the wind or comes out of the sea in clumps like seaweed. He says they bewitch him like mermaids, though Owen says that's daft because they're only girls and walk on two legs like the rest of us.

Rhys has tried to show Jakey how to get a girl's attention, advising him to wear his board shorts lowslung like London boys. This is risky on a surfboard; someone might see your arse. But poor Jakey's face is like a dimpled shortcrust pasty made with extra lard before it is put in the oven. For all his talk aboard the *Maria*, on dry land Jakey is like a nervous witness under cross-examination. Rhys, by contrast – with his strong cheekbones (according to Lianne, his first girlfriend), sun-kissed skin, green eyes, dark ginger curls and freckled chest strong from carrying a hod of bricks and a hundred daily press-ups in the yard – is a champion at turning girls' heads. He has an easy way about him and more often than not catches the wave, although he has been known to wipe out with those clever girls from Exeter University whose eyes glaze over when he opens his mouth.

Dav, on the other hand, likes boys, and he is none too keen on getting a drubbing from the fury of waves. That's no skin off Rhys's nose but he would rather they were the *same* so they could stick together, catch a party wave into shore, go fishing for girls in a pack. Like, 'Here's my smart little brother, he will blow your socks off with the things he knows. Will you come with us for chips?'

Late July, when Rhys found a girl, Owen and Dav had followed them into the dunes to play bingo, the rules of which Rhys learned after he'd kicked their spying backsides.

There were five points if she flicked her hair, to a maximum of twenty because some girls take this too far.

Ten points if she gave him a shove with her hip sideways and he fell in the sand, on purpose-like, so that when she helped him back up, he could flick her foot from under and make her land on top of him, ha, ha.

Ten points if she stayed there and thumped his chest and tried to pin his arms down, laughing all the while.

Ten more if, further down the beach, she honked with laughter when he dropped to one knee, a ring pebble, hole through its middle, for her finger – Rhys keeps a few in his pocket; they are not hard to find – and asked her to marry him there and then on the beach in front of God and the sunset.

Fifty points if they kissed. One hundred if they snogged.

A thousand if they *did it*.

This has not happened yet, though Rhys has claimed otherwise, showing his brothers the condom he carries in his pocket like a trawlerman's holy talisman. Dav says Rhys believes his own porkies when it comes to girls.

But this year, Dav told his brothers that he fancies boys. Owen, for his part, had no quarrel with this because, although girls are okay in his school, he's seen teenage ones hitting boys hard and snatching their chips. Maybe they're only joking, but it cannot be nice. He has decided never to kiss, but at least if you kissed a boy you wouldn't risk getting make-up on your face.

'Have you got a boyfriend yet?' Owen asked.

'No,' Dav told him. 'I'm going to wait till university, any road – away from here. Like at Nottingham.'

'What's Nottingham got to do with anything?' Rhys asked.

'It's personal,' said Dav, meaning right now he wasn't about to tell his brothers he planned to leave them one day for far-flung inland places.

'What about us?' Rhys said. Phil Fisher warned him this would happen. That they would all become *scattered boys*.

At first, Dav didn't tell anyone he was gay, maybe because Owen was going through this phase when he wanted to know whether people were *this* thing or *that*, like goodies or baddies, rich or poor, one thing or another, so he would know who to trust and who to run from.

In May last year, the brothers had been down on the beach, no clouds in the sky, the sea a sheet of polished glass, when two lads jogged shirtless out of the dunes. One was brown and lean as a footballer on the telly. The other was tall and white. They were grockles, of course, wearing their best trainers in the sand – not knowing it takes a single solitary grain in the sole to pull the glue – and the white lad's shoulders were pink from too much sun after no sun at all. Also, their socks were white and pulled high.

The lads slowed to a walk, arms falling loose round each other's necks, like teammates do, like anyone does to his mate who scored the goal, deserving the wrap of legs, arms and sometimes a great sloppy kiss on the top of their head that says, 'Well done, my son,' better than words. Their arms dropped as they came close to where people were – the town, the prom.

But instead of coming apart – a shove, a punch, a laugh, like, 'Mate, good session. Same again tomorrow?' – Rhys had to look away because, sweat shining on their chests, they kissed.

Shit, Rhys thought, and looked to Dav to share a laugh. But Dav was staring at the scant line of hair leading down to their fancy running shorts like he was holding his breath under a wave, though he was sitting land-locked and dry. Rhys looked back to the boys in time to catch two fingers meeting, curling, till their hands swung together as one fist.

Rhys said, 'What the hell? Is Lythcombe turning into London?'

'Soppy boys,' said Owen.

The brown-skinned one turned his handsome head their way and crossed a smile to Dav, the way the sun throws light and heat when it comes out after being behind a cloud. Dav punted a nice smile back and on the boys walked.

Seeing this, Rhys drilled his ankles into the sand, wishing he could do the same with the rest of him, ostrich-wise. Dav's beacon face was lit red like a signpost, a cardinal mark, a blazing advert for what he was.

'Okay,' said Rhys, feeling a pulse of rage. 'So now I've got a bumboy for a brother.'

Dav swallowed the way kids do when they see a kiss in a film with their parents sitting close. 'Don't call me that,' he said.

Rhys tucked the board he'd borrowed from Jakey under his arm. 'I'm going in,' he said, heading for the water.

Later, in their dark bedroom, Owen asleep, Dav tried to explain what learning you are gay feels like, and Rhys had tried to listen.

'You know...' said Dav. 'You know when a high-tide wave breaks over your head and there's nothing you can do to stay on your feet and you turn over and over and upside down and the sea...'

Rhys knows the moment when there is no knowing of up or down or back or home, and lifeguards fidget, wondering if they should go in, till shaking swimmers stumble up the sand, their skin sandpapered raw, baptised.

'Well, that's what seeing them lads kiss felt like, Rhys. Can you understand? A proper drubbing.'

By way of answer, Rhys laid a soft pillow over his previously joint-favourite sibling's face, to prevent Owen waking to the sound of knuckle on cheekbone. Dav, for his part, lay still and quiet, and closed his arms over his head against his brother's blows.

Rhys spent the rest of that week looking for the visiting gays of Lythcombe: the long of the beach, two campsites, the caravan park, board shop, chip shop, coffee shop, pub, harbour, and the Point, white foam breaking on the cliffs.

He found the brown one sitting with a Black lady on a bench on the prom, looking at photos on her phone. 'Delete that one, Mam,' the boy had said. His accent was from very far away, north even of London. 'Delete it, now. I hate it.'

'You look fine,' said the lady. 'And it's a nice one of Joe. It's my picture and I want to keep it. When you're away, it's all I've got.'

'Don't tell me you spend all day sitting on my bed crying, looking at my baby pics.'

She started laughing now, smile lines round her

eyes. 'Anthony, Anthony, Anthony. When you're at uni, that's exactly what I do. I sit on your bed and cry and look at photos of you.'

He snatched her phone and she snatched it back and then they got up and put their cups in the bin. Before they went, the boy winked at Rhys and said, 'Mams, eh, what can you do?'

Now, you cannot slug a boy in front of his mum, can you? It would have to keep.

When Rhys next saw this so-called Anthony, the latter had knelt down next to the brothers on the sand, uninvited, and said, 'You're local, aren't you?'

Rhys balled his fists.

'How do you know?' said Owen.

'From your castle. You know the sand to water ratio here. For structure.'

This made Owen happy. 'Are you a brickie?' he asked. 'My brother Rhys was going to be a brickie if he finished college. He'll tell you about mortar mixes.'

'That's cool, but I'm not a brickie. I'm reading Maths at Nottingham.'

'You can't read Maths,' said Owen. 'It's made out of numbers. It's not a story.'

'It is a story. It's the story of everything.'

Dav was itching to know what Maths at Nottingham was, but that would have to wait because at that moment the boyfriend turned up in a shirt and tie and pulled Anthony to his feet. 'We're going for lunch,' he said. 'Time to get changed.' And they kissed again, not such a long one this time.

Owen said, 'Are you boyfriend and girlfriend?'

They laughed. The white one said, 'No. We're boys, so boyfriend and boyfriend.'

'What will you eat?'

They looked at each other. Anthony smiled and said, 'Not sure. It's my mam and dad's wedding anniversary.'

'There's nothing here but the chip shop,' the boyfriend said.

Seeing Rhys glower and squeeze sand in his fist, Anthony said, 'He doesn't mean to be rude. We'll probably try somewhere in Plymouth.'

Then the boyfriend said, 'See you around, boys,' and they held hands and left.

In the end, Dav had to wait till September to ask a teacher what reading Maths at Nottingham meant.

It was confusing but Rhys explained it to himself like this: boats have sonar for inshore waters, and the sonar makes a picture of the seabed out of sound, as bats do, and whales and hospital machines.

Ping... ping... ping... it goes, to the bottom and back. And the answer creates a shape, a mirror of what is there but cannot be seen so there's no risk of running aground or hitting underwater outcrops, like a reef or wreck.

Rhys understood then that this moment was a sonar image of Dav's future, pinged back to him. Anthony's mum and the way she looked at her son as if he was her greatest thing in the world; the photos of him on her phone, a stop-frame reel from boy to man; his boyfriend and the way his boyfriend looked at him as if he was the loveliest thing in the world; the ironed shirt on his boyfriend's back, his tie, their smile, the fancy food they were about to eat, the waiters, his dad and the conversations they would have about Maths at Nottingham and who knows what else nonsense too.

'So there's nothing here but the chip shop, is there?' said Rhys later, in the dark, Owen snuffling his little-boy snores. 'So, you're going to piss off to Nottingham or London and leave us?'

It was too much air to take in all at once, too much water to hold in one hand.

Two months later, in the July, Rhys met Lianne, the then love of his life. It was the week of the Rip Curl South West Championship and she had been watching over her brother, the way Rhys watches over his brothers when Phil Fisher is away. Though from Berkshire, miles from the sea, Lianne had creamy tanned skin and a head full of ideas for her future and enterprises that she hoped would save the world. Rhys, for his part, had never given much time to thoughts of wrong or right, to fairness and its opposite, till the Saturday he was teaching grommets in Mr Barker's Sunrise Surf School Special Kiddies' Class, Lianne's little brother among them.

When the lesson was over, with not one but four blue foam learner boards tucked under his long strong arms, Rhys and his wet-suited ducklings came in from the sea and saw: *Hi Who Are You?* written in the sand. A blue glitter-and-gemstone toenail underlined the 'You' as Rhys passed, head down, to cold-shower the piss out of his suit.

Rhys has since wondered if that second word might have been *How* not *Who*, letters jumbling as they do when he reads. But at the time 'Who are you?' was not a question he had been asked before, unless you count the time his foreman, who thought nothing of talking shit, had found a turd and a slug of 2-stroke aflame in the mixer and enquired of Rhys, 'Who do you think you are, you filthy fire starter! Get off my site!'

Rhys stopped by the sand-words and instructed his little 'uns to run along before he wrote a reply – *Only Rhys* – at the end of her question, and she laughed and he laughed and he knew then in his heart that she was the one for him. Which she was not. But she could have been and should have been too, because what she wrote next was, *Can I see you again?*

That put a smile on his phizog.

By late afternoon, Lianne and Rhys were sharing chips and a can of Coke on the breakwater. Rhys treated her brother to an ice cream cone, these being months when he was earning, so the little boy sat with them too, and laughed at Rhys's jokes, especially the ones he did not understand that made Lianne bat Rhys with the flat of her hand till he held her wrists, gentle-like, for he is a gentle man, to stop the tickle.

And when she wriggled free, instead of running, she looped a finger in Rhys's salty ringlet hair and told him he should get it braided with beads by someone good at style, such as herself. She was very forward about such things, including commenting on Rhys's dad's old Levellers T-shirt that he had borrowed that day: 'Vintage, I like it.' And his 90s boardshorts: 'You're different, like you don't care about materialism.'

Telling Dav about Lianne later, Dav said this was a bad omen for future love, but for Rhys it was the first time a girl was kind enough to let him know what changes were needed so that she would find him good enough. Granted, Phil Fisher knows nothing on this subject and is content if his sons turn out in clean togs; beyond that, he does not give a flying crap about the way they look.

What is more, Lianne had asked Rhys about his family and what they did, which gave him a chance to invent the life he wanted – a better life by far.

'My dad's a fisherman,' said Rhys. 'Like my grandad and my grandad's grandad, man and boy. We keep our boat in the harbour. I could show her to you if you liked. She's called the *Maria*.'

Although the *Maria* was, strictly speaking, Jakey's dad's pocket trawler, Rhys could always text Jakey for the keys if Lianne fancied a spin.

'And your mum?'

'She looks after old folks in the care home. You know the big white house on the way out of Lythcombe? Sometimes...' He laughs, the way he sees boys laugh about their mums. 'Sometimes – if she's not on shift, that is – she comes out with us and cooks bacon butties in the galley while we're throwing out the ring-nets. "Stop rocking the boat, Phil!" she goes. "I'm cooking!" You don't have to pay for seafood when you're a fisherman, but when we get sick of fish, Mum makes the best sausage stews. And there's nothing she don't know about rabbits. Now, did you hear the one about the man who walked into a chippy with a twelve-pound bass under his arm?'

'No.'

'He said, "Do you sell fish cakes here?" and the chippy lady says, "No." So the man says, "Shame. It's his birthday today".'

Lianne frowned. 'I'm vegan,' she said.

'Sorry to hear that.'

Soon, Lianne led the conversation to new places. Away, that is, from jokes and towards important matters like microplastic pollution and government spending, so her little brother went off and started looking in rockpools. Till this day spent in her company, Rhys did not know there was more to be cross with than he already had, but Lianne showed him what he had missed. And that was when he learned about anger and its twin brother, blame.

A lot of people in Lythcombe will say that Dav is the more mature brother, but that is because they do not hear the mean things he says behind Rhys's back, nor do they know how slow he is to change his mind about Rhys's business, and quick to call his girlfriends minging cows, and say they were never on Rhys's side.

Take Lianne again – the first to douse the flames of Rhys's over-pumping heart. He had been dead set on the idea of breeding puppies till she poured cold water on his dreams, saying it was immoral to breed dogs when so many of them ended up homeless and abandoned.

The first time she dumped Rhys in front of his mates was two days into their courtship, when he started talking about rabbit hutches. She only took him back after he promised to go vegan – no meat, no fish, no honey, not even his leather belt – as a token of his very serious respect for her feelings.

One sweet cyclonic day, Rhys had borrowed Jakey's board for the Rip Curl South West qualifying heats – a glassy four-foot high-tide break off the harbour spit. Instead of hiding his phone in his towel, he gave it to Lianne and while he was surfing, she looked up his phone history and saw fox-proof hutch designs. She dumped him as he came out the water, saying in her educated voice, 'You want to keep animals in cages? That's up to you, but you won't be doing it with me.'

Granted, Rhys cried in his bed for a whole secret wasted day like a total dick and Dav came in with jammy toast and rubbed his back and said nice things like, 'No great loss, mate. Stupid cow's going home tomorrow, anyhow.'

And, 'What a muppet to miss your roundhouse off the lip.'

And, 'You're our local champion. You're going to

smash the Rip Curl Championship next week, you'll see.'

And, 'I've got a bag of lugs off of Declan, if you want to go fishing.'

'Anyhow,' said Dav about the rabbits, when none of the above made anything better, 'Lianne doesn't know how well you'd keep them. She doesn't know how happy they'd be – everything they ever wanted right there. Clean water. Dry straw. Dandelions picked fresh, just for them. She's not worth it, Rhys. She doesn't understand creatures the way you do.'

Rhys's crying further abated when Dav found these next words, set here for the record: 'If you ever become a farmer, she's not the kind of girl who'd get her arm bloody when you're lambing, is she? Not with those nails.' Warming to his theme, Dav went on, 'And besides, can you see Lianne reversing a tractor up the slip like Mrs Grundy? If you're going to be a fisherman, you're going to need to eat fish, aren't you? Fishermen can't be vegan. You're going to need the kind of girl who'll catch macks on the beach, right?'

At this, Rhys's eyes dried. He sat up. Dav was spot on. Rhys couldn't give up a mackerel buttie, now could he?

But nor would he make the same mistake again and lose a girl he was meant to love.

Three Xannies and a tin of cider into an evening and Rhys will tell you he does not blame Owen for killing their mum, but sometimes it is hard not to. Backalong, Phil Fisher made him and Dav promise never to tell Owen that their mum died giving birth to him because he was too small to understand the reasons why.

And those reasons, Phil told him, included – and this Rhys will never forget, still less forgive – Westminster politics, Her Majesty's ministers, members of parliament, civil servants and the House of Lords. Between them they decided, in their wisdom, to relocate the nearest Accident and Emergency department and the maternity ward thirty-two miles north-northeast of Lythcombe Bay to Exeter.

Before the hospital closed, not mother nor baby ever died under local care. The A&E and maternity wards were moved to make savings but the Fishers were not saved. This is burned into the deepest part of Rhys's mind, like a bullock brand or seaman's tattoo, till the day he dies – a date he expects sooner rather than later, given the banging benzo headaches he gets in the afternoons when he wakes.

Rhys has concluded that one thing babies do not know when they start this life is how things will turn out in the end. They have to be patient. We come here bawling, he knows that: the first time we sniff the air, new-born, we wail and cry. Rhys has seen it in the park – how babies and toddlers spend a lot of time snivelling and not knowing what to do, like when to sleep and what to eat, spitting out food when they are hungry, dropping their carton of juice on the grass when they are thirsty. How can they know that soon, their hands will start working the way their brains instruct, their legs too, and they will be running and climbing and their mouths will say sounds that mean something and they will get teeth in the right places and chew toast instead of sucking it?

And surf. They will surf, too, unless they grow up hydrophobic like Dav, of course.

Phil Fisher has not told Owen that while he was being born, Siân Fisher, who smelled of the wild strawberries that grow on the tor, died; that is, her body broke and could not be restarted. One day, Owen will surely come to wonder if he is to blame because there are no pictures of him with her, unless you count the laughing one of Phil Fisher in his best Marks and Sparks shirt when it was new, his hand on her big belly.

'It happens to ladies in childbirth, not very often,' Phil had told Rhys. 'One in twenty million, which is the same as nearly never.'

Except, 'Not our never,' said Rhys, because they were the unlucky one in all those lucky millions.

After meeting his friend Dodo, Rhys learned that such deaths were more common than you might think, at least since the NHS was 'gutted by savage and reckless cuts'. Hearing this, Rhys tried to imagine by what knife a hospital might be gutted and what its insides would look like. Dodo had searched it up and has given Rhys the figures: one in ten thousand mums die in childbirth in the UK, and in parts of Africa, one in a hundred.

Those babies have a reason to cry.

If Rhys says any of this aloud, Dav tells him to, 'Shut it, or else,' but deep down, Rhys knows numbers will not change the past. His mum never saw Owen walk and talk and run and stand on a surfboard in nearly three-foot waves, which means Rhys never got to see what she must have looked like watching *him* walking and talking and standing on a board and bringing home a gold medal – the pride of Lythcombe.

Rhys has studied mums in the park, to see what his would have been like. Some frown like skippers negotiating paddleboarders in the harbour when their sprogs do basic stuff for the first time. Others take pictures on their phones to keep for another day so they can compare, like Phil Fisher does: little Rhys in his baggy nappy against big Rhys on his Kawasaki.

He has seen a mum sprint to her kid and get there in time, like Spider-Man, before he falls from atop the monkey bars. Not all mums are like that. Some see their little 'un trip or slip and they look tired and carry on chatting or say, 'Get those shoes dirty and I'll—'

At school parents' meetings, Rhys watches mums and thinks his would have been more of the Spider-Man ilk, shooting a sticky web from her palm to scoop him away from the forces amassing against him – in particular, the numbers and letters that dance.

'See that grade 1?' she would surely have said. 'It's only a scribble from a 9. Here, get me a pen...'

That's his idea. And as the only Fisher, except for his dad, who can remember what she was like, he's probably correct. Dav was little and Owen was inside her for their time together, nine months cuddled close, fed, swimming day and night; what a holiday, though not so long as a seal pup.

One snowy winter, they were riding bin bags down the tor and running back up again like howling wolves, their T-shirts steaming. Phil Fisher lay in the snow and Rhys and Dav fell in next to him, *whomp*, breaking the crust, not so cold as you might think, at least not for Owen on their dad's chest, always hot, arms enough to beat the wind, his prickly neck smelling of Brut.

Owen asked, 'What was she like?'

'Your mum?' said Phil Fisher.

What a stupid thing to ask, thought Rhys. *You see her in photos every day; she was very pretty.*

'Yes,' said Dav, leaning close. 'What was she like?'

'Well,' said Phil Fisher, 'she would've hated this, for a start.'

'Why, Dad?'

'Gorse here. Ditch there. Granite scarp. Sheep shit.'

'Maltesers!' Owen giggled.

'Shut up and listen, squirt!' said Dav.

'She would've called us in and chewed my ears off for putting you in peril. She'd have a bale of cotton wool from the old folk's home ready to wrap you up in, my boys.'

Rhys imagined their mum's fingers cold from snowballs, warmed sausage-hot in Phil Fisher's hand. If she'd been there to put Owen's socks on his feet, he would not moan.

'Right, then,' said Phil Fisher. 'At least put your

coats on, lads. It's what she would've wanted.'

So they did. It was very sweaty but they did so all the same, because it made them closer to what she was like.

SIX

After meeting Dodo in September, Rhys collected more black bin bags from under friends' mums' sinks, unlocked galleys and the household cleaning shelf at the SPAR. He knew that most of Lythcombe was owned by absentee landlords so the two rolls Dodo supplied would not cut it. But since hiding the bags in a disused lockup in the yard while Phil was last home, he had almost forgotten about them – though not the colour of Milly's eyes or the way she had looked at him when he had agreed to help.

Dodo's signal to distribute the bags, the first step in a series of protests against unbridled capital greed, came at midnight on the 16th of October while Jakey was ring-netting pilchards with his dad. From the harbour, Rhys could see the wheelhouse lights of the *Maria* zigzagging like a pisshead in the bay as it hunted the ghosts of shoals on its sonar. A cruise ship inched past, east to west, every porthole lit up like Christmas, a column of soot belching from its rear stacks.

Rhys sent Jakey a text:

> Job's on.

In seconds his friend had replied,

> Sorry, mate. Bloody beauties tonight

and waved his phone torch to Rhys, who was sitting on the breakwater.

By one in the morning, after running up and down his seaport town with a bin bag full of bin bags, Rhys had to visit the SPAR stockroom for reinforcements. That was when one of Declan's little brothers, Kieran, in Owen's year, was passing on his birthday e-scooter – his dad was a man unable to keep money in his pocket – and saw Rhys slipping out of the stockroom window.

'What are you doing?' said Kieran.

'What are *you* doing?'

'I asked first.'

'Direct action.'

'Nicking bin bags?'

'Borrowing. It's symbolic.'

Spray filled the air from the high-tide waves licking up the prom. The wind combed their hair flat.

'What's "symbolic"?'

'Something that stands for something else.'

'Like what?'

'Like what holiday homes are doing to Lythcombe. Like saying their greedy owners need sticking in the bin. You're not going to tell on me?'

'I won't. You're Dec's mate. Let me help you?'

'No. You should be in bed.'

'I'll tell.'

'All right then, but I'm seeing you home after.'

Rhys showed Kieran how it was done: holding a bag to the sea air till it was as big as a lobster pot, tying a knot and sticking the knot end in the letterbox. All the while, he kept an eye on the *Maria*'s roll and yaw, for the forecast was Moderate becoming Rough. Soon, there was not a door on the seafront that did not have its own black marker-buoy bobbing in the hooley. Rhys wrote *Sons of Devon* on a few doors with a bit of soft beach brick. Kieran added some smiley faces for good measure.

But the problem with bin bags is that, whilst they may be direct, they are almost certainly not irreversible. On their return, Rhys saw that some had already drifted from their fixings and floated down the promenade before trammelling on lampposts where they flapped like turbot in the mesh of a tangle net.

Going past Mr Barker's shop, the boy said, 'You used to work for Mr Barker at the surf school, didn't you?'

'Ay.'

'You won the Rip Curl South West Regional Championships, but nowadays you're—'

'Done. Let's get you home.'

Later, when wind and bags were spent, Rhys sat in the lee of the quay on a mess of pipes and lines, waiting for the *Maria* to finish chasing the shoals and come in. The tide was out, leaving the boats on higher moorings, barnacles and seaweed on their rudders and keels exposed for all to see. A gull, woken early, stood at his side and together they watched the *Maria SE56* via Rhys's Automatic Identification System app. On his screen, the *Maria* going after a shoal, was an arrow that left orange circles like a toddler scribbling over Lythcombe Bay.

After a nap, Rhys listened to the shipping forecast, issued by the Met Office on behalf of the Maritime and Coastguard Agency at 05:00. Plymouth was a southwesterly, three or four becoming variable at times; Moderate or Good. Biscay was still seven or eight, becoming Rough or Very Rough. *Dad'll be delayed at Santander,* he thought. *They won't sail in that.*

'Where's my bloody black bags?' bellowed Jakey's dad, Mitch, as he brought the *Maria* past the harbour arms and saw Rhys sat on his bollard. 'They were in my shed last week, and now they're gone. Ron and Skippy's, too. What are you boys up to? I'll find out anyway, so you can tell me now.'

'Don't know,' said Rhys. 'Can I help you pack and stack?'

'Not this time. I've got repayments on these new nets and Jakey comes cheap.'

'Child labour,' said Jakey, standing taller than his dad in his yellow gumboots, his meaty arms throwing Rhys the mooring rope. Rhys tied her off, then dropped the water and diesel lines to Mitch.

'I don't want paying,' said Rhys. He climbed down the ladder, skipping the last rungs to jump on deck. 'I don't have anything else to do, so I might as well. Where's this lovely pilchard, then?'

The early gull caught the heads mid-air as father and son worked on deck, throwing the bodies to Rhys, who ran up and down to the fish room below to chip new ice from the block. No one talked, but they fell into a rhythm until it was done, packing the fish in a pretty herringbone pattern that had earned Rhys high praise from a college teacher on his tiling unit.

When Rhys came up for the last time, there was a whole flock of seagulls bickering on deck. Jakey had saved two tea mugs of fish heads for him, 'For that pussycat of yours.'

Rhys chucked a head in the water and a dark silver shadow swam past and swallowed it whole, coming up a moment later to gaze at the three fishermen with sad-dog eyes.

'Don't listen to Sally Seal,' said Mitch. 'You encourage her and she'll help herself on deck. Make the place smell... Help us get these ashore, then.'

While Mitch checked his nets and updated the ship's online log, Rhys and Jakey worked on the boxes – not an easy thing to carry on a jetty ladder at low tide. So many fish, Rhys marvelled how they live in the sea with the *Sally*s and *Maria*s at them all day and night. And how, in most cases, when the brains are out, a thing will die and there end, but seafood of all kinds rise again; every now and then on his way up the vertiginous ladder, eels protested in their icy boxes, thrashing against the lid, and the crabs carried up earlier could be heard scratching as they climbed over each other for the exit.

When the catch was all stacked on a pallet for the forklift, Mitch stuffed the pockets of Rhys's hoodie with two fistfuls of pilchards and instructions to fry them up in a little butter for his dad and the boys.

'Devonian sardines,' Mitch said. 'There's no breakfast finer, though I hear the Spanish like them with tomato sauce so you could try a bit of ketchup. I'm sure Phil knows all about that. Sorry about your pockets. I'd have put them in a black bag but they're hard to come by.'

Kieran's words weighed heavily on Rhys. It was true that he had won the Rip Curl South West Championships last July and no hand could erase the *Express & Echo*'s printed words: 'local hero'. For once, things had seemed to be going his way. A storm had shifted the beach, lifting grit, sand, shingle and dune and throwing them down, easy as you like, a mile along the bay, stirring the water into a tidy six-foot swell in time for the finals. The breaks were more like concrete bucket-rinse water than the polished diamonds the Cornish boys had known since babyhood. Unable to see the bottom, not knowing if reefs might spike their boots and shred their ankles, they took to the waves like ageing grockles hobbled by hydrophobia.

Of course, Rhys showed them how it was done on his sweet Gerry Lopez, hand-finished in Malibu and worth a penny less than four grand if you had bought it from Mr Barker's shop.

Before the horn sounded the end of his twenty minutes of catching waves, Rhys knew he had made enough banging turns to win the competition: namely, a breathtaking, death-defying, gravity mocking set of freestyling dives over the horizon and back again.

That's when he should have come in, but, like all surfers, he thought, *I'll go for one more*. In his head, he was already spending the £2000 prize purse and hearing Mr Barker's gushing praise as photos were taken for *Carve* magazine, making Mr Barker's surf shop the most desirable in Devon.

But tragedy was about to strike. Rhys wiped out on what he claimed was a buoy displaced by the storm or other flotsam in these waters. The force of his falling broke the leash and his weight descended, splitting both fibreglass and varnish.

Rhys's surfboard was lost, winning him a whole heap of hassle because when he made out it was his board that was not entirely the truth. It was a borrowed board he'd found sitting lonely and dry in the surf shop, the perfect length for the conditions – unlike Jakey's longboard leaning by the showers (which was three inches too long) or the shortboard that Phil Fisher had bought him, which was too short, had no fins and a fissure down the stringer.

The gold medal meant nothing to Mr Barker, so

fixed was he on profit and capital. By way of reparation, he confiscated the £2000 prize and Rhys's old board as down payment for many years of labour – which Rhys would've done had Mr Barker not also sacked him from instructing at his surf school.

Thus Rhys was sentenced to sit the rest of the summer in the dry dock of a windy parking shed – and the summer following too – watching grommets on blue foamies bobbing in the shallows. From that day, no girl caught his eye except through window glass, and then only as they stooped to find small change spilled in the sandy footwell of their parents' car, looking past him for a space.

Worse than that, Rhys was forced to take up a construction apprenticeship in September that involved being too close to the wrong kind of sand – that is, filthy sand in the mixer, lime and grit and piss-coloured water – and never near enough to the beach, not even for a pasty at lunchtime.

Broken boards are more than disasters – more than loss of prize money, branded beanies and sunscreen samples – to those young and handsome who have perfected the art of sea, the poetry of waves, the choreography of the ocean. No, broken boards constitute a loss of pride. And pride, once gone, is hard to recover.

Rhys has always been hopeful. Putting lost girls and broken boards behind him, he hatched his plans for a breeding programme of lop-ears. Most people are very bored with French bulldogs and the like, of picking up dog shit and staying in all day so the pup does not feel lonely and cry. With rabbits, you can leave them a bowl of food and water and a bit of hay and they will not mind. They are friendly too, though they seldom know their names.

He has a stack of nice-smelling pine pallets from his dad and will be ready with a prototype hutch, once he has the pocket hole jigsaw and the two-inch coarse-thread screws he needs to finish the job. When these items became available, he will be pursued by riches like that boy in South Wales who breeds unusual lizards, African land snails, mice and Asian cockroaches and sells them all round the world. With too many global orders to keep up with, that Welsh lad has abandoned education, henceforth and furthermore, to work. A lot like Rhys, who plans, with his future great earnings, to fix his Kawasaki, get Dav a new bike that is the right size for his height and bestow upon Owen his own breeding pair of bunnies to name their babies as he pleases, no matter how batshit.

And as for his dad, Rhys swears that when he has sold the small-mammal business as a profitable going concern, Phil Fisher can hang up his regulation European driving kit bag and take up with him on his next venture. No need to drag his trailer across the continent. He can stop here in sunny Devon with his boys.

But if these things don't work out, there are other paths open to Rhys's talents, like line-fishing from the beach to sell macks to the gastropubs of Salcombe and odd jobs with a value in barter: a wax change for the loan of a board, fish for eggs, a gutter clean for some fresh-baked pasties.

A family he knows on the Jubilee estate are farmers without a farm, keeping their pigs, hens and sheep on parcels of spare land, paddocks, lay-bys and abandoned back gardens. They swap meat for grass-rent with some landlords – that is, freshly slaughtered, ready-sausaged in vacuum-packs for the freezer. The rest is honest profit.

He can see it already: a modest flock jostling about his wellies, bleating for their tea.

Come by!

The day after the bin bag action, Dodo called Rhys to thank him personally for his work and sent a video to the group to explain that the absence of media attention was because the system is rigged. He also reminded Rhys about capital and the problems it wreaks, such as 'indefinitely rising house-price bubbles', 'permanent unemployment' and 'staged foreign conflict'. This Dodo knows, having had a private education leading to Modern History and Philosophy at Oxford, out of which he nearly dropped on principle when he saw the ills of it – and also to piss off his father who Dodo says has profited his whole life from injustice and misery.

Rhys scrolled down the replies and saw Milly's lovely face in a thumbnail profile image below Dodo's pronouncements.

> Sterling work

she commented about the bin bags, though it had not made the papers or shaken the world in any way except for new notices asking people to be more careful of their rubbish disposal and to remember that fortnightly collection dates were available to download on the council website.

It did not matter that Mitch had started calling him the Lythcombe Bag Lady. It was enough that Milly was happy with him. *If you liked that*, Rhys thought, *I can do more and bigger. Just tell me and I will do and do again. I don't give a shit what neighbours say about teenage litterbugs.*

> We will make them lissen we will never go back

ran Rhys's comment in the group chat, not attempting the word 'irreversible' in case the spelling of it let him down. Milly added hearts and fists to his words, making the day a better one for all the boredom and skintness of having no job.

Then Dodo called again to ask him if he was ready for the next level.

'I was born ready,' said Rhys.

The next level turned out to be an invitation to Dodo's house in Exeter, where Milly also sleeps, to discuss Mebyon Dewnans' future stratagem in person – *mano*

e mano, as Dodo put it; no longer *in absentia* nor *in periferia*. 'The working classes,' he said, 'must be placed front, centre and to the fore of decision making.'

Getting yourself to the front and centre is harder than it sounds when you're shackled by Stagecoach South West's scanty timetables and have to thumb a lift, but all the same, Rhys asked Phil, who was home for the weekend, if he could see a friend in Exeter.

Phil said, 'Go on, let your hair down. Don't forget we're fishing in the morning. Come home direct if she's not nice, we'll save you some tea.'

Rhys wanted to tell him it was not only about a girl this time but could not find the words. He wished he could think a bit more like Dodo, still more talk his clever way of talking; big words chasing more big words, each neck-and-neck like a string of sheep coming off the moor or a race of ponies or a shower of whitebait in the glittering shallows.

Dodo was soon to be published, his poems telling truths that will hurt his bond-trading dad more than knives when he sees them on the paper of a proper book.

Rhys has since learned you must never trust a poet to tell you stories, but we'll get to that.

That first evening in Exeter, Dodo talked mostly about the sundry contents of his terms at Oxford. Rhys said nothing; his memories of education are filed under 'Forgotten', along with the humiliations of his first construction site placement – Level One, Bricklaying Principles – when he was sixteen.

It was there, as the builders were eating their lunch, that Rhys had stood in the muddy foundations of a building halfway between two states of being – *plan* and *built* – and marvelled at how a house begins as straight lines on blue paper, drawn by an architect's unmuddied hand. Somehow it then becomes a home with a family – in Rhys's mind exactly like Jakey's, his sister Liz slamming her door, and their mum singing; lovely Sarah, with her great wobbling boobs so soft that you would throw yourself off your bike in the hope of her medical ministrations.

Though Rhys had been standing on that building site in windblown mizzle, he fancied he could hear a mum telling her sproglets to take off their shoes and come in the kitchen, where she was ready with some jammy toast or slices of banana, and a kiss.

It was only a stupid building site, only mud and cursing and grit and all kinds of hardcore, but Rhys could see what it would become. *That there'll be the kitchen*, thought Rhys, much like Sarah's, old Nelson farting in his dog basket and the oven hot with a fish pie, secret slices of hard-boiled egg hidden beneath its creamy folds. 'Are you hungry, Rhys? Sit down. You are more than welcome.'

This house will build, thought Rhys. *Flowers will be planted*.

'Stargazing, are we?' said the foreman, eating his pasty. The other builders laughed. 'Now, you get that row done and clean your tools then you can have your manky fish sarnies.'

The men laughed some more, hugging their sides and holding each others' arms for support. Rhys's insides turned liquid. Later, he found his lunchbox filled with quick-dry cement, turning out a sculpture that would win a London art prize, but, 'Where's my bloody sandwiches?'

Rhys did not know, then, that they were all oppressed by the iniquities of our capitalist-imperialist system, none more so than the Portuguese subcontractor who mashed his fingers and couldn't go to hospital on account of his visa expiring.

It's a good job Dodo liked talking. Milly did not speak much, but she was a painter – walls and doors mainly, with slogans of great importance, and also wild landscapes; don't ask which way up they should go.

After smoking a joint with Dodo, words came to Rhys. He told his new friend about what happened to their A&E and Siân Fisher and the maternity ward closing. Soon as this was said, Milly roused from her benzo doze and ran to Rhys's side, her fluttering footsteps as light as smoke. She laid her head on his shoulder, her hand on his knee, and left them there while Dodo sallied forth on the reckless capitalism that had caused the Fishers' misfortune.

Dodo did not seem to mind her closeness to Rhys one bit, which is the opposite of how Rhys would have felt if he was Dodo and if Milly was his girl. He would have cracked the ashtray on Dodo's skull, tipping ring pulls and ash and spliff ends over his cream sofa. Instead, Dodo took a bubbling toke from his watery bong and – proving he was the better man – passed it to Rhys as a token of their great friendship which, though they only met in September, was true and for ever, like brothers.

Dodo's girl, Milly – or Millicent, a beautiful name – smelled of almonds and ladies' soap; as far from Mr Vadic's 2-in-1 blue shower gel (99p a bottle – good for hands, feet, hair and balls) as a hand-finished Lopez is from a plastic Bic off the factory line.

Her hand fell from Rhys's shoulder and rested atop his left biceps, fingers curled round to know what a hard-working motherless man's arm might feel like, before they dropped back to his knee, light as a flower. She looked at Rhys with eyes like rain-swollen clouds. 'I just can't bear it!' she said, pupils wide as Thing's in the night.

Rhys put his big mitt on her delicate paw, gentle-like, and told her he was okay. 'It was such a long time ago. I was tiny then, a little boy,' even though it was not, nor ever would be okay, not by a long shot.

Nor was it even a long time ago because Rhys remembers the day like yesterday – the ambulance four hours late for his mum and Phil Fisher drained of all he was. Rhys is the same boy still, never to grow the way he should inside while his outside charges on regardless, long legs and strong chest and a new red beard on his chin.

Rhys wanted so much to kiss her long hair and then her lips, though she was Dodo's girl, just to take away her sadness for the boy he had once been.

It was wrong of Rhys to enjoy this moment. Who knew girls would be like this – kind to him for the thought of his mum? He resolved never to use this knowledge to his advantage unless unavoidable; to employ other tactics first, like his smile, rescuing little 'uns from rip currents and, failing that, making them laugh and sharing a cone of chips. He takes no credit. Phil Fisher gave him the secret formula: 'Tell a joke. Listen. Be nice.'

Girls in Lythcombe can be pretty but, at twenty-one years old, Milly was stunning in that white cotton blouse that floated on her delicate limbs, no make-up on her face but the cherry lip balm she applied after every draw of weed. No crop tops or Lycra leggings from Topshop for her, but linen fairly traded in India from the stems of hemp and a bamboo scarf from a cooperative in Indonesia (she showed Rhys the label) 'for the better protection of the ecosystem, avoidance of ocean plastics and conservation of marine treasures'.

Also, she had been to art college and would never look at a boy like Rhys.

Love, like waves, is not so bad as fire, though both try to keep the good air from your lungs long enough to kill you. So what, then, is to be done when breathing is not an option, when you are roiled and rolled under and your skin sand-blasted on the seabed?

As a surfer, Rhys has experienced what it is like to be held under for what he knows will not be for long but feels like for ever, the water a mess of white and shell and quartzite grain. The prickling lungs. The bursting. The holding on. There is no more to do but wait.

If you start swimming, how do you know which direction is up?

You might go the wrong way, make fatal errors of judgement, catch a current unknown to any but fishes, your half-eaten body finding the coast of Jersey or France. But if you don't fight, instead let yourself go limp and bedraggled and lifeless, the sea will sooner or later spit you out like a cork float or seine buoy. Such a turn-up may be to your advantage, in a sweet lull between sets so you can catch a full breath and tug your leash and slip on your board for the next. Then again, it may emerge you only long enough for you to take less than a quarter-breath before the crashing weight of another breaking barrel drags you back to the bottom for more.

While girls are complicated, a minefield of potential error, one true fact remains – if Milly saw Rhys sucked beneath the waves only to surface again and take the next and the next and the next, she would have no need of Dodo's poetry.

Dodo is the best man Rhys knows and his ideas the finest. But because Dodo is an artist – if you count poetry as equal to paint – he seldom goes outside into the fresh air. Milly would do better in light, is Rhys's considered opinion. She would do better in sea and wind and with sand underfoot. Exeter is too skanky for a girl like her because in Exeter there is no proper horizon and her horizons should, by rights, be endless.

If only Rhys had a board to surf and a car to drive Milly in. He'd show her the harbour break at the turn of the tide – crests tumbling, rolling, curling – and she would see his sun-brown arms casting out, duck-diving under the invisible line from which the sea spits out or chews up those it deems unworthy. There would be no going back.

She would see Rhys for what he was: more water god than man, light-footed on the waves.

SEVEN

When thinking about Milly, Rhys tries to remind himself that he is a boy no more and has already attracted the attentions of a grown lady, a departure that loosed its moorings a couple of months back, on Rhys's seventeenth birthday. Plans had changed because Phil was away driving, so Rhys was having a laugh with Jakey on Tinder, the dating app where you can invent the characters of rich men called Keith who drive a BMW M4 finished in Estoril blue, and send ladies pictures of your privates until you are blocked.

After a third tin of Strongbow, Jakey gave digital birth to Kenneth, with his nice Subaru Impreza who tests champagne for a living. When Kenneth was reported, Rhys came up with Kurt in his mint-condition split-screen 1966 Land Rover, a good Dartmoor custodian-farmer with thirty acres and a side-hustle breeding lop-ears for pets. The ladies flocked for Kurt's bunnies, till Jakey spoiled it by sending one of them a high-definition photo of the underside of his scrotum.

The moderators were quick on their feet. Poor Kurt was banished instantly.

'Why aren't you laughing?' said Jakey.

'I am laughing,' said Rhys, who was not. He was thinking about when he was six, walking with his mum up on the old coast path, now subsided into the sea, and they had found a rabbit in a piteous state.

'Now, put that down,' his mum had said. 'It's got myxomatosis.'

Rhys marvelled at the softness of its fur. He was too young to see it, but the bunny was not at its best; mange had eaten scabby patches of coat bare and its suppurating eyes were raw. It had no further use for life, sitting as it was, hunched and waiting on the cliff for jaws or beak to call it a day.

'He's crying,' said Rhys. 'Can we take him home?'

'No, love. There's nothing we can do to make him better. It's one of those things. Now, turn your back, my love, and put your fingers in your ears.'

He turned. Half a minute later he felt her hand on his shoulder. The rabbit was gone.

'There. Done. It's for the best. He didn't feel a thing, promise. It is wrong to let them go back to their burrows and make their brothers and sisters ill.'

Not long after, his mum came home from her night shift at the care home with a cardboard box. Inside were two pretty lop-ear girls, very soft and small.

Despite it being time for school, Siân Fisher took Rhys and the box out to their yard, where Phil Fisher had built a hutch made of pine pallets, with a run and a sleeping place, chicken-wire sides and a hinged felt roof. Rhys stuffed the sleeping place with straw and fixed up the water feeders. When it was ready, he took the gentle lop-ears, careful as you like, and put them in the run.

'It's not hard to make a rabbit happy,' said Siân Fisher to her son. 'But there are a few things they cannot get for themselves. It's up to us to make sure they have a dry home, food and water, and to be told nice words. That's it, nothing more. If we go up the lane once or twice a week and pick dandelions, they'll be happy.'

Rhys called them 'Mrs Kevin' and 'Ginger', because he liked the name Kevin and Ginger was ginger.

'Good names,' said Phil Fisher.

'None better,' said his wife.

Siân Fisher could have taught the Longleat small mammal keepers a thing or two about rabbits. It is a shame she had not been alive and with them the day Phil Fisher took his boys on safari; she would have calmed Phil right down when the officious gatekeeper instructed him to park in the deliveries bay on account of the Iveco's prodigious size.

Not only that, had she been there, Siân Fisher would have turned it round in her husband's mind, telling him that having to ride the complimentary shuttle bus was a blessing in disguise, considering the corrosive qualities of macaque shit on a lorry that, in fairness, belonged to Freight Logistics Ltd, for which damage they would have been liable, as per usual, with scratches and sundries taken out of his pay packet.

And what's more, going round the small mammal

enclosures, she could have told Owen the things she had told Rhys when he was small. Rhys remembers her words well: 'There are many fancy kinds of bunnies in the world: the Harlequin, Rex, Angora, Lionhead, Dutch, Polish and the rest. In the wild, they live in big families. They like spending time with friends who will have a game with them, groom them and look out for them, but they need a retreat option, too, so they can get away from a bad situation.'

Mrs Kevin and Ginger were clever bunnies but they did not always like being picked up and fussed and could hold a grudge for hours. But Rhys was very good with them. He knew that neglecting a rabbit leads to suffering and pain, and that some can lash out with claws and teeth if their needs are not met. Small things are not to be underestimated, any rate.

Just over ten years later, celebrating his seventeenth birthday on the *Maria,* not wanting to remember, Rhys swallowed a half of Ketamine, rinsed it down with a good slug of cider and began fashioning a new profile for 'Kenton' on Tinder. Kenton was a European pilchard; that is, a small herring-like fish. He found a good specimen in his catch album: the pelvic fins well-behind that of the dorsal, with the last two soft rays on the anal fin being larger than the others. Its upper parts were olive-green, with blue-gilt flanks and a silvery belly. It was as rich and good-looking a fish as was ever caught in a net.

What did Kenton want out of life? To swim, mainly, and follow his brothers.

Was he looking for love? Yes. And no. A safe place to keep his thousand eggs, perhaps.

Kenton the Pilchard got a match.

> Are you really a fish?

... messaged the lady.

> Yes,

wrote Jakey.

> A European pilchard... Sardina Pilchardus of the genus Sardina.

> No thanks, arsehole.

'Don't worry, Kenton,' said Jakey, wiping tears of laughter from his eyes. 'Plenty more fish in the sea.'

It was then, Jakey bent over from giggling, that Kenton got suspended and Rhys said, 'Let's do one for you, Jacob Grundy. The *real* you.'

'Me?' Jakey wobbled his belly and kicked out his gut-stained galoshes. 'Who's going to want me?'

'They'll like you more than Kenton.'

'Would you put a bet on it?' said Jakey, the hope in his eyes dulling as he arrived himself at the answer. 'No, mate. Let's do one for you. For a laugh-like.'

Jakey had some nice shots of Rhys roundhousing a

glassy six-foot wave at the Rip Curl Championship, and they searched up the one of him in the *Echo*, cropping out Rhys's dad and brothers because it would put the ladies off, seeing their Toby jugs.

'Gurt handsome,' said Jakey. 'You'll have all the girls sighing over you.' This being something Siân Fisher used to tell Rhys when she was flannelling his freckled face before bed, Rhys reached for his Rizlas and eighth of resin to put it from his mind.

'What year shall we make your birthday?' said Jakey.

'Make me over eighteen-like. Twenty-five sounds about right. You work it out.'

While Jakey performed the calculations on his phone, Rhys considered himself at that great age. Perhaps he would be a husband – a dad with a bit of a belly like Phil Fisher. Would he be fitting granite worktops in people's kitchens or loading hods on residential extensions? Or would Jakey's dad have retired by then, leaving the *Maria* to his only son, who would say, 'Come and work with me, mate. I can't run a pocket trawler on my own, can I?' And when they got back, over-brimming boxes for processing, perhaps the King's Arms would be open, a warm place, the fire lit and fishermen buying each other ciders and telling tales about the weight of their catches. In that case, Rhys imagines, he would shake Jakey's hand and say, 'Not this time, mate. My good lady wife is waiting for me with the little squirt. There is no place I would rather be than by her side.'

Jakey turned his phone to Rhys. 'There, the fourteenth of September 2000. That'll do. Now, what name are you going to call yourself?'

'Kevin,' said Rhys.

'What – like your old rabbit?'

'Can he not come back as a pro surfer? A surfer with a farm?'

'Nah. You've got to be you, mate. Stick your own face on the hook, you juicy lug, or the ladies won't bite.'

Jakey swiped right on the first two hundred ladies. No matches. Rhys rolled another joint and all thoughts of rejection were soon forgotten until, later that night, in his bed, Dav and Owen sleeping, Rhys summoned the app and found he had a message from Caroline, a nice-looking forty-nine-year-old divorcée from south-west London who liked yoga.

> I'm down on holiday. Fancy a coffee?

Reading Caroline's message was, for Rhys, like seeing a new map of his world, one in which teenage girls in crop tops, chewing gum, their hair straightened or else curled, who looked at him and then rolled their eyes at their mates and laughed till his balls shrivelled, were set to the margins and a new world of grown ladies was brought to the fore.

Caroline was a grown lady and she liked the look of him. This was new.

They arranged to meet at the café at 3 p.m. Caroline, hair coiffed so that the wind would not trouble it, took off her bug-eye sunglasses and smiled with very white teeth to see him waiting at the table where he had nursed a complimentary glass of tap water for the last hour in case she came early.

'So, you're a local,' she said. Rhys nodded. 'God, lucky you, living here! I'm heading back to London in a few days.' She sighed. 'Six and a half hours. Minimum.'

From this point, Caroline did the talking and if she thought Rhys might look a little young for his age, she did not let on, telling him instead about her ex-husband, Henry, who she admitted she still loved, and their teenage kiddies, Rafe and Crispin, kept safe from emotional storms at Winchester, where she sometimes goes to watch their rugby competitions when her schedule allows. They are doing quite well, although Rafe was considering dropping Latin.

She had retreated to Lythcombe for a week of yoga and no make-up, having found a spiritual seaward Airbnb on the foreshore. She would not give its name on account of personal safety, but Rhys knew the one, a good spot for line-fishing at high tide where he had seen more than a few grockles out at the crack of dawn with their roll mats and easels and laptops open on the pebbles, not a sprat to show for their labour.

Mindful of Phil Fisher's advice, or fearful he would make an arse of himself, Rhys held his peace and all the while she was telling him this, he listened and listened and listened. It took a long time but eventually the wind went out of her sails and she stopped, looked into his eyes and whispered that 'sexual loneliness' had crept into her nights. 'I yearn for someone to touch my body,' she said.

'I know how you feel,' said Rhys, blushing, because he cannot even touch himself when he wants to, not with his brothers farting in their bedroom and their socks two foot from his face.

Sweeping her cold half-drunk decaf oat latte aside, she stroked Rhys's rough breeze-block carrying fingers with her gel nail. 'Say something nice to me,' she said, slipping her hand under the table now to Rhys's strong hod-carrying thigh. 'Even if you don't mean it.'

Rhys swallowed. 'You are very pretty.'

'Thank you, Kevin,' she said, heaving out a great sigh. 'How refreshing.' She fluttered her hands by her face, the way Lianne did when she was drying her nails. The gesture, Rhys thought, was unnecessary, Caroline's nails already being done, so its meaning was unclear. For now, he sat as still and quiet as old Admiral Nelson, Jakey's dog, awaiting further instructions.

'Most guys send dick pics,' she went on, 'or they seem normal and you go on a date and…' She made a funny face. 'You know, before we'd even ordered the hors d'oeuvres, the last one said he liked my tits and asked for a shag in his sports car.'

Rhys's ears went salmon pink. He composed himself. 'Did he tell you the marque?' he said in a soft voice to the tabletop.

She looked delighted. 'Guess which.'

'I don't know.' Rhys forced himself to meet her eyes like a man. 'Maybe an BMW M4 or something, Med blue, alloy wheels?'

Caroline shrieked with laughter. 'Finally, someone who gets it! Guys online think women actually care about cars. And they don't listen, not like you. I might have to visit Lythcombe more often.' She took a nibble of her tea cake and set it aside, though by the looks of her she could do with eating a fair bit more. 'What about you? You're some sort of local surf champion, right? Do you give private lessons? Maybe we can come to some kind of arrangement?' She brushed Rhys's cheek. 'I would pay well for your time.'

Now, anyone in Lythcombe would tell you that once invited, Rhys can talk on the subject of surfing for hours, so it is no surprise that, before negotiating fees, he began with his early days, Phil Fisher pushing him on a two-foot bodyboard in the milky shallows, ending at the Rip Curl South West Championship, the pinnacle of his career, while Caroline massaged his inner thigh and listened to his repertoire of techniques and moves, gasped at their incumbent risks and nodded at which of them were best suited to the contemporaneous conditions.

'Anyhow,' finished Rhys. 'Long and short of it is I won two thousand quid. My photo was in the paper.'

'Bravo!' Her strokes lengthened under Rhys's board shorts till the tip of the nail of her middle finger nearly reached his privates. 'Who was watching? Any female admirers?'

'No. Just Dad and my brothers. And Jakey, that's my mate from school.'

She brought her hand back slow, returning it to the tabletop, and smiled and wobbled her head at the same time. The way she gazed at him then, or rather *inside* him, it was as if she could see the transparent shape of an absent Siân Fisher, not on the beach, not watching him.

Rhys bent his head, feeling very small, and searched for something manly to say in the foamy dregs of the hot chocolate she had bought him, saying, 'My treat, whatever you like... With marshmallows, cream *and* sprinkles? Funny, that's Rafe's favourite.'

Caroline sat up and held her handbag and coat over her little boobs. A slight frown flickered over her face. 'You're not twenty-five, are you?' Rhys shook his head. 'How old are you?'

'Seventeen.'

Gathering a breath, she said, 'And does your mother know you're here?' Her voice was light now, more like Jakey's mum asking if he wants beans with his bacon.

'She passed. When I was little. I still think you are very pretty.'

Like Caroline, Milly was a sophisticated lady. And, also a bit like the way Caroline had looked at him in the café, Milly's eyes burned at him from her place on the sofa in Exeter, though Dodo was the one speaking.

Dodo said, 'Every age has its revolutionaries.' The French had theirs, very bloody. The Russians, too, very cold. Lately in England, insulation revolutionaries blocked the road and nearly got run over by angry Range Rover mums trying to get their squirts to school. And before that, there was Swampy playing badger in tunnels, and backalong still, Guy Fawkes with his fireworks trying to blow up Westminster.

Rhys took his word for it. Dodo has dealt in revolution since the day he was born. He has tied himself up in trees and crawled down muddy tunnels and flown secret drones over Exeter airport (where he won Milly's heart) to stop fossil fuels burning up our world. He has stopped lorries transporting Dartmoor ponies, still living, their eyes rolling, throats parched, to France to be turned into sausages. He says haulage drivers are the worst. They will pull anything for their lords and masters, no matter whether it is plastic crap to fill the shops at Christmas, only to be followed by hauling more plastic to landfill a month later, then crates of chicken ready for the argon gas – all carried out by the working class with 'blatant acquiescence'.

Rhys was also invited to consider the many miles of aviation fuel burned in our greed for an out-of-season grape. Or worse – an avocado.

'Avocados,' said Rhys, after Milly had spoken her piece on the subject of imported groceries. 'Hate the things.'

Though, of course, Rhys hated lettuce more.

Rhys knew then he would never tell Dodo, if questioned, about Phil Fisher's Iveco, nor the baby-leaf in his trailer. It was partly shame but also because, very soon, he would right those wrongs and show that a son can be braver than his dad. Rhys will not pull a load of blatant bloody lettuce for anyone. He will not be the kind of man who leaves Plymouth freight terminal on the only seventeenth birthday his firstborn would ever have.

Rhys then remembered the time Lianne had asked him who he was and concluded this was a sadder question than he had first thought. Truth was, he did not know. He felt worthless, a nothing – a failed apprentice when he should be a warrior.

In the reckoning of himself, Rhys found he was not the words, but the dot that comes at the end of them.

.

Like that. Here comes another, in case you missed it:

.

But with Dodo, Rhys could be more than something small – he could be a hero of the revolution.

EIGHT

It is a mizzling day in Lythcombe Bay, at the end of the October half-term holiday. Being a Friday, Phil will be driving his lorry down the ferry ramp in Plymouth later today so Owen is bouncing off the walls. Rhys and Dav have taken him to the park, where there is a wooden play frame in the shape of a pirate ship for little 'uns to climb. The playground also has monkey bars, a swing, a slide and an obscene sculpture by a famous local artist of a sea serpent titled *Leviathan*, sponsored by the European Union. After ten years of Devonian rain, salty air and the work of teenage NEETs high on acid, it now looks more like a great stiffy and therefore has no place in a children's playground.

Once they've arrived at the park, Owen makes for the climbing frame, uttering the hideous howling monkey cries they heard at Longleat.

Across the park, the so-called 'Regeneration Zone' men are out again with their tripods. Rhys knows a surveyor when he sees one. They lurk on building sites wearing wax jackets over their suits and ties, and hard hats for no good reason, as if they think the sky will fall on their heads. These last months, they have come sniffing around Lythcombe. When Phil Fisher asked what they were doing, they told him they were there to ensure that rigorous housing standards were met. 'Well, that's good, then,' said Phil Fisher.

Rhys sits on a swing, crumbling resin into a joint on his knees while Dav sits on the bench looking at pictures on his phone of pretty singing boys to pass the time. He is zooming in on Harry Styles's tattooed torso when Owen brings him a notebook he found under the slide, a bit soggy from the weather, to ask his considered opinion. Owen thinks it is a spy book because it's full of codes.

'You might be right,' says Dav, knowing it is not a spy book because, at least up to this point in his life, dramatic things do not happen in Lythcombe. But he plays along. 'See those numbers? If we had an enigma machine handy, we could tell what the enemy was planning.'

Owen reads aloud: 'Ninety-seven, thirty-nine, forty-one, Daffodil Cottage, check pool pH, six three two one... Dav, what's the enemy planning?'

'Invasion, probably. What else things do enemies do?'

'Wait!' says Owen. 'Do we have an enemy, then?'

'Ask Rhys.'

Being long past school where we are 'all friends together, children, no unkind words please', as Mrs Hill would say, Rhys knows a thing or two about enemies.

'Ay, squirt, we do,' he says. 'Construction sites have the worst.'

Rhys gets a text from his dad in Plymouth harbour.

> Sorry, lads. Back of the queue in customs. Be a couple of hours.

Rhys walks away to light his spliff while Owen sits on the swing peeling more soggy pages apart.

> **8462 Fisherman's Cottages** – check zip wire.
> Turn off heating manually.
> **2391 Foundland Park House** – check no dogs.
> **0905 Long View Farm** – check hot tub pH.
> Use the 300-count Egyptian cotton.
> Replenish complimentary fruit bowl.

Soon Owen goes back to his game of monkeys while Dav turns pink at the sight of Jung Kook's lean abs. Happy days.

Apart from the surveyors out sizing up the Jubilee estate, no enemies come that day, not the sort you can see, any rate. *But that's the trouble with Dav and Owen*, Rhys thinks, *they cannot see.*

In Rhys's mind, they are like fledgling terns bobbing about waiting for their dads to come vomit up some tea. They think they're safe. They don't know that dolphins and osprey don't mind a change from fish now and then.

One day he hopes they will see them – the forces out to make their lives lesser than they should be – and they will thank their brother Rhys for taking direct and irreversible action.

When the brothers get home, Dav tells Owen to give him the code book. 'It's important,' Dav says. He knows full well it's some cleaning lady's notebook. He will put a notice up in Mr Vadic's shop so she can get it back.

'No,' says Owen. 'It's mine. I saw it first.'

'Shut up, I'm older,' says Dav, and hides it from Owen under the floorboard where Rhys keeps his skunk and the emergency fiver, and there it stays till the night of the Lythcombe riot when the meter runs out and the electric fire cools and Dav needs somewhere warm to study for his tests, thinking, *If I pass, they'll give me a university mentor and I'll read Maths at Nottingham.*

And leave his brothers, no doubt, his brothers who love him. But this is yet to come.

Owen's inflated expectations for his ninth birthday started to cause some concern for Rhys and Dav, like watching a lilo drift offshore towards a reef. What they needed was money, but being off-season in Lythcombe, with a cold sting in the air, there was no work to be had servicing the grockles with car parking or glass-collecting in the pub. So, on their way home from the park, with Phil still at customs in Plymouth, they decide to try the evisceration line at the fish processors, where their mates' mums and nans work, hands faster than the eye can follow.

'You wait here and crack this,' Rhys tells Owen,

sitting him down outside the fish factory with his Rubik's cube set to chaos. 'We're auditioning for a part.'

'Hope you get it,' says Owen, who already knows his lines for the Christmas show.

Earlier that week, Rhys had assured his middle brother that it was not to be a permanent arrangement, so would in no way affect Dav's studies and Mrs Morris would keep an eye on Owen for a few hours if Phil was delayed, like today.

They would, he had calculated at the rates being offered on the noticeboard, only need to work two weekends to get the items Owen had been busy sketching – a new rod, a 6x6 speed cube of fiendish difficulty and a tarpaulin for the roof of his pallet palace – plus one further Saturday for the things they'd need for a tidy party.

'Sausage rolls,' said Dav, making the list on his phone.

'Ice cream,' said Rhys. 'Balloons filled with that stuff…'

'Helium.'

'That's the one. Don't forget party poppers. And something healthy – carrot sticks and hummus.'

'What kind of weirdo likes freaking hummus?'

'Granted. Scratch that.'

'What about cake?'

'Ay, chocolate, nine candles. We'll bake it ourselves…' *Like Mum*, he thought, *though it will never be as good*. 'Enough for the whole class, any rate, and all his friends invited… Invites!'

'Check. Are we doing party bags?' said Dav, smiling at the thought.

Rhys spun round, eyes wide. 'Ay. Proper presents inside, too. Tidy stuff, like. No expense spared.' They walked on, savouring the moment it would be, the looks on the kids' faces. The looks on their mums' faces. 'It will be a party so wild, folk will be talking about it for years, like, "Remember when Owen turned nine?" they'll say. "Now *that* was a party!"' His face fell. 'There's thirty-two of them in Year Four. Might take another week.'

'That's okay,' said Dav, clapping Rhys's back. 'We'll do it.'

Now, with Owen waiting outside, Rhys and Dav have a few minutes to impress. They step inside, their ears filling with the sounds of scraping metal, running water, a great clanging and the low vibrating hum from the generators. It smells like the fish room in the *Maria* and the floors are slick with blood and mucus.

The brothers stand to the side as fish agents hurry past in orange gumboots and white coats, then fall in for a health and safety briefing.

Next comes the fish. Rhys winks at Dav to say, *We've got this.*

'Remember, you cannot eat the guts of a fish,' says the lady-foreman, a tiny woman of advanced age. 'Guts will spoil the meat so must be removed. It is not difficult to do so.'

Rhys knows this much and more but listens all the same, the factory feeling very still and firm under his feet, no gulls squawking or fighting overhead. A lobster crawls round a tank, its pincers taped shut. The strip lighting hurts his eyes.

'If your fish is live-catch, you will need to subdue it first,' she tells them. 'Use a blunt object to strike the head to make him unconscious. Puncture his brain with your marlin above the eye. Jiggle the spike to cut through his thinking; this is the most humane method. Watch how Melanie does it.'

Declan's mum smiles at them and takes an ice-sleepy skate. *That particular fish*, thinks Rhys, *will never swim again*. As her blade goes in, the guts come out.

Seeing Dav wince, Rhys squeezes his brother's arm and says, 'Pass the parcel. Fizzy pop.'

'Diet Coke?'

'No. Full fat.'

'Bloody hell, they'll go mental.' Dav swallows and focuses his attention on how the skate's white flesh comes off in strips. 'I can do this.'

'Rule number one,' the lady-foreman says in her squeaky voice. 'Never work under the influence of drink or drugs.' She gives Rhys a long look over the top of her glasses, as if she has just seen him an hour ago rolling spliffs on the swings in Jubilee Park. 'It will addle your brain and cause harm to yourself and others. Now, take a fresh apron and stand by this station…'

The brothers take their places at a row of sinks.

'Not you, Dav. You're underage for knives.'

'But…'

'Wait for your brother in the office, please.' She turns her attention to Rhys. 'Right. Rinse that there bream under cold water. Grip his tongue and pull down hard to rip out his gills. That's it. Proper job. Go on. Now stick your knife near his tail. Spread his sides, careful, now. Pinch those organs between thumb and finger and pull them nice and slow and gentle-like. If he has a kidney, scoop it out with a spoon; look for a small bean-shaped organ. If his head isn't fully off, give it a little twist. Rinse. Discard your gubbins in the grinder. Good effort, well done. Now wash your hands.'

Rhys takes more care over the job than he does on the *Maria*, showing off his skills to Declan's mum, who watches him with the side of her eye. Not a fish spoiled, not an incision awry; his cuts are as precise as a surgeon.

Owen is lucky to have a brother such as Rhys with all the things he knows and can do.

'So do I have the job?' Rhys asks on the way to the office where he joins Dav. He can already feel the carbon fizz of a new-opened bottle of pop up his nose, the headache of thirty-odd squirts tearing up Jubilee Park, Owen taking a long run-up and headbutting Rhys's stomach in the way he does when he is at his most pleased.

'You were magic,' the lady-foreman says. 'A little slow, but you you'll speed up with practice. You can start next week.'

The following day is Saturday, the last of the half term

holiday. Phil is finally home. He's had a sleep but he can't stop. He's driving again, only locally in a dinky 7.5-ton lorry for John Lewis. He will take Sunday off for fishing, he promises.

The brothers are on the harbour break, waiting for the tide to drop. Most grockles have towelled off and gone home but three old men roll up in a brand new VW day van. Their sliding door whispers open on its well-oiled rails and they pull on mitts and suck their bellies into 4mm winter suits. The swell has turned mean and it takes a special kind of muppet to go in.

'Complete door knobs,' says Rhys, watching them roll neoprene hoods over their bald slapheads. 'It's like they're putting on condoms.'

'What's condoms?' says Owen, legs dangling over the breakwater, holding his spade and bait bucket.

'Nothing you need to know yet,' says Dav.

The sea is nasty. Too rough to fish, the brothers bring in their lines. All the same, the men start paddling out behind the breakers where they sit on their mint boards and chat like full-bellied gulls after the fleet has come in.

'Are they going to get on and catch a wave?' says Rhys, his red forelock flattened by the mizzling rain.

'You can do better than them,' says Owen. 'Least you can stand up.'

Rhys pulls Owen's yellow sou'wester hat that once belonged to their grandad over his eyes – a way of saying, *Thanks, mate. Appreciate it.*

'I mean, if you still had a board,' says Owen. 'Like,

if you hadn't—'

'Shush now,' says Dav, nudging Owen's little ribs. 'Don't remind him. It pains him. He knows.'

As a former local champion, surfing is something Rhys would like his brothers to master. Owen had been making excellent progress, till Rhys lost his job with Mr Barker. Dav, though fifteen now, has never been light to his feet on the drop. He can't do a bottom turn or carve off the top, not like Rhys by the same age; easy in the air, cheers from the beach, fifty quid in your pocket, thank you very much. As a surf school instructor, Rhys stood by his brothers, pushing them into the green and yelling, so they can hear over the waves things like:

'Now, surf like there are girls watching.'

'Paddle! Paddle! Paddle! Stand up!'

'… Yes!'

'Oh…'

'No worries, mate. Try another.'

One day, Dav may be able to make a bottom turn, but he will never dance like Rhys on the shoulder, toes to the nose. This much is evident. All the same, the winter sea in front of them now would spit most surfers out. The sideways squall locks everyone behind misted-up car windows, bars of rain on the glass, not an ice cream or football in sight.

'Idiot,' says Rhys, but not about the surfer who has just caught his edge and wiped out. Rhys is still thinking of his championship surfboard. That Gerry Lopez Lightning Bolt would probably be his best ever surfboard of all time. But boards don't work out for Rhys, no matter how much he tries.

A lady gets out of her car, hunches forwards cupping wind-battered ears. Hand-scrambling her way up the breakwater stones, those that keep Lythcombe safe, she yells at one of the wetsuited dots in the sea and waves her arms like she's bringing in a jumbo jet. Waves thunder back like double-bladed Chinooks taking off.

A container ship on the horizon looks a bit choppy too. Its rusty deck will be swamp-washed, like the brothers now when this big one hits. *Woosh. Slop.*

'Tide's going out. Let's get on with it,' says Rhys. 'Lugworm don't dig themselves.'

'You two go,' Dav tells Rhys. 'I'm going for a run.'

So Rhys takes Owen along the beach to find ugly lugs for their promise of fish. They will all go out on the *Maria* tomorrow so will need as much bait as they can get.

The rain is lighter now, visibility moderate. A crack in the clouds grants compassionate release to a grey winter sun, ankle-tagged on bail till spring. Owen's sou'wester falls over his eyes. The oilskin is cracked but keeps him dry and makes a good sandcastle mould when called for.

'Remember when Mum came home from wiping bums at the old folk's home,' says Owen, 'and brought us Chinese crackers in a bag and sweet and sour chicken and egg fried rice and we ate till we burst, which you did, all over the sofa? It reeked to high heaven and Dad had to carry you out to finish the job in the yard.'

Rhys shakes his head and says, 'No, I don't, and neither do you. You weren't even alive.'

According to his school results, Rhys is not very good at remembering, but it is more the case that he prefers not to. For example, he doesn't like to remember the humiliation of that building site or the day he won the Rip Curl Championship and came home boardless and broke. Most especially, he doesn't care to remember when he was Owen's age and their mum was around.

'Who says I wasn't alive?' says Owen. 'I was swimming in her insides, listening to every word said.'

Owen claims it sounded like grumbling explosions in his ears, and when she ate, he tasted the same, and when she slept, he kept watch. 'Fists at the ready,' as Phil Fisher says, 'little prize fighter he was.' And when their mum held Rhys and Dav, Owen says he held them all too, a smidgen away from their heads on her belly.

'Shut up,' says Rhys, not liking this bit remembered. 'Go find a cockle with two legs.'

But Owen is not easily dissuaded, telling Rhys next what happened when Phil Fisher had put on a soppy song and pulled their mum up to dance, arm's length, on account of Owen being inside her belly, taking up all the room and dancing too. Dav joined in, his beat more like dancing in a metal mosh pit, jumping off the sofa.

'You held out, Rhys, till Mum yanked your arm and said, "Let's go, big boy. Show us how it's done. For me, my love?" You danced then, you did.'

'No, I didn't. You're daft as a carrot, you are.'

'Did. Dad said.'

Owen doesn't know when to shut up. He tells Rhys how their mum had said, 'Will you look at that? Only boys can dance like that. It's a lovely thing when a boy dances.' And hearing her words, Dav had slowed his tempo to that of Rhys and they joined arms the way Mr and Mrs Fisher were joined, ballroom-style, beam-jointed, load-bearing ply, and swayed.

'Tell me what Mum was like, again,' Owen asks Rhys, now digging for lugs in the mud-sand, gale over, the rain slight now, tide receding. 'Tell me the story about another time we had. If you don't, I'll tell you anyway. I *was* there.'

The hills behind Lythcombe are no trouble at all for Dav. In summer, he takes the back lanes, loses the queue of caravans going west, and half a mile later all engine sound is muffled. Grockles call it 'Peace and quiet at last', but it's far from that, because you will most certainly hear all manner of noise. A blackbird's brain-splitting song. Pony-stamp. Gorse-rattle. Buzzard-mew. Bullock-bellow. A sheep bellyaching for her lost lamb. Wind crackling your ears. Grasshoppers humming with their legs.

Skylarks fill the air with their trill racket and Owen is usually whining, 'Slow down!', miles behind, because he is too a-feared to ride his bike.

Dav does it three times a week, this dash up the

lane to the tor and back. The sweat to the top is worth it for the sea sparkling in your face – like a golden Saxon hoard – and the moor at your back, granite rocks all around. Stick your head in close and you will see that granite is crusty with jewels.

'If you could crack those diamonds out, you'd be a rich man,' Rhys told Owen once. 'Lythcombe Natural Healing sells them for £2.50 a teaspoon. They call it quartzite – for spiritual protection and regeneration-like, but what do they know?'

You can also count nineteen sorts of lichen growing on the rocks – a tiny world of colour, like the Barrier Reef on *Blue Planet*: some bearded, some flat, some like red matches, others orange, yellow and silver; a seabed tipped out on the hill.

Higher up, on the open moor, collie dogs can sometimes be seen galloping wide round a flock of sheep, the farmer in hot pursuit on his quad bike. Ravens circle till crows mob them, swooping at the last when they see the ravens' prodigious size and think, *Flipping hell, I'm out of here.*

'What a place to live,' says Phil Fisher, when he is home for the weekend. 'What a place to be alive!'

Here, hill and moor pull northwards, purple-green, smudged with pine. Rhys often sticks Owen on his crossbar for the freewheeling ride down. One of these days though, Owen is going to have to learn to pedal himself, like every other little squirt in Mrs Hill's Year Four. Go to Jubilee Park or the sand flats and there they all will be – quarter-grown boys and girls, off and away on their wheels. Brake-burning, sole-scuffing, suicide-cornering, skid-stopping.

Anyhow, when his bike broke, Dav took up running, inspired by the copies of *Runner* magazine and *Men's Fitness* he keeps under his mattress.

While Rhys and Owen are digging lugs on the beach, Dav likes a bit of time for himself. The thin soles of his trainers feel every stone but instead of slowing down when the gradient bites, he runs faster, his pulse fit to burst. For all his clever, mathematical ways, Dav is, in this respect, Rhys's equal and a fine athlete, if a tad on the skin-and-bony side.

Who needs a bike, when you've got a good set of lungs?

At the top, by the old farmhouse now used by grockles for their holidays, he takes a screenshot of his time. Door to moor in 00:18:36. He looks forward to showing Rhys, who's never bettered twenty minutes, even in the days before weed blackened his lungs.

To celebrate, Dav dunks his salty hair in the granite trough set in the hedge, covered in moss and brown ferns and fed by a spring from the hill so the water is clean and cold, then he splashes his pits and dips in his head again. His brain freezes.

He comes back up and watches the view for a moment, imagining the long-gone barks of sheep dogs holding back-and-forth arguments between the now-ruined smallholdings hugging the hill, in the times when they were still farms run by father and son. He dips one more time. Then a car engine makes him pull his shaggy head out of the trough, spraying water like an advert for ladies' shampoo.

Dav's mouth falls open when he sees the vehicle. It is an open-topped sports car, old-fashioned suitcases on the back seat. It pulls out of the farm driveway past two pig feeders filled, not with the boiled scraps and other swill that were once its purpose, but with plants, now bedraggled in the late-October winds off the sea. Having no interest in fine cars or women, Dav cares not that it is an Audi TT convertible driven by a pretty lady.

It's the man in the passenger seat who has his attention.

He is very handsome, run Dav's thoughts. *Is he her boyfriend? He looks like he's been to university. He'll have clean hands, too, no doubt. Soft, they'll be, never smelling of fish. What might it be like to kiss a man like him? I will find out one day, if I go to university.*

The car stops. 'Hi!' says the lady. 'Are you local?' Dav nods, water soaking his top, pulling his eyes away from her man and his nice clothes. 'Oh my God, lucky you, living here! This is our special place. You know when you work so *hard* and you just need to...' She smiles painfully. 'Escape?' Dav nods again, knowing full well that feeling. 'We're heading back to London now. Unfortunately.' She sighs and pats the man's knee. 'Seven hours.'

Dav hopes the man will look up from his navigation app so that Dav might see the colour of his eyes.

'Eight,' says the man, not looking up. 'Traffic.'

The lady takes a last look at the view, smiles and presses a button. The roof of their car folds over on itself like a slow barrel wave made of origami. But before it lands, the man looks at Dav and says, 'Enjoy your run.' Dav's cheeks burn red hot. He would run all the way to London for a man as beautiful as this.

She presses another button; secret electrics click and Dav is witness to this slow-sliding of security gate across a luxury rental property set up only for the purposes of unearned wealth. As it whirrs shut behind the car, letters wrought in iron by the hand of a smithy spell out *Long View Farm*.

The cleaning lady's book, thinks Dav. *I must remember to get it back to her.*

Truth be told, had Dav picked a different route for his run, it would have saved the Fishers a whole heap of misery.

NINE

While Dav is running up that hill with no problem, Rhys is walking with Owen along the beach.

The smell hits them first, then they see the dead fish.

'Leave it,' says Rhys, when Owen stoops to stroke the scales, like you would a poor rabbit or ferret or other such pet found dead or sleeping. 'It reeks.'

'So would you,' says Owen, 'if you were put on dry sand and your proper place was water.'

'My proper place *is* water.'

Sand is no place to die and no place to live if you are a fish, yet it doesn't feel right laying him to rest with his own kind – a watery grave, stripped to the bone by the sharp teeth of his cousins. Owen finds two sticks to flick the dead fish over the seaweed left by winter storms and gets it above the tideline, so that the sea cannot wash it away.

Though it stinks worse than Phil Fisher's socks after a week sleeping in his cab, a gull eyes the fish, his grey baby too – hungry-watching, brave-planning.

'Just you try it,' says Rhys to the gulls, knowing

Owen will not give them his new fishy friend. 'Shoo!'

Rhys waves his arms and the birds hop to the air – a few flaps, a safe distance.

'Where do dead fish go, Rhys?' says Owen. 'Into heaven?'

Fish cannot shut their eyes so it looks at the boys and smiles a lipless smile. Rhys wonders at the fish's life, the things it had seen: ankles, children playing, seabirds paddling, the pink bellies of lilos, windsurf masts leaving the water, plop of wakeboarders landing and gone again. And surfboards, as perfect as girls and easier to touch, and feet strapped in big-wave boards, the paddle-dip-glide of kayaks and rowing boats, jet skis' tantrums like a wasp nest, silent yachts (very peaceful), catamarans flipped on one hull, leeward clinker lines tinkling. The big whomping slow prop-turn of cruise ships, container ships, super-trawlers, ocean liners.

And surfboards again; the way water parts and comes together again around a fin.

All that in a lifetime. Makes you think.

'I'm sorry you had to die,' Owen says. 'I'm sorry you were born a fish and not a boy.'

Who can blame him? What a world fish live in, running from one danger to the next, fleeing for their silvery lives. Did they think the cliffs a land-wave come to smash on their heads?

'Are you done yet, mate?' says Rhys, standing guard to stop dogs and greedy gulls taking Owen's fish-friend. 'I'm freezing my balls off here.'

'Wait! Get us some shells?'

Rhys chucks Owen a nice half-scallop and some empty limpets, once alive, now clean as a whistle. Owen sets a limpet-hat over the fish's upwards eye to make it dark and help it sleep. He leaves a crack of light in case it gets scared.

'He needs a name,' Owen tells Rhys. 'I'll call him Morris.'

'Good name,' says Rhys, looking for sea glass. 'Mrs Morris drinks like a fish.'

'Good night, Morris-fish,' go the words of Owen's song. 'Morris in a bed of sand, seaweed blankets, shells around. Good night, sleep tight, don't let the sand fleas bite.'

'Shall we tuck him in with sand, now?' says Rhys beside him, counting smooth buttons of sea glass into Owen's hand like a magic kind of coinage.

'Morris-fish, good night,' he says again, decorating the grave with red, green and yellow sea glass. 'Hope you dream of what fishes dream of when their holidays are starting and their waters are quiet and their dads are come home from Spain.'

'Tidy,' says Rhys. Then he throws Owen atop his shoulders so the boy can ride with the bait bucket in his hand like 'Bill Brewer, Jan Stewer, Peter Gurney, Peter Davy, Dan'l Whiddon, Harry Hawke and Old Uncle Tom Cobley and all!'

The rain gone, the sou'wester swings from its string down Owen's back.

'And Old Uncle Tom Cobley and all! And Old Uncle Tom Cobley and all!'

From his vantage point on Rhys's shoulders, Owen next spots a dinky rolled-up carpet, half buried in the stones. It belongs to Mr Vadic, the special one he uses for his five-a-day prayers. It was nicked from the storeroom a few weeks ago by one of the town junkies, the last time they broke into the SPAR. Mr Vadic had been very upset and put his phone number on the noticeboard and bus shelter because his carpet was special in a religious kind of way, though you wouldn't know it now, being all manky with sand and seaweed. Rhys tells Owen what he had once learned in religion and philosophy lessons about how Muslims roll their carpets out to Mecca.

'Where Sarah plays bingo in Torquay?'

'No, squirt, the holy place.'

'Is Torquay not holy?'

'Not in the same way.'

The brothers turn their faces east, where the sun comes up. Rhys decides he will rinse the carpet in the freshwater stream and shakes it out; very pretty, it will be, a world in itself, wet reds and golds like sunset. Then, 'Holy crap!' cries Rhys, jumping like he has stood barefoot on a weever. 'Pardon my language, squirt.'

'What is it?' says Owen, scared to see his brother like this. He looks. 'It's only a crab.'

'A big 'un,' says Rhys. 'Hiding in the carpet. Took me by surprise, is all.'

The crab gnashes its pincers at them. But the trick with red edibles is to not be afraid and grab them by their backs. Granted, they can snip a man's finger clean off his hand, but if you do it quick, those choppers can't chop you.

Owen calls the carpet crab a 'grandaddy' – perfect for tea: soft white flesh, dash of vinegar, slice of bread. 'Crab sarnies!'

'We're putting him back,' says Rhys. 'Doesn't feel right.'

Owen, who knows that Rhys flees from boiled crustaceans in case he pukes, says firmly, 'I found it so it's mine.' He frowns, but before he can add, 'Please?' Rhys seizes the crab, quick as a flash, and walks to the low-tide rocks. The crab's legs wave hello to the sea and off he gallops into the deep of a pool.

The carpet comes up tidy, clean of sand, cold stream-water run over the threads like new. Rhys sticks it on spikes of marram grass to dry, and the brothers finish filling their bucket and set their rod. With mackerel, you can't always tell if it's a shoal or sunlight catching the waves. Not many jump on their lines today.

Back on Rhys's shoulders, Owen moans about how they could have sold the crab at the pub, or at least have swapped it for some chips.

'I know we could have,' says Rhys. 'But it was living in a holy place for weeks. If you don't respect that, what've you got? Come on. Time for shopping.'

Mr Vadic's SPAR on the seafront is located three boarded-up shop windows down from the chippy. Mr Vadic had a wife once, who died of war long before the brothers were born, so they have something in common, even if they don't speak of it. The door swings fast, as if to slam, hisses and slows at the last when the cylinder kicks in to save fingers, and mums tell their kids, when they flinch, 'Don't be a dafty. Nothing'll hurt you.'

Rhys would like to hear this said to him once in a while.

Mr Vadic runs a tight shop, one kid at a time, so Rhys tells Owen, 'Wait outside, squirt.' That way, Owen won't see the tin of sketty hoops he will stick down his pants, to go with the chips they will get next from Angie. He leaves the prayer mat outside for now, in case he is caught and accused of stealing that too.

Rhys waits for his neighbour Mrs Morris to get her vodka, and the man from the end house his lottery ticket, and the bell to say they've gone – ding for in, ding for out. He hides the sketty and goes to the till to buy a 30p Freddo.

'Good afternoon, Rhys,' says Mr Vadic.

'Is it?' says Rhys.

'We're alive. It's not raining any more. A piece of cliff came down last night. The fossil hunters are back. Good for business.'

Rhys knows the fossil hunters. They dig in the rocks like they're on the allotment, little rakes and mini-spades.

Mr Vadic taps his head. 'They should wear helmets.' He shuts the till. It makes the sound of a shovel in gravel. 'Rocks could fall on their heads.'

'Yeah, well,' says Rhys, 'they're in a hurry. Two or three tides and sea takes everything.'

Mr Vadic smiles as if he knows about how that feels,

the way time goes too fast, and then not fast enough, like tides that sprint and rake.

Rhys meets his eyes and says, 'You're right, though. Some people don't have enough respect for cliffs. They think they can go up there and muck about and falling won't happen in real life.'

Rhys pays for the Freddo. Mr Vadic slides a double Mars bar in with the change. 'I'm running a special offer today,' he says. 'Buy one Freddo, get one chocolate bar and a tin of Heinz Alphabetti Spaghetti free.' He comes round the counter, turns the sign to *closed* and points to his watch. 'Time,' he says.

'I'm sorry,' says Rhys, shame burning his brow. 'I take things from you. Sometimes.'

Mr Vadic nods. 'It's okay.' That's a smile under his bushy frown. 'I know you Fishers. You are good boys.'

Rhys posts the carpet under the metal shutters as they go down. Inside the carpet, Mr Vadic will find three silver-blue tiger-striped macks, ready-filleted and wrapped in the very latest edition of the *South Devon Express & Echo*.

The next day is the last Sunday in October. It is no more than a 5 on the Douglas scale (Moderate sea, winds Light) so, as promised, the Fishers go out on the *Maria*, an inshore pocket trawler, their rods on the stern. As usual, Jakey has taken the wheel and his dad is cooking bacon butties in the galley while Phil Fisher chews everyone's ear off about excise paperwork, visas,

European Certificates of Professional Competence. Rhys and his brothers watch the rod-tips for bites.

They are all present and correct, fishing together the way Rhys likes – none left ashore or on another continent. Such times don't come often but they do happen.

First, they get six dogfish, skin too leathery for a keen knife to cut, so they chuck them back except for a small one. 'Dispatch it, squirt,' Rhys tells Owen, guiding his hand while the fish flaps and gasps. It takes Owen a few goes with the priest tool to make the dogfish give up its hold on life. Rhys gives his brother an encouraging smile to lessen the small loss you sometimes feel fleeting across your soul when you kill a thing.

'Good man, squirt. Now we wait for the big one.'

'Pacific yellowfin tuna?'

'That would be a bloody miracle. We're not in Honolulu, mate.'

'Colossal squid?'

'Don't be soft.'

'But I read about them…'

'Rubbish,' says Jakey from the wheelhouse. 'They don't live in these parts.'

'Anyway,' says Rhys, 'you'd need to be a sperm whale to get one of them.'

Jakey laughs. 'Sperm, ha, ha!'

'Whale,' says Rhys, thumping Dav's arm, Jakey being out of reach. 'Sperm. Whale.'

'Moray eel, then?' says Owen.

'Indubitably,' says Rhys, cutting nylon knots in a broken lobster creel while he speaks, a dark look in his eye.

'What's that mean?'

'Don't know, but it sounds good.'

'Your brother's been spouting all kinds of shit lately,' says Jakey. 'Like he's swallowed a dictionary.'

Rhys laughs but then straightens his face. Revolutionaries would not laugh, not with all the wrongs they had to right. In Exeter, Dodo said he must be alert at all times and in all places. It was coming: direct and irreversible action. It will take toughness, the quality of manliness; *vertù*.

Rhys points his knife at Owen and says, 'Keep your fingers in your pockets when we bring it in, squirt, or you shall have stumps for hands for the rest of your days and your willy will shrivel and die. That's what happened to Dav.'

At this, Rhys and Jakey put their mitts in their life jackets and laugh at Owen, very close to the way the men laughed at Rhys on the building site, though Rhys does not see it at the time. He presses home his point, looking all the while at Dav. 'How will you learn to ride a bike without hands?'

'I can ride a bike,' says Owen. 'A bit.'

'Going to turn out like Dav, the rate you're going.'

'Dav can ride a bike. Why are you being mean?'

The swell smacks the hull. Bow and stern take turns to dip and rise, and cormorants hit the sea like arrows where they disappear, holding their breath while they flap and swoop and glide the same way they do in air but beneath the waves.

Jakey's dad comes up from the galley for air. 'All friends together?' he asks, sounding like Mrs Hill, and gets no reply. The boys glare at each other, Dav holding back tears and Owen frowning.

By now, Phil Fisher has gone a bit green round the gills so Jakey's dad, who never gets sick, finishes his buttie for him, adding a smear of ketchup to the fish gubbins on his apron. He chucks the crusts overboard then rolls himself a fag. 'Only the one, Phil, don't tell Sarah.'

Phil Fisher waits till the fag is licked and lighted before he snatches and crumples and chucks the roll-up into the sea.

'You asked me to stop you, Mitch Grundy, so I will.'

'Now, Phil...' Jakey's dad gives Phil Fisher a look like he is set to punch him in the guts. Threatening, if you did not know he was Phil Fisher's best and only mate from school, all the others having gone to places where better-paying work is found. 'I didn't mean it when I said that. You're no mate to punish me thus.'

While the dads wrestle by the anchor, the rods twitch and Rhys brings up another dog.

'Nine point three,' says Jakey, who can tell the weight of fish by looking. 'Put her back.'

Then Jakey opens the throttle to new waters, far from land, though they can still see the lighthouse and Lythcombe Picture House where Phil Fisher used to take their mum before it shut and junkies broke in and lifted the chairs to make their velvet beds. Rhys was disappointed that his dad never cared to comment on the decline of the South West, though it was obvious to anyone with a basic understanding of historical materialism. That was his dad's problem. He had no idea, nor Mitch, nor Jakey, nor his brothers. They were only happy if the fish were biting and their nets came up heavy.

Three rods twitch and bend over the port stern; will it be the same fish as before?

'Take the spool,' Phil Fisher tells Rhys. 'Let her out a bit. And be nice to your brothers – give Owen a turn.'

Owen shakes his head, wanting very much all of his fingers for all of his life, and his willy.

'Owen's scared,' Jakey tells Rhys. 'He's got a skill issue.'

'I don't have a skill issue,' says Owen.

Jakey laughs. 'Owen's a Cornish seagull.'

'I'm not Cornish!'

'He's turning gay like you, Dav.'

'Cut it out, son,' growls Mitch from the galley hatch. 'I'll have none of them phobias on my boat.'

Jakey starts the motor to find new waters but a grinding, angry sound fills their lugholes and the *Maria* stops dead, throwing her crew against the rail. The straining boat moves sideways, if anywhere at all. What will become of them now?

Rhys looks to Phil Fisher for an answer, but he wipes his sweaty balding head and says, 'I dunno, lads. We've been caught by a big 'un. Can you not bring her round, Jakey boy?'

Jakey's dad throws himself below and comes back frowning in his orange gumby suit and tosses a Crewsaver jacket for Phil. When Jakey sees his dad blowing in the top-up tube that inflates the chambers if you don't want to waste a gas canister, he throws the gearing into reverse again. Nerves look set to snap.

'Well, brave boys,' says Mitch, lifting Owen bodily by the shoulders of his junior Crewsaver and shaking him to see if he would slip through. 'I love you all. It seems we have met our match.'

This is news to Rhys, who has fished with this man his whole life and never before witnessed this trembling, this breaking of spirit, nor that of Phil Fisher, at least not in public.

'We are doomed,' Mitch says. 'It's right to be scared.'

Sweating now, Jakey tries to shift the boat; engine screaming, stern driving dangerous-low in the water, too weak for what holds her in its teeth.

'What is it, Dad?' says Rhys. 'What's got us, Uncle Mitch?'

'A colossal squid!' says Owen.

Phil Fisher winks at his youngest. 'Right on, the very same, that can swallow a vessel whole, suck out its marrow and spit out the crunchy parts.'

Rhys tightens his straps till he is white for want of breath. Jakey, for his part, looks to his dad, who swallows, his jaw set, and then peers over the edge for signs of the creature. Jakey gets his best knife but, wet fingers fumbling, it spins across the deck. His dad brings down his boot to stop it going over; he was never the best at football either so the knife flies out through a scupper hole in the gunwale – that bit on the side of a boat that lets waves reunite with their kind, back-sweeping over the deck into the arms of the sea. The knife glints flat on the surface while it gets its bearing, then, remembering it is a heavy thing, lets itself sink.

Rhys is scared now, he won't mind admitting it.

Mitch looks over the gunwale again, pointing at the root of their stuckness, Phil Fisher too, and their laughter cracks open the clouds.

'Rhys. Jakey.' Phil Fisher turns the windlass to weigh anchor; up it comes, dripping in weed. 'Here's your colossal squid. Whitebait you are, lily-livered, the lot of you.'

Jakey's dad puts his hands on Owen and Dav's shoulders. 'These here young 'uns excepting. You were gurt brave, lads.'

Rhys glowers at his dad, then turns to the open ocean thinking dark thoughts. *I am the brave one*, he thinks. *Me alone. You just can't see it because you're not here most of the time. But one day you will. You wait! One day, I will do something so bold you will see it in the papers and say, 'There's Rhys, my son, gurt brave'.*

But there is no time for speeches, silent or sounded, because a column of pilchard comes on the sonar and there is work to be done – rod-lines in, ring-net out. Mitch circles the shoal. Seine-strings drawn, the water boils with angry fish unused to nylon walls in their dominion.

Rhys teases their gills from the net and throws their

flapping bodies into the ice boxes till his fingers go numb. Mitch promises him a cider and whatever Dav and Owen are drinking.

'A barrel of rum to fill my tum!' sings Owen.

'No, son. I was meaning something soft.'

'… that's the life for me!'

The *Maria*'s eel-hook gets no use but they catch some bream on the way home, three kilo the biggest. Jakey's dad fillets them so fast, his fingers working 'like a bloody brain surgeon's', according to Phil Fisher. Bream is very tasty roasted skin-on crispy with buttered bread. Not a single bone. And neither dad chews Rhys's ear off when he jumps from bow to quay before they get a hawser round the bollard.

Later, in the King's Arms, Phil Fisher says, 'Now, listen, Dav and Owen. If Rabbit-Heart Rhys and Shakey-Jakey here ever start on you again, you have my permission to call them "colossal twits" and the like.' He scruffs Owen's curls and locks Dav's head in the crook of his arm. 'You're all right, son,' says Phil Fisher, smacking a great kiss on the top of Dav's hair. 'You keep doing you, as folk say in America… You, too,' he says to Rhys, pulling him in, his haulager's pits none too fragrant after a day at sea. 'Don't worry about Dav. Just concentrate on being you.'

Rhys resists the hug, wanting to show his dad he is not happy. How can Phil not see that Rhys is older and stronger and different in every way?

But then his dad says, 'A little bird told me you got a job at the processors yesterday. Good on you, son.

I'm proud of you.'

The pub is full of friends and that half of cider is warming his insides. Mitch and Dav are now up on a table singing along to Lady Gaga on the jukebox. Jakey is showing Owen how to throw peanuts into his mouth and the squirt keeps missing.

Phil will be off to Spain again tomorrow. Together times like these don't come often, so Rhys leans into his dad and forgets himself awhile.

*

Two days later and Phil Fisher is well on his way to Murcia. After school, Dav has gone for a run up the hill and Rhys is taking Owen to Angie's chippy.

'I was Mrs Hill's Tuesday Hero today,' says Owen. 'How long till my birthday again?'

'Fourteen days.'

'You mean thirteen, because today doesn't count. Will I get my own rod?'

'Maybe. Wait and see.'

'I will! You're smiling, and that means I will. Is it going to be the one I showed you on Amazon?'

'Maybe.'

'You're smiling, Rhys.'

They reach the chippy. No queue in winter, the brothers go straight into the warm. The windows are steamed up so Owen draws faces on the glass. 'Why are we here?' he asks, Year Four champion of the stupid question.

'We're here for chips, mate.'

Owen hangs on Rhys's arm till his brother's shoulder aches. 'Stop it, Owen, please. You've got to grow up a bit, now you're nearly nine. We're having beany chips today but you've got to behave.'

'Like at school?'

'Ay, there too. Work hard and do your homework.'

'Like Dav?'

'No, not as much as Dav. He takes it too far.'

'Dav says if I do homework I can get a year-round job that pays. He says I should leave Lythcombe when I'm grown. I'm too smart to stay.'

'Why should you live somewhere else? Our ancestors were Vikings. We belong by the sea.'

'All right, my lovers?' says Angie behind the counter. 'What will it be?'

'Small cone, please,' Rhys says. Everyone knows Angie fancies Phil Fisher, in spite of his great belly and aversion to razors. Rhys once heard her say, 'He'll end up alone if he waits too long, and that'd be a shame.' He wonders if Angie might keep Phil Fisher home, but her arms are spotted with oil scars like white foam caps not quite cresting on a moderate sea, and besides, there's talk of the chip shop shutting down soon, such is the cost of raw materials, like oil and spuds, and the means to heat them.

'Did you hear about the fishing closure that's coming?' says Angie behind the fryer. 'Just announced. Eleven weeks. All vessels.'

Inside, Rhys is a kettle coming to the boil. He was supposed to be starting work at the processors. He has a rod to buy. A party to give. *How the hell can you turn nine without a party?* You can't. Not properly. Not the way you should.

He puts £1.20 on the counter, his hand shaking.

'Lots of vinegar, please,' says Owen. Angie wipes her apron and winks at the squirt. Taking the 20p, she slides back the pound to Rhys, makes up a large tray and throws in an extra scoop.

'Growing boys,' she says. 'When's your daddy home?'

'Soon,' says Rhys.

'Eighteen minutes and twenty-three seconds to the farm,' says Dav when he gets home. 'Better than last time. Have you got my chips?'

Rhys is already one Strongbow and a benzo down and mutters, 'We should be farmers.'

He's in a dark and dangerous mood, smoking a spliff to help him digest the chips and the prospect of eleven weeks of thumb-twiddling, ordered in their wisdom by the Association of Inshore Fisheries and Conservation Authority on so-called environmental grounds, to let fish stocks recover. The fleet, day boats and trawlers, will be confined to port; there'll be no fish processing, so you can go home. No box washing, so off you trot, and no auction sales. The King's Arms will be closed for the foreseeable. The directive is tantamount to three months of no work and no income. Sixty jobs gone. Sixty families waiting for manna to fall from heaven or credit from the outer reaches of the universe.

No job, no rod, no cube, no tarp, no party; it has all gone to shit.

'Yeah, we should be working the soil,' Rhys goes on. 'Our soil. Like it used to be, right? Herding with our own dogs and shearing. Not your French bulldogs and chi-wow-wows. Proper dogs.' Rhys has been practising a passable shepherd's whistle; green skunk exhaust billows from his lips without the intended sound. 'Come by!' He coughs. 'Away!' He would quit smoking weed if it did not so soften the ragged edges of his pain. 'Sheepdogs herding sheep. Our women spinning the wool we cut, weaving.'

'Our women. *Right*,' Dav says, trying to not laugh.

'Shut up, Dav. Weaving the wool into jumpers. Droving ponies on the moor. We should be doing that too – not haulage, not lorries. And we should fish where we like and how much we like and what size we like. That's why we left the European Union, wasn't it? We should be eating lobster for breakfast and scallops for tea.'

'Mate, you're allergic to shellfish.'

'It's not about me. It's about heritage. We should be harvesting the sea with broadswords in our hands. That'll send a message.'

'What message is that then, Rhys?'

'French boys! Stay off our scallop banks!' His voice goes quiet, almost crying-like, given that scallop banks have a lot in common with life. The shifting, the buggering off, so that when you go back it's all gone, nothing left, the whole colony on the move. 'And we should be farmers, Dav, did I say that? Living off the fat of the land.'

Rhys's head falls onto his brother's shoulder. Dav strokes his red curls the way he strokes Thing the cat, and says, 'You're all right, mate, you're all right.'

'We should have farms and tractors, and horses waiting round to pull the heavy shit, like backalong. We should have a green acre each, to reap and sow and plough and dig up and all the other stuff farmers get to do.' *Like stamping their boot into troughs in winter,* he thinks, *to break the ice and let thirsty beasts drink.* 'Ask yourself, Dav, can a field be stolen or lost or carried away? How much land does a man need? It is a man's birthright, yet too much in one set of hands is patent theft.' He remembers what Dodo told him. 'To each according to his needs, you see. From each should come something, mate, something or other... ability.'

He worries he may not have said any of these last things aloud. It is hard to tell.

'Rhys, you're wasted, mate. I'll get you some water.'

'Shut up! You asked me to explain!'

'Then, explain.'

'Owen's party's off.'

'You what?'

Rhys's phone pings: a message from Jakey. He reads it and says, 'I'm going out. Someone's got to do something.'

It has started without him: direct and irreversible action.

PART TWO

Revolution

TEN

Tuesday night turned out to be no more than a few drunken boys shouting at seagulls and a couple of upturned wheelie bins. The Lythcombe riots warm up on Wednesday morning, when the bus shelter is paint-sprayed, three cars dented and Mr Vadic's SPAR window smashed. Soon, Rhys's former classmates are running down the prom atop the roofs of cars, torching the public litter bins and making a general nuisance of themselves. They are angry. They will not take their place in the silences of history, with their CVs full of yarns and misspellings. Their muscles are designed for more than sitting around watching daytime telly.

Lythcombe's off-duty police officer, PC Michael Curtice, calls Plymouth for backup. 'The big boys are on their way,' he tells the teenagers smashing windows on the high street. 'And they won't be nice like your Uncle Mick. Go home, lads. Come on, now. None of us like what's happened... Jason! Adam... Put that back, Declan! Now, Connor, I know who you are and I am duty-bound to call your nan.'

As news of the closure gets out over the course of

the day, other boys turn up. Some are box washers, wearing their chlorine-fragranced white galoshes in protest; others are sons of mothers who work on the evisceration line; and sixteen year olds hoping for their first trawler season, practising the angling of their navy beanies in bathroom mirrors.

None are fleet owners or part-investors, these last having indemnity against financial losses. Lythcombe has none of that, just three months of hardship ahead. The closure directive is about sustainability, they are told. But answer this: how can families be expected to sustain the unsustainable? Do their needs count for nothing?

In Jubilee Park, boys douse *Leviathan* in red diesel and set light to the pirate ship, a beacon of their slow-burning anger from the last closure, when their dads watched them on the swings for want of employment. Seeing their work was good, the town boys, the same ones who beat grockles at football on warmer days, shout, 'Oink, oink!' and freewheel Mick's car into the window of Lythcombe Natural Healing & Souvenirs, manufacturing a whole carpet of crystal out of sheet pane.

Rhys is not present himself at this moment but as soon as hears the commotion, he hot-foots it out of the Fishers' flat, a biting feeling in his belly like men of yore would have felt upon joining some crusade or other war, like Rhys's new favourite historical personage, Michael An Gof, a Cornish blacksmith who marched an army to London to kill some King Henry over taxes, and whose name is immortal, at least on Wikipedia.

More shop windows shatter, another burning car rolls down Main Street, and Rhys's ginger nut and freckled arms stand out clear as day on the council's parking enforcement cameras, a head higher than his mates who are more sensibly hooded and masked, hoicking up their pants. He lobs a traffic cone at a police van. It bounces off. No harm is done to the reinforced glass, like a trawler wheelhouse in a storm.

A neighbour comes out wrapped in a dressing gown. 'Pack it in, Rhys,' she says, but he cannot hear her. Next, he tries to wobble a brick out of someone's front garden, unlocked bikes against the coal box, toddler's slide on the grass. Rhys stomps at that wall, working masonry out with his boot as if he had never studied construction or spent hours breaking his back carrying hods of bricks, stacking them flush on pallets. And when the wall does not move, he grabs a For Sale sign from a front garden. Roaring, he javelins the sign – *Let us find your forever home!* – at the armoured police van inching forward in the break of battle.

After the talk and talk and more talk, the taste of action fires up his forearms and he wants more. Dodo and Milly don't even know about this yet, but they soon will. At school, boys like Rhys are always either too big or too small; too big when they move and too small when they open their mouths. When people see the news, they will see him front and centre, the magnificent size that he is.

Half-scared, half-brave, he recites Dodo's words in

his head. *There is no basis to property other than what a man needs. Therefore a cap should be set on what a man can have: no more stone and mortar than he can lay, no more soil than he can turn.*

No, thinks Rhys. *This is our town.*

An unmarked police car arrives from Plymouth as he's throwing a pine fence panel on the road to add to the burning barricade of picket wood and garden gates. Four officers roll out with their batons and cuffs, collaring the first boys they see. Little 'uns, out on their bikes when it started, throw stones or else hang off the arms of those trying to arrest their big brothers.

Rhys watches this for a moment, like a light-stunned rabbit in the road. At first, his eyes are lit by defiance. Then they are clouded by a memory of Children's Services and he thinks he sees a cardigan-clad social worker bundling Dav and Owen into her car. His vision fogs; it must be the smoke.

How can I think about breaking the law? What if they take Owen? he thinks and runs from the riot, stumbling into Connor's nan on the corner on her mobility scooter.

'Rhys, lad,' she says, taking his hand. 'I'm so glad you're here. Have you seen what they've done to the swings? Took us a year to raise the money for that rubber. Now what are kiddies supposed to fall on? Be a good boy and push this thing. My battery's gone.'

'Someone's got to act,' says Rhys when he gets home, feeling the sting of failure. 'They can't just close

Lythcombe down. What about all those super-trawlers dragging their mile-long nets? They don't close offshore processing ships, do they? They go for the little boats operated by dad and son and best mate. Screw that, we will not go down quietly.'

'Why can't you write to our MP like a normal person?' Dav asks. He accuses Rhys of forgetting the miles Phil Fisher is driving so they can get what they need and some of what they want. Then he asks if Rhys thinks that acting like a complete dickhead might be the quickest way to bring their dad home. 'They'll have CCTV,' Dav warns. 'You stick out like a sore thumb. They'll come for you and then they'll come for us. Did you think about that?'

Rhys combs his hair in the bathroom, even though there will be no females on the frontline, the fish processing ladies being mostly of grandmothering age and ill-disposed to civil disobedience. The water leaves a grimy high-tide line in the sink, at which sight his heart aches for summer. He would rather throw down a towel on the beach with a girl, to pass the time in laughter and kisses than revolution. All the same, he must go back. What if word got out that his main contribution to the fight was helping an old lady with a flat battery get home?

'Or maybe,' says Dav, 'you don't think at all.'

Rhys pushes his brother out of the bathroom. 'I only came back to see you were okay. Shouldn't have bothered.'

'Rhys,' says Dav, other side of the slammed door.

'You think no one's going to dob you in? How many of your stoner mates will keep quiet when they put up a reward? None of them, that's how many. And then Children's Services—'

Rhys shoulders past Dav to the front door. 'Shut up! Shut up!'

'You'll get a record. If you don't, I'll still tell Dad. You can't carry on like this. It upsets people.'

'No, *you* upset people,' says Rhys, eyes hot and cold, afraid and not. 'You don't get it, do you?'

'I do. But you don't fix things by crapping in your own bed.'

'Some things are more important. Without action there can be no re—' Dav snorts a laugh. 'Ah, piss off, Dav.'

On his way out, Rhys kicks the recycling bin over his Kawasaki, stripped to bits on the slabs, waiting for eBay to come good, knowing it never will; two simultaneous states of expectation essential to the control of the proletariat, according to Dodo.

Dav goes to fetch his brother's coat but Rhys has ripped the yard gate off its post, swearing and cursing, and is gone before he gets the chance. Owen appears, snivelling, by Dav's side. If Rhys had known he was there, he would have moderated his language.

'Just me and you,' says Dav, messing up Owen's ginger mop because that is the Fisher way. 'Don't worry. Rhys is going through what is known as a rebellious teenage phase. He'll soon realise he's being a muppet and come home.'

'What if *you* do a teenage rebellion?' Owen says with a twitch of alarm in his eyes; to lose one brother is bad enough, but losing two would be a disaster.

'I don't have time to be a normal kind of kid,' says Dav. 'I've got too much on to strop out.'

'Like what?'

'Like my tests tomorrow for the mentoring scholarship. Like Maths at Nottingham. Like making the tastiest tea ever. Come on.' Dav turns Owen by the top of his head back inside the flat. 'Tell me, how many sketty hoops can you fit on a fork?'

The tipping point comes when you least expect it. You can put up with shit for ages, not even knowing it's shit – and then something goes pop, and another thing and another. For Dav, not much later that same night, it went like this...

Owen spills a mug of water over Dav's phone. The screen goes weird. Dav can't use it to search up what to do if you get water on your phone, nor can he call Rhys for help. Then the tin opener starts going round and round with no teeth to bite – not the worst disaster in the world, but tins are what they have for their tea each evening and the budget variety don't come with built-in pulls. Then the room goes dark, much like being dragged beneath a wave on an overcast day, blanketed by low cloud and a good layer of bladderwrack on the surface. The storage heaters are already cold, that being a saving, so Dav stays by the electric fire as it fades from pale yellow to red to grey. Such things happen to the Fishers most winters but since prices went through the roof, it is a weekly event.

'No problem, mate,' says Dav, because he knows how to feed the meter. He gets the emergency fiver from under the floorboard.

But Mr Vadic keeps short hours off-season so they will have no top-up till morning.

Shit me! says Dav in his head, for he, like Rhys, would never knowingly swear in Owen's company. But this is the night before his all-important test and Dav has set his heart on revising. His future depends on it – and you cannot revise without lights or a charged phone or when you are cold and hungry.

Dav goes upstairs to talk to Mrs Morris – if she isn't pissed, if he can get her to come to her door, and if that door will open for the things that block her way: stacks of junk mail and floor-to-ceiling 90s phone books. 'The world's numbers are in them,' Mrs Morris says, 'every person you could imagine – a micro-computer in one book!'

Dav will ask Mrs Morris if he and Owen could stop round hers a bit, just to do his homework.

Then, later, they can go back downstairs to their flat; they'll be okay in jumpers and coats under the covers, just for the one night. He will have to sleep in Owen's bed, in case his little brother wakes screaming blue murder in the dark.

It'll be like a polar expedition, he thinks, *without the sea ice and fatal blizzard.*

Mrs Morris doesn't answer.

Owen catches Dav's arm by the front door as he comes back. The floorboard squeaks. 'Don't leave me,' he says. 'You're rebellioning, when you said you wouldn't.'

He hangs on to Dav. The little squirt's feet skid along the lino corridor from the front door to the kitchen, Owen the skier and Dav the *Nautique G25* towboat.

Sleety hail smacks the sheet of plastic in the missing window; draughts sneak in to nick the last of their heat, so Dav goes back to the front door to stroke the peeling duct tape down. The floorboard squeaks again.

'Mate,' Dav says, not fancying polar exploration, 'why don't me and you do some rebellioning of our own, the two of us together? An adventure-like?'

And here hinges the tragedy, because Rhys cannot simultaneously be with his brothers, taking care of them like the good brother he always tries to be, *and* away fighting for their futures.

Rhys has predicted that Dav's fine memory will be their undoing. Sure enough, there in the cold corridor of his flat, Dav recalls the tight-fitting shirt of the handsome fellow in the Audi TT, his fancy man-perfume wafting out of the open-lidded car. He puts the fiver back under the floorboard and takes out the code book.

Long View Farm. How to get the key out of the key safe box and how to work the heating. How to get a little order back into chaos.

'Enemies!' yells Owen, delighted.

*

In central Lythcombe, a second riot vehicle arrives from Exeter. Its lights illuminate the darker corners into which the town boys have dispersed, against orders to remain where they were in full view. There is no ringleader to hunt down, though they will one day claim it is Rhys, who has spent the last thirty minutes skirting the skirmish, arguing with himself whether to wade in.

Dodo didn't say anything about a riot, Rhys thinks, but he does remember hearing about the 'bottled rage of the proletariat'. Should he get stuck in again? But what use will he be to the struggle if he is arrested? And how exactly does burning the playpark further their aims?

He is now at the processors, standing outside the box wash. A sign says:

Our dedicated colleagues steam clean and scan each box for bacteria. At the end of the line, boxes are neatly stacked, ready to be returned to their boats in time for their next trip to sea. Cracks and other defects are logged and failures discarded.

We're no different to those stinking boxes, thinks Rhys. The authorities want each man and boy to be neatly stacked for the duration. Cracks and defects and failures discarded.

Smoke rises near the schools. He watches two boys

get caught and cuffed by the harbourmaster's office, and feels Jakey's hand on his arm.

'Are you tripping, mate?' hisses Jakey. 'Get a wiggle on, pull your hood up. Adam's dad has topped himself. It will get proper nasty now.'

*

Dav takes Rhys's forbidden racer and climbs the hill to Long View Farm, holding Owen fast on the crossbar so the squirt doesn't fall. Behind them, smoke plumes out of Main Street. The climbing frame lights up the park, while police cars, fire engines and ambulances flicker, electric, through the Jubilee estate, like those tropical fish you see on the telly. Riots look very attractive from a distance.

'Is it Bonfire Night already?' says Owen.

'Ay,' says Dav, also thinking the lights and spits of fires are like bioluminescent algae. 'Exactly that. Fireworks.'

Dav and Rhys had first seen the twinkling flashing algae one night when they were ten and eight. Owen was only a toddler. He was fast asleep.

'Gid up, boys,' said Phil Fisher to Dav on the top bunk and Rhys on his blow-up bed. It was dark through the curtains. 'Put on your trunks.'

Dav hung over the edge, looking down at Owen.

'Don't fret. Mrs Morris is here to watch Owen. Let him sleep.'

Five streets down, they saw the moon, bright as a full-beam headlight, and small waves cresting in

Lythcombe Bay. That would have been special enough by itself, but there was more.

'What is this, Dad?' said Dav, riding piggy-back. 'What are we doing?'

'Bioluminescent algae, lads. Our visitors.'

The moon lit a path down the slipway and soon they were up to their knees, magic footsteps in midnight shallows, the boys' hearts beating fast, afeared as they were of lion's mane jellyfish, sharks, colossal squid, hungry humpbacks, piebald orcas (say no more) and lost anacondas from the Amazon.

Phil Fisher drew his hand in an arc across the surface of the sea. 'I've been waiting to show you this,' he said, proper chuffed. 'I nearly took you last year, but you were too young.'

Flashes of light threaded round his fingers and dissolved like a magic trick. Rhys's brain sparked with questions, like, 'Where does it come from? How is it made? What is it?'

'It's a glow-in-the-dark love letter, son,' Phil Fisher told him. 'Sparkiest fellow gets the girl. Mind you, it could be about protection. Hungry fish comes along and flash-bang-skedaddle!'

'What do they look like?' Dav wanted to know.

'Ah, that's the problem,' his dad said. 'They're so tiny you need a microscope to see them. You can't see one till you touch it, and if you touch it, it's gone. We're seeing what's left behind.'

'Algae poo?'

'Maybe. No deeper now, Rhys. You're shivering.

One more minute and we're going back to bed.'

Phil Fisher stooped; Dav scrambled up his front and Rhys his back. His skin warmed them both and he waded to shore.

Walking back, the town was very quiet and theirs alone. At home, Mrs Morris took Thing back upstairs to her flat and Phil microwaved mugs of milk. Dav sat on his dad's lap and Rhys pressed close next to them on the sofa and they drank their milk as slow as they could, not wanting the night to end.

Owen has not seen the algae as yet, their own private fireworks, but Phil Fisher says he will take the little 'un when the time comes. Till then, Owen must make do with these fires of Rhys's, colours burned into his retina for ever.

Down at the port, where Rhys is holed up like a fox, the *Maria* is Baltic. In the trawler's ice room, frozen drips decorate the pipes like Owen's snot candles, and hoar frost spikes the boxes. Jakey tosses Rhys a Gumby suit, good for ten hours protection against hypothermia in fully submerged conditions, proving beyond reasonable doubt that the pair of them are like men overboard and lost at sea.

In a survival suit it is very hard to roll a joint; Rhys's fingers are too fat and when he takes the gloves off, his fingers are too numb to feel the Rizla. But when it is done, he starts to feel better and reaches for the matches, only to find them too damp to light, a further disappointment. Also, Jakey's emergency cider tinnies have two centimetres of icy rime and no fizz.

'Adam's dad?' says Rhys. 'The union man? How so?'

'Locked himself in the white-fish freezer when he heard the news of the closure. Corporate manslaughter, they're saying.'

'Bastards!'

'Adam is calling it assassination but everyone knows it's suicide,' says Jakey. 'He closed the door, sat with the coley and waited for death to come.'

They raise a tin to Adam's dad and to Nelson, Jakey's arthritic Alsatian, not dead but threatened with being sent to the RSPCA in Exeter.

'Can they not just keep Nelson in a kennel, till the closure's lifted?'

'They say they are not a hotel.'

'I can't believe your dad would do that to him.'

'Not Dad. Dad loves Nelson. Mum's the one saying it.'

Rhys thinks about losing dogs and what you can do to make money when things are turning to shit.

'What about Brixham?' says Rhys, jabbing a knife through the ice to get at the cider. 'The box wash pays £10.20 an hour there. You can get a stack of Pedigree Chum for that.'

'It's not that simple. Nelson's thirteen now – he's not insured and he needs vet's stuff. Metacam for his joints. Any rate, we'd need the bus to leave at four in the morning to make that work. Brixham starts at five.

And Dad's checked already. They're not taking anyone on. Closure's the same there. Forget it, mate. The old boy's nearly dead, any road.'

It is hard to tell if those are tears on Jakey's face. All the same, Rhys punches his best friend's arm in lieu of a hug.

ELEVEN

The lane is quiet. Long View Farm appears before them, mica glinting in its ancient granite walls. Dav takes out the code book for instructions and looks for lights coming up the lane. It is late. Surely no grockle will rock up at this hour, but what if a burglar alarm goes off, despite the code?

Will that make us burglars? he asks himself. *Is wanting to be warm a crime?*

He finds the safe box in the side door of the triple garage, above a sweet abandoned Gerry Lopez Hawaiian Pipeliner. If he'd been there, Rhys, who knows the cost of a surfboard just by looking, would tell you it would fetch a good £2000 on eBay, even on a slow day. Yet here it is, left sitting on its fins by some muppet who has no idea of its value.

The code-book numbers work a treat; the front door opens and a boiling waft of potpourri-scented air hits their chill faces. There are no hammers on spikes or hungry pit bulls, no laser beams, electrified traps or other security precautions. To leave it so unguarded, its owners cannot know about Lythcombe's junkies and other skint characters.

The house could get burgled in real life, thinks Dav, *not just borrowed by two cold boys.*

The owners have left the radiators on like they are millionaires.

'Inside,' Dav tells Owen, closing the door. 'You'll let their heat out. Money doesn't grow on trees, you know.'

All things considered, Long View Farm is extremely bloody nice, thank you very much. Dav does not write that in the guestbook by the front door.

'They must do a lot of sitting down,' says Owen, counting the chairs and sofas while Dav goes into the kitchen and finds a bowl of fruit on the table. There is also a loaf labelled 'artisanal' in a chrome bread bin, milk in the fridge and honey in the cupboard. Owen comes in and fiddles with the touch screen on the fridge. It spits out ice cubes. Another button grinds ice into slush like the lane outside.

'Get a mug,' Dav tells him.

Dav mops up the slush and puts the tea towel on the Aga where it turns crispy. This gives him an idea – he has remembered to bring Binty, that filthy rag that Owen cannot sleep without, but has forgotten clean socks so he washes the pairs they have in the sink, confident they will be dry by morning on the oven, along with their trainers and his phone, coming back to life.

Dav adjusts the positioning of the socks and his phone judders. He smiles at Owen.

'That'll be Rhys, then.' But the screen has no words,

only a pattern of lines. Who knows how far away Rhys and Phil Fisher are? *What if I cannot reach them?* thinks Dav. *What if they cannot reach me?*

'What does he say?' asks Owen.

'He says he's fine,' Dav lies. 'And Dad, too. Now, where were we…' He sees it is 9 p.m. 'Shall we have a midnight feast, then?'

Although by rights Owen should be put straight to bed, Dav gets a tin of sketty out of his school bag and borrows the lady's tin opener, washes it, dries it and puts it back in the drawer tidy-like, proving he is not a vandal or a wrecker or a thug, no matter what people are saying tonight about Jubilee boys. He fills two glasses with water. The toaster cooks four slices at once. They fill it twice over and sit on stools made out of stainless steel dairy churns around a table made from an old stable door on legs. Owen worries the horse will go cold with no door on its box. He feels sorry for the owner of Long View Farm, too hard up to afford a proper table, not even a free one from Shelter.

'Mate,' says Dav, when Owen misses his plate again. 'No crumbs! We want the nice owners to invite us back, don't we?'

Dav, wanting Owen to grow up with some sense of right and wrong, hopes to hide from him the true legal status of their visit; namely, breaking and entering a property without seeking or receiving permission.

'Let's check out the hot tub in the garden,' says Dav. 'Luxury it will be, and nice-smelling. Good for cleaning your skanky feet, mate.'

When they take off the dripping cover, Dav's first thought is: *Rhys has got to see this!* Because things are never so much fun without his big brother who, if he were with them now, would do a daredevil backflip into its boiling centre.

Dav's second thought is: *I hope he is okay, the dickhead.*

The Vicks VapoRub smell of the water makes Dav's heart flutter, recalling a time when his mum had laid her cool hand on his head, checking him for a temperature, her brow furrowed like low tide.

Owen shakes his head, thinking the dinky pool is some kind of pot for boiling the shrimp catch, so Dav goes in first, in his boxers. 'It's a hot tub,' he says. 'Come on in.'

When Dav presses a button and bubbles start, Owen dips his skinny body; there are more buttons to press, other kinds of bubbles, and he laughs and pushes Dav's head under. The water soon fixes their stinky feet and soothes Dav's back that aches from wheeling Owen up the hill.

They are pink as boiled lobsters by the time they get out.

The storm of the riot has not yet blown itself out. Indistinct shouts and half-screams, the crackling sounds of fire and pouring water make it down *Maria*'s steep galley steps into the ice room where Rhys and Jakey will try to sleep later. Rhys kicks himself for not having taken some video footage of himself, before the police came to help PC Mick sort out angry boys. He could have posted that to the group; how Milly would have smiled to see those flames – undeniable proof that he, a Welsh warrior, was taking action.

Instead, shivering in the icy bowels of the *Maria*, their balls shrivelling despite the survival suits and with sirens sounding across Lythcombe, Rhys and Jakey retreat to the central theme of their life – not the merits of steaming black ink off of cuttlefish boxes, or overtime rates at the processors, being sore subjects in view of the Closure, but cars and girls.

'Hey, Rhys. Would you rather lick fresh mango juice off a Brazilian girl or Ben & Jerry's off an American girl?'

'What flavour?'

'Cookies.'

Rhys gave it some thought. 'Brazil, then.'

'Would you rather a V8 Mustang 4x4 or a V6 Audi TT convertible?'

Rhys considered the question. 'Depends on the season. What good's your average TT going to be in Devon come winter? My turn. Say you were a deckhand on a luxury yacht,' Rhys went on, 'would you rather shag a different stunner in each port – two months between them, mind – or one on-board average girlfriend every night?'

'I don't know. On-board I'd say. But would you rather have a snog from Paige or a feel of Chelsea's tits?'

Rhys's mind snags on Jakey's words. Perhaps it is

the cold, or the fact that Dav had not long chided him that it was 'objectifying' to speak thus about females. He had told Owen, 'Don't listen to Rhys's misogynistic maunderings. He has been hit on the head by a fin too many times.'

'Mate. Maybe we shouldn't talk this way. Would you like it said about Liz?'

'Are you going all Dav on me?'

'No,' says Rhys. 'I just want a girl I can talk to. Have a home. Something real.'

Rhys wants to talk to Jakey about Milly, but it would sully his love to speak of her now, lest saying the words, 'I have met that very girl,' makes Jakey laugh in his face. Far safer to talk about Dodo and the unequal distribution of property, there being a connection to Nelson's fate and poor Adam's dad in the coley freezer.

'I have heard it said…' he begins but falls asleep to the stages of Arctic sea ice forming, the product of his cold-teeming brain: *pancake, brash, ice cake, floe, fast.*

'Where's Rhys going to sleep?' says Owen, upstairs at Long View Farm.

Dav does not want to frighten Owen so he says, 'Let's see. Which room d'you think he'd like? Take your pick.'

The code book said 'sleeps 8', but the place could accommodate sixteen, if you count the three sofas in the sitting room, the one in the kitchen by the fireplace and the big one on the balcony landing.

The brothers choose the room they'll share, the biggest with its own bathroom like that of a king in a palace. Dav unpacks. Owen's smile drops, remembering his Spider-Man PJs are not enough. He wants home, that's all, and his own bottom bunk and his own Spider-Man duvet. He does not like this room at all, what with the old shears and iron horseshoes hanging over the bed that might fall off and gash them in the night. What kind of person needs to fleece a sheep in a bedroom?

'Dav, I want to go home.'

'Do you want to change room?' Dav asks. 'We can do that.' He follows Owen's gaze to the farm implements on the wall, 'Is it them? They'll not fall.' And when that does not work, Dav says, 'Please, Owen, I need to study. It's too cold at home.'

Owen places the side of his fist against the window. At home, this time of year, it freezes on the inside so he can print the side of his fist on the panes and then dot his fingertips above the print. It comes out like a mini-yeti footprint. A few more makes it look like a yeti has walked across the glass and his brothers used to say, 'Oh no! The yeti is back!' all scared-like. There is no ice for this game on the inside of Long View Farm's triple-glazed windows.

'Who lives here, Dav?'

'Rich people.'

Owen traces the horizon with his finger. Ships hover, like kestrels in the bay, going nowhere, prop blades beating in nothing if they beat at all. Rhys once told him that when clouds mix the colour of water, the vessels you see above the horizon are flying. 'See how their hulls drip as they go?' said Rhys. 'That's a warning to low-flying planes to get out of the bloody way!'

Owen's teacher, Mrs Hill, says it's lovely to tell the class about your adventures, so tomorrow, when he gets to school, he plans to tell her about the ships he sees from the nice farm bedroom, the soft bed with too many pillows, gurt big towels and a cupboard full of bog roll enough to wipe ten backsides for ten years.

Dav points at the ISS space station, flying through the night sky. 'That's home for seven astronauts,' he says. 'Did you know most of them have Maths degrees? That's a wonder!'

There are so many wonders it's hard for Owen to keep still, let alone sleep. New things every day, like finding stuff and losing it again, making towers, Thing licking egg off his fingers, mackerel throwing themselves onto his hooks, a trapped ladybird the wrong side of the window soon rescued, a bloom of moon jellyfish in the bay, rabbits in the future. All things found easily on earth, Rhys would tell you, not flying though the heavens on the back of a university degree.

And now this luxury farmhouse with its creature comforts – secret tins in cupboards, bananas on a plate, buttons on the fridge and how does this floor get so hot? Toast and toast and toast and a tub too small to swim in but steaming as a mug of tea.

'Can we go in the tub again?' Owen asks after brushing his teeth twice and once more for luck. 'In case of cavities,' says Phil Fisher, when he's home, mindful that Lythcombe doesn't have an NHS dentist any more.

'No, it's bedtime,' says Dav. 'You've got school in the morning.'

Owen tucks himself up inside a nest of scatter cushions, nose on Dav's hip. Dav leaves the telly on because Owen finds the flickering light a comfort.

'Turn over, squirt,' says Dav. 'Don't watch, it's only stupid boys on the news.'

'Why are they stupid? Let me look, I heard sirens—'

'It's nothing.' Dav mutes the telly. 'Sleep, now.'

Owen is quiet for a while, before finding he can switch the bedside lamp from low to bright to dazzling and back to off again with a tap of his finger on the shade. For Dav, this is like trying to revise in the middle of disco night at the King's Arms so he tells him, 'Cut it out. Go to sleep.'

Owen snuggles against Dav's leg with Binty, and Dav sits up with his revision books, the lamp on low, the telly on mute, keeping half an eye out for Rhys turning famous.

Even though the bed is family-sized, Owen starfishes the lot of it. When Dav's formulae are done, he sleeps on the edge, knowing if he falls it will be onto soft-tasselled throw cushions and deep-pile carpet, such is the life rich grockles live.

But Dav is restless. He wakes before daylight,

thinking nonsense like, *Why does Owen's heart go so much faster than mine, like a mouse or a baby bird?* And, *What job pays enough so you can afford to buy a fridge to spit crushed ice at you when you are hot and a six-slot toaster to make artisanal toast when you are hungry and a hot tub to boil your balls when you are cold?*

What job indeed pays enough for this view: the low moon through the blind, the sparkling lines of waves? Whatever it is, it would not be termed a *job*. Jobs are things like hod-carrying, car-park attending, box washing and glass collecting. No, it would most likely be termed a profession.

One day, I will have a profession, thinks Dav. *After Maths at Nottingham. And nice things and maybe a boyfriend.*

And then he gets down to it with his sums for another couple of hours, after which he watches a bit of telly with the subtitles on, Owen gently snoring by his side.

Chief Inspector Karen Wills from the Devon and Cornwall Police is being interviewed by Sally Spiers. In the background there are burning bins and burning cars and boys running.

Sally: Why is this riot happening?

Karen: We believe radical elements are exploiting the labour dispute at the Lythcombe processing factory.

Sally: Processing?

Karen: Fish processing.

Sally: Go on.

Karen: Yes, radical elements are exploiting the labour dispute and the vulnerable state of grief in this community after the tragic death of Alan Flower at the plant. We urgently ask the general public to come forward with information.

The Chief Inspector then turns, looks down the barrel of the camera at Dav and asks, 'Do you know any of these criminal young men who are wantonly destroying their community? Do you know their whereabouts?'

'Nope,' Dav tells her.

He has never met Adam's dad and he never wanted to work at the processors – with a Maths degree, you can buy a thousand rods for your little brother – but one thing is clear. Later, once the powers-that-be have had a little think about the lessons they have learned, they may agree on this: beware of spoiling young men's futures; they will become a flapping, snapping moray on the deck, electrics firing long after they've been clubbed on the head.

In the moment before Rhys wakes in the frozen belly of the *Maria*, where he and Jakey spent the night sheltering from the heat of the riot, he mistakes the chill air for a cooling summer gust up by the lighthouse and imagines he is lying on sea-pink turf watching guillemots, the onshore wind blowing the hair out of his eyes, arms wide, hands out, as close to the edge of the cliff as flying.

He wants to ask his mum from what tropical places these Atlantic clouds grab their bellyfuls of water – those called *cumulonimbus, altostratus, cirrostratus, nimbostratus* – and why they drop their freight here and seldom take it elsewhere, and how waves turn glassy, Slight to Moderate to High in landward swells and back to rippling peace, their heavy tumbling crests worn away with the effort.

The cliff he dreams himself atop is high as a flying drone. Birds wheel, winklers winkle, jellyfish bloom, bubbling boiling waves froth like a video on mute. Far below, seals bark and cough and slide back to the sea. Rhys would do the same. Why stay where you feel like aggregate – that is, sand and concrete and rubble – when you could be a dancer elsewhere, a water poem, a swift, a spark of silver to spook anglers on their spots?

He looks up and there is Owen on a horrible steep section. *This will not do*, dreams Rhys, because the drop dizzies and Owen is like an hour-old colt on the moor, tripping on his feet.

'Mum!' he cries in his half-sleep.

But Siân Fisher can't answer, being long-since sunk without trace in a pot the size of a crab bucket down at Plymouth crematorium.

He feels a soft kick, cushioned by the life-sustaining layers of his Gumby suit, and opens his eyes. 'Wake up, Rhys. We've got to get going.'

Rhys wipes the exposed part of his face, sending shards of frozen condensed breath snowing from eyelash and brows.

'Bloody Baltic,' says Jakey, knocking the ice off Rhys's survival suit and melting the fastener with his breath.

'Bloody frozen,' says Rhys.

'Bloody starving, mate.'

'Bloody let's go, then.'

It is five o'clock on Thursday morning and Lythcombe is quiet. Rhys is jumping on stiff legs from the *Maria* to the quayside when he gets a text message from Dodo:

> Your little riot was a start but we need to dig deeper. Let us take a knife and cut this land in two and see what worms are eating it inside.

The port is still: grey sky, grey water, grey docks, no bow waves to disturb the surface, no engines to ruffle the air, none of the winching and cranking and clanking and men shouting to 'Get a bloody move on, fish do not catch themselves'.

'Come for brekkie at mine,' says Jakey. Rhys would normally say yes, but since there's a closure, he thinks of Sarah at the table, her eyes red, and Jakey's dad looking like a thunderhead set to discharge its ions.

'I don't know,' says Rhys. He needs a smoke to get him through the morning after the night before. 'What if your mum and dad know about us breaking stuff last night?'

'Stop worrying. They'd've been watching *Strictly*.'

'But what if they hear us coming in?'

'They'll be expecting that. I told them I was staying at yours.'

They head through the docks, past the harbourmaster's office into town. At the edge of the estate, now fenced off by police, they pass three men with a tripod.

'What are they up to?' Jakey says, after giving the suited surveyors a polite nod.

'Costing the damage?' says Rhys. 'Though it's not like the council to be so fast.'

'These ones were here last week. Liz thinks they're planning on levelling Jubilee and starting from scratch. They're going to gentrify us out of Lythcombe.'

'They can't do that,' says Rhys. 'We live here.'

But even as these words left his mouth, he remembered that Dodo had predicted this would happen. For all its ruin – poor ventilation, leaking roofs, rising damp, black mould, condemned balconies, broken steps, lofts so sieve-like they heat the stars – they are living on top of a bloody gold mine.

There are some streets they cannot walk down, given the presence of the emergency services, but in a roundabout way they reach Jakey's house, one of the bigger ones on the estate with an unauthorised extension for Liz's bedroom. Jakey's dad being a popular man in these parts, no one has reported it to the council.

It's too early for Sarah to be cooking and with Nelson too old to make a fuss, Jakey and Rhys creep up the stairs to Jakey's bedroom where they find a spare lighter and open the window, wide as it goes. Last night's unlit spliff is a bit crumpled but soon straightens out and they fill their lungs with its medicinal draught, an elixir of forgetfulness. Then, top to toe, they doze on Jakey's Hulk duvet till the smells of bacon and sausage and smoked fish bring them down for breakfast.

'Are you hungry, Rhys?' says lovely Sarah in her flannel dressing gown and apron, stirring a sausage stew with a focus more often seen in oyster or scallop shuckers, minding they don't lose a finger. 'Sit down and eat.'

If she was thirty years younger, Milly or no Milly, Rhys would marry Sarah tomorrow.

'Are you feeling okay, Mum?' says Jakey, swinging back in his chair like Mitch and scoffing in Rhys's direction. 'Is that *stew* we're having for breakfast?'

'No, love. The stew's for Adam's mum.'

Halfway through his bacon buttie, Dodo sends Rhys a text about 'New Tactics' but direct action has left an unpleasant taste in Rhys's mouth. It seemed like a good idea at the time, but now, in the warmth of Jakey's kitchen, he worries again about being caught, sending Dav and Owen back into the toxic orbit of Children's Services.

Out of respect for Sarah's breakfast, Rhys mutes his phone. Dodo can wait. At any rate, Rhys will have to go home first and see to his brothers. With Phil Fisher not back till tomorrow morning and his mum in heaven and sausage stews doing the rounds the way they did when he was seven, Rhys swears he will take care of Dav and Owen and keep their futures tinder-dry.

There's no one else to call them in, so they must call themselves.

TWELVE

At Long View Farm, morning comes without warning. The alarm on Dav's phone does not go off as set and the first of his two tests is due to start in half an hour. He has no phone numbers to call the school, nor means of getting them, and if he is not at that test, he will have to stop in Lythcombe for the rest of his days.

I could still make it in time, he thinks in a panic, *if I leave Owen here and bike down to school.*

It would be the work of ten minutes, fifteen tops – one hell-for-leather freeride down the lane, through Jubilee to the school – but he cannot leave his brother, who needs him to supervise his waking, dressing, feeding, cleaning and delivery unto education.

It is over. No point hurrying. Dav swallows his tears and pulls their neat-folded uniforms out of his school bag. He scans the bed for hair and crumbs and goes to wipe off the piss Owen often leaves on the bog seat. It is clean.

'Owen, mate,' says Dav, trying to sound happy. 'Well done. You got a clean shot.'

'I used the kids' one,' says Owen, pointing to a low

sink that might be for washing your feet in. It does not have a flush, so Dav gives it a rinse and wipes it with a bath towel which he puts back neat on the hot tubes.

In the kitchen, he grabs two bananas from the fruit bowl and shepherds Owen into his coat.

'No, you cannot go in the hot tub again. You're late.'

'You're late, too. Your test.'

'Not no more.'

In the garage, Dav returns the key to the safe box. Just as the brothers are nearly away, their school uniforms hidden under their coats, they hear the electric gates whir and the unmistakable first-gear whine of an engine labouring up the steep driveway. A van, it turns out, its livery emblazoned with

GUEST-READY 24/7
Serving 150 square miles of the Devon Riviera from Plymouth to Torquay
For All Your Key Exchange, Laundry & Cleaning Needs

The boys stand by the garage door as the van circles the rusty plough and its rotten flowers. An older lady lowers the window. She waves. Owen waves back.

Caught red-handed. Will she call the police?

'I'm so sorry,' she says. 'I didn't know you were staying longer. I was going to do the changeover, but I'll go now. The new guests aren't due till next weekend so no hurry. Is everything okay? Anything you need?'

Owen shakes his head, solemn-like.

'Warm enough?'

The squirt gives her a shy smile. 'The hot tub is very... hot,' he says. 'Thank you.'

To Dav she says, 'Tell your parents to just check the online bookings calendar. It's often possible to extend, off-season. Though if I were you,' she looks in the direction of town, a mess of smoke curling in the bay, 'I'd be making a break for home.'

Her eye catches the open garage and she frowns. There is the Gerry Lopez, lying wax-side down on gritty concrete in a state of rank ignominy. Though she is more used to changing sheets and cleaning up after grockles, it is clear by her wincing expression that she recognises nobility when she sees it and feels the injustice of its treatment in her bowels.

'Now, boys,' she says, teeth gritted like the cold-water wax which will need changing now – a morning's work. 'You're very welcome to borrow the old board, just hang it up in its cover when you're done. Enjoy your stay!'

That morning, the school run is not what Dav is expecting. Though his heart has turned to granite knowing he has missed his test, he keeps a good grip on Owen down the hill and, in town, makes him get off over the bits of pavement covered in glass, to save Rhys's tyres.

'What's going on?' Owen asks.

Mr Vadic is taping up his broken shop front with

flapping bin bags while the council men, out on the wrong day, sweep glass down the gutters with long brooms. Mrs Morris is sharing the war memorial bench with a telly crew. One end of the bench, made of blue recycled plastic, has melted like an ice cream in summer. She raises her vodka bottle, they raise their Costa coffees, and Dav and Owen wave. A tree in the park is still smouldering, and fire engines wail around it like at a funeral.

The brothers pass the carcasses of cars eaten by flames, their skeletons like beached whales, next to a motorcycle-fish picked clean to the bone. Good job they did not hear all this last night. Long View Farm guests are well-insulated, like being in the chippy in a storm, rollers breaking on the prom, the news on mute. Good job the town is 'only a film set', as Dav says now, seeing Owen's tears brewing. 'Nothing bad has happened for real, they'll have it back together again in a jiffy.'

He sounds like their dad. 'Time heals,' says Phil Fisher, but what boy would not sooner have Jean in the school office with her tin of biscuits or Sarah with her pillowy bosom, or a paramedic with his stretcher, than flipping *time*?

A tented incident room structure is being built in the park, where bricks and splintered wood litter the beds. The same flowerpot Rhys threw sits upended in the road but there is no time to right it. Police officers narrow their eyes at Dav, who is the same age as some of the perpetrators, though they should know by the gentle way he carries Owen over the glass, going back to carry Rhys's bike over the same, that he is not the type to take direct and irreversible action.

Says Owen, 'But why did they have to break *everything*?'

'Like I told you, they've made it look like this on purpose. It's not real.'

Dav holds Owen in case he loses his balance on the crossbar or wastes time gawping at the so-called film set, actors lurking in police costumes.

'Extras,' explains Dav, 'learning their lines.'

No one is hurt, he soothes, no more blood than Owen's ketchup trick – the one when he says, 'Call the doctor! My finger's bleeding!'

But when they see the charcoaled bones of the climbing ship, Owen finally sheds a tear.

He hopes the film people have a brother who can saw and hammer and joint and joist as well as Rhys, more wood coming soon in Phil Fisher's Iveco to finish the job. No ship to climb on, the Union Jack still smoking on its metal pole, Mr Vadic's window broken, strangers everywhere like it was July. *They have made a proper mess of things*, thinks Owen. *Film set or not, it is very scary*.

At the primary school gate, Dav wheels Owen past mums with buggies still chatting to the office staff where he writes Owen's name in the late register and braces himself for a bollocking.

'Dav Fisher!' says Jean the secretary, wobbling in for the hug. Then, in contravention of school lateness policy, she offers them orange squash and calls Dav a 'darling big brother'.

'So many kiddywinkles are off.' She swallows to ease the catch in her throat. 'They're frightened, poor babies. Did you see the playpark? I don't know what's come over this town.' She opens her tub of homemade biscuits Owen's been eyeing since he came in. 'Sugar helps with shock,' she says, and pats Dav's head. If he was a lamb and she a ewe, she'd be licking his ears by now. 'What year are you in now, Dav?'

'Ten, Jean.'

'Got a nice girlfriend yet?'

'No, Jean.'

'He's a gay,' says Owen, still holding Dav's hand and looking pleased to know more than a grown-up.

'Ah, well. That's nice too. And how's our surf champ getting on with college?'

Dav shakes his head. 'That didn't work out. He tried an apprenticeship, too, but, you know. See you at three,' he tells Owen. 'Be good.'

'He's always good,' says Jean, ruffling Owen's mop, smile-crying. 'Like his big brothers.'

Dav takes himself to secondary school next, which acts with a compassion for lateness it never showed Rhys. 'You don't have to write an excuse,' says the office lady when Dav takes the late-sheet clipboard and Biro string. 'Not today.'

'Horrible,' says Dav's tutor, escorting him to the lesson so he does not get a detention for bunking and lose his lunchtime. 'So much glass! We moved the test to this afternoon, in light of the disturbances.'

Dav laughs, then wipes the smile from his lips and arranges his face into a frown. 'Thank you, sir.'

The tutor's hand hovers over Dav's shoulder before he changes his mind, like a butterfly taking off as soon as it has landed. 'We know how much the mentoring scheme means to you,' he says. 'You can do it, Dav. Don't let the rioters stop you. They will be brought to justice. They will be locked away, every single nasty little one of them.'

At lunchtime, Dav looks up Long View Farm on Airbnb on the school library computer and discovers they had been sleeping in five stars. *Highly recommended and beautifully furnished getaway, set on an elevated spot within the grounds of a non-working farm.*

If you paid for it with money, it would cost you two grand for the weekend. His loud snort summons the librarian. Thinking Dav must be an avid student of Leisure and Tourism, she calls him 'diligent' for working through all the stress. 'I'm so sorry,' she says, tears in her eyes. 'I've been informed about your… situation.'

'Excuse me?'

'The pastoral team put up a list. We're making reasonable adjustments for Jubilee estate students, where the fires were worse.'

The librarian pulls over a wheelie-chair to help Dav, who is now showing an interest in sundry rental properties via Virtual Tour and Screen Show Mode. According to the professional data retrieval tool later used by Devon & Cornwall Police, he was on it for an incriminating total of twelve minutes and thirty-six seconds.

'Imagine that,' she says. 'How the other half live, eh?'

'Toasty,' says Dav.

Foundland Park House has a swimming pool and croquet lawn. Shepherd's Nook stares at the sea and is perfect for writers and artists, and also people wanting to meditate or do yoga. Fisherman's Cottages has a fifty-foot zip wire and a sofa swing in the garden, the thought of which makes Dav's toes curl. There would be no relaxation to be had on a swing waiting for Owen's ambush to spill him to the grass.

'Where is this place?' says Dav. 'How are grockles supposed to find it?'

The librarian explains that tourists must book and pay to get the address. She shows Dav the online booking calendar with plenty of winter availability. 'It's off-season,' she says. 'Holiday lets make their money in summer.'

Dav nods. *Like us Fishers*, he thinks.

When she goes, Dav does a quick search on social media for Fisherman's Cottages, Lythcombe, South Devon. Allegra from Alton in Hampshire has posted a photo.

> Seals waiting for fishermen. Took this from the kitchen window.

Chen from London writes:

> Kiddies loving the sand. That's
> Fisherman's Cottages, right
> on the cliff!

So, by triangulation of his very own cliffs, coves and moorland, Dav copies their whereabouts into the back of his maths textbook. He is not planning to steal, only borrow for a time. Like he and Owen did last night, for warmth.

He's never been in trouble or a bad kid, nor, while we are about it, is he a thief or burglar.

He just has these tests in his mind, is all, and it's easier to think when you're warm.

After the test and school is done, Dav sees what his tutor meant when he said, 'So much glass!' The Lythcombe boys must have turned wild in the night. Mrs Morris's kitchen window is smashed, red paw prints snaking across the yard, over the low wall and up the coal shed onto her balcony.

'Poor Thing,' Owen says, and climbs his pallet palace to see inside. 'It's all right,' he tells his brother, who is down below him. 'He's licking his paw. Hey, Thing.'

Thing meows once, a short cry.

'Can you see Mrs Morris? Is she okay?'

'Yes, Dav. She's waving at me now.'

Just then, Rhys opens the broken gate. He's cold, hungry. Also, he still has a whiff of fish guts and rotting bait about him.

'All right, numb nuts?' he says.

'No thanks to you,' says Dav.

Owen wants to tell Rhys about the luxury tub, hot as a half-boiled kettle, the ice machine and the tidy Gerry Lopez board in the garage. *Rhys will like the sound of that*, Owen thinks, it being his hobby and vocation. But Owen doesn't get a chance because Rhys takes on a nasty temper, an angry northeasterly in his sails and, ignoring his brothers in the yard, starts cleaning himself up in the bathroom, shaving his top lip and the parts of his face where he has a beard. As he puts on deodorant to make Milly like him more, Owen sticks his head round to ask if he has seen the film set.

Rhys says, 'I've got no time for film sets. I'm going to Exeter,' so Owen then tells him that his tooth is wobbling. On a normal day, Rhys would be interested.

In earning times, Rhys had once stuck a slippery tenner under Owen's pillow and claimed the tooth fairy had borrowed his felt-tips to write the note Owen found, in twirly pink letters, saying Owen must return the nine-quid change under his pillow 'quick as you like'. That tenner was a box of tricks to Owen. Small wonder he kept forgetting to pay the fairy back. In the end, Rhys had to carry him to Mr Vadic and make him get change. 'Fair's fair,' said Rhys. 'Get a Freddo. You don't want to piss the tooth fairy off.'

Another time, Owen had a razor-sharp tooth that

would not fall out for three weeks and his blistered tongue never learned the lesson of it. Owen worried his tooth was there to stay, a sharp little knife in his mouth. Then it came, just as Rhys said it would. 'A baby tooth can't stay in your mouth for ever. You either swallow it or it comes out freely of its own accord.'

This time though, Owen is glad his tooth is only starting to wobble. He tells it to wait in his mouth till Rhys is back from Exeter and their dad home from his Spanish lettuce because, after Long View Farm, who knows where he will sleep next? *Better off in my own bunk with my Spider-Man pillow,* thinks Owen, who loves his matching duvet and curtains, and the little Spider-Man stickers on the walls. *The tooth fairy knows where to come.*

Rhys, now sweet-smelling for Milly's nose, bids his brothers farewell. Dav is sweeping up the yard. 'I'm going to Exeter,' says Rhys again. Dav gives his brother a frosty shoulder so Rhys snatches his broom and chucks it into the corner. 'Little git, don't ignore me.'

'Don't be angry with us,' says Owen, now back in his palace. 'We had no lights last night. And it was cold!'

Rhys's anger folds in on itself like a slowing wave, its energy spent, shattered on rocks three thousand miles from whence it came, hot off the coast of Argentina. He holds out his strong arms to catch Owen, who jumps down.

'I'm sorry I didn't come home,' says Rhys. 'Look...' He shudders, in need of a Xannie to steady his nerves.

'It was not supposed to be like this. I couldn't stop the boys from starting on the park.' He turns to Dav. 'It was my responsibility and I clean forgot the meter. Last night was messy, you see. Declan got arrested.'

'Kieran's brother?'

'Ay. I wasn't going to let them get me, so me and Jakey stayed on the *Maria* last night. We froze our balls off.'

Owen laughs. 'What did you catch?'

'Pneumonia, mate.'

'Serves you right,' said Dav, 'for being a dick.'

'You have no idea what you're talking about. There's a closure on. That's what started it in the first place, what the arrests were about. *They* started it.'

'But Rhys—'

'Don't look at me like that. I'm doing it for you. You'll understand when you're older.'

'I saw you,' Dav says. 'On the news.'

Rhys looks to Owen but he is climbing the palace. 'You saw nothing,' he whispers. 'The time has come and I'm going to be very bloody busy. Anyhow…' He switches to normal volume with a note of brightness. 'I'll top up the meter on my way out. Keep your heads down while I'm away.'

'Are you going out on Jakey's boat again?' says Owen. 'Can I come?'

'No, mate,' says Rhys. 'Like I said, I'm going to Exeter. But don't tell Dad.'

Owen looks at Dav, uncertain. 'Won't Dad want to know about the hot tub?'

'Nice one.' Rhys laughs, thinking Owen has made his first sarcastic joke. The flat is cold, but it was colder on the *Maria*. 'In truth, it was more like an ice tub than a hot tub, mate, herring guts in the hold.' Owen jumps from the pallets again into his arms. 'No, lads. I'll kip on Dodo's sofa tonight and be back quick as you like.'

'What'll you do in Exeter?'

Rhys bends to set Owen down, then rises to his full height, taller than Phil Fisher and Dav, who will never catch him up.

He feels expansive. 'Planning, mate. Planning.'

Seeing Rhys smile, Dav gets out his phone and shows his brother the lines. 'Can you get it fixed in Exeter?'

'I will buy the glass and fix it myself. How was school?'

Owen gets in first, saying, 'We did fractions.'

'Nice. Did you do two big ones or lots of little ones?'

'Lots of little ones. And I wrote a hundred and six and a half words about Home. We were supposed to do one hundred but I went over. I stayed in at playtime to finish. Mrs Hill gave me a star.'

'That's because you are a star, mate. Let's call Dad before I go and tell him we're fine.'

Monitoring the conversation for unhelpful truths, Rhys holds the phone, cramming their dad on board the *Pont-Aven* and their three ginger-tops into the screen.

'How are my boys?'

'Good, Dad.'

'How's school?'

'Good.'

'Mitch told me about the closure. Sorry about that. That's why haulage is a good bet, Rhys. Have you made any further applications for entering education, employment or training?'

'Sort of.'

'Good lad. How's Mrs Morris?'

'Good, Dad.'

'And Thing?'

'He's all right. When are you home, Dad?'

'Well, we left on schedule. I'm somewhere in the middle of Biscay now,' says Phil Fisher, far from where he'd rather be. 'If the Bay behaves herself, I'll be home in the morning and we, boys, shall go out.'

'Out?'

'Yes, boys. Out. I was thinking of us watching the Surf Championships up in Croyde. Mitch has promised me some of his red diesel now he won't be needing it. Can you hang together a little longer? Till Croyde?'

In sore need of a steadying joint, Rhys thinks, *So you will humiliate me by making me watch, will you? I don't want to watch, I want to surf.*

How can he stand on grit sand, earth-bound and washed by rain when he should be a competitor and then champion, unindentured by land?

Seeing Rhys's face darken, Dav says, 'Don't worry, Rhys. We've got something lined up. A Gerry Lopez, mate! Totally genuine. No one's using it—'

Owen snatches Rhys's phone and runs round the

flat yelling, 'Croyde! Croyde! Rhys is going to win a million pounds!' but 3G cannot abide vibration, so by the time Rhys extracts it from Owen's hand, Phil Fisher's face is frozen in a grim smile. Rhys gets a text:

> My connection's gone. Love you boys. Thinking about you day and night.

> Stay together.

'Will God look after Dad at sea tonight?' says Owen, who frets about Rhys and their dad when they're not there, and Thing, if the cat does not come down the stairs to their flat for a few days, and he worries about Mrs Hill from school, too. He worries, in fact, about anyone who is not in the same room – and Binty, of course, if that scrap of cloth is not festering in his hand.

'No,' says Rhys. He feels he is poised on his board, tightening his resolve, ready for the drop. Owen should start growing up a bit, face facts, but when his brother's eyes turn glassy with fear, Rhys lets the wave go under him and changes course. 'I meant yes.'

'But you said *no* first.'

'That's because it's both. There's an element of luck to it as well. God's got to be in the right place at the right time. You can't be everywhere, can you? It's like whitebait, mate. Remember when they were throwing themselves on the beach?'

Now Owen understands what Rhys is driving at. Whitebait don't whimper or cry when cornered. They fight their hardest, not knowing if a hand will come down to save them. The brothers once saw them hunted into the shallows by a pack of mackerel, panic roiling the surface of the sea like a boiling kettle. Reckless, they jumped from the waves, as a man from a burning building, then flapped on the sand, gills gasping, tails slapping, out of bounds and out of air.

The gulls moved in.

Those u-bending bodies of the whitebait started to fold like the Fortune Fish you get in a Christmas cracker, you know the ones: moving means you're jealous; if it flips over, you're a liar, but if head and tail move together, *ha ha, muppet, you're in love*.

A nice-looking lady in a flowery sun hat said to her kid, 'Quick, put them back, they can't breathe.'

As a volunteer lifeguard, Rhys could never abide the sight of a mum in distress. 'Get them,' he ordered, and his brothers obeyed, grabbing and chucking, following the shoal down the line of the beach, silver alive and kicking in their hands.

Plop! went those babies into the waves and away they swam, grateful probably, for the good God Owen and the great God Dav and the greater God Rhys, for their fish-slippery fingers, their monkey grip and thumbs. Cheated of their meal, the slick macks had already moved, empty-bellied, on down Lythcombe Bay.

'But we might not have been there,' Owen had said at the time, looking stricken. 'What would have happened then?'

Rhys tries not to be critical to his dad's face, but now the call is over he says, 'Bloody salad, bloody closure, bloody environment, bloody capitalism, bloody Westminster,' and storms out, holding the front door wide in order to slam it closed more loudly.

Later, he will be heart-sore that he never asked how Dav's test went and whether he thought he was in with a chance, but a secret part of him is certain of Dav's success; smart kid that he is, Dav will solve every problem they throw at him. One more test tomorrow and when he gets back, Phil Fisher will throw a party in the street for his middle-born son, not seeing that passing those tests is the fastest route to losing him for ever.

Though Rhys would refute the allegation, at seventeen he is still a boy, and the breaking kind at that. When Phil Fisher returns from hauling lettuce across Spain tomorrow, after puking his way over the Bay of Biscay, Rhys plans to confess what he has done in Lythcombe, both the wrong and the right of it. Besides, if he doesn't, Dav will tell Phil what he has seen. How can you keep a riot from your dad? The Home Secretary has issued a statement. The Prime Minister is monitoring the situation and Phil will see footage on his cabin telly, angry lads wheeling torched council bins down the high street like chariots of old.

Rhys plans to say, 'We broke this,' and show Jakey's TikTok – the shattered glass – and, 'We burned that,' and show him the charcoal climbing ship and the melted bench. He also plans to say that his brothers had nothing to do with it, safe in their flat where they were told to stay – because sprogs can't choose, can they? They have to follow those in charge. That is the rule and the law.

All things considered, though some call him a 'bad influence' and others a 'menace to society', Rhys would say his brothers are lucky their elder knows what's good for them. His rules include: getting to bed by ten (nine for Owen), no high surf and no sleeping in the dunes in case of pissheads and junkies. As for having a bit of what they like, this includes but is not limited to bonfire teas on the beach and mile-long football.

The rest is what it is. The neighbours are not happy with what happened last night in Lythcombe – the rage and the mess – but like Phil Fisher told the headteacher on the day Rhys was expelled, 'Kids make mistakes, then grow into adults and make stupider ones still. No harm done if you don't do it again.'

To himself, Rhys makes the promise that he will never pick up the bricks and stones and commemorative coronation planters in anger again. Next time, it will be different. Next time it will be slick. It will drive home its point. Car fires and broken glass may look impressive but they are also, according to Dodo, inefficient and counterproductive. Vandalism, as a political tactic, leads to side-eyes of hate from neighbours and former friends. Especially when you forget to write the explanatory placards. It also leads to arrests and investigations and bitter recriminations, cold brothers sleeping in darkness – not to mention a night hiding in the stinking bilge ice and rough-folded seine nets of Jakey's trawler, too damp to light a spliff.

Rhys turns at the door and throws a 'Catch you laters,' at his brothers. He is already away in his mind, stiffening his resolve to do more and do better, even as Owen begs him to stay.

Mistakes were made in Lythcombe, Rhys freely admits in conversation with himself, on his way through the estate to the bus stop. But no more.

✱

Not too long after, Dav is holding a crying Owen on the sofa. 'Don't be an angry idiot like Rhys,' Dav tells him. 'Don't spend summers in a car park shed and be without work in winter. Your future will be better so don't cry. Dad'll be home soon and we'll go to the tor and make things out of snow and take bin bags to slide on. And when it gets warm again, we'll have a picnic by the lighthouse and go down to the cove and bury Dad's legs while he snores.'

'And what about Croyde? Dad promised.'

'He didn't exactly promise. Any rate, you can't make adults hold promises. He said, "Stay together and we'll be all right".'

'Like kings?'

'Ay, like kings. Who else is like us?'

This will not be enough for Owen so he reaches for the shell that goes with him and Binty, thinking the two put together have powers. Except now he remembers that he left Binty at Long View Farm. Dav says they cannot go back now the flat is warm – Rhys kept his promise to top up the meter; the electric fire is working, the lights have come on.

Owen makes a wish in his shell for Binty. Holding back his tears, he says, 'What if I never find her?'

Dav reaches over and wipes his brother's eyes and the dribble of snot running into his mouth. 'All right, then. We'll fetch Binty.' And thinking about Croyde and making Rhys less sad than he already is, he adds, 'And while we're at it, let's take up that lady's offer and borrow the Gerry Lopez. Proper job, eh?'

THIRTEEN

On the bus to Exeter, Rhys considers writing a poem for Milly about surfing. He wants to explain why those ten seconds on your feet on a board on a wave are as long as a lifetime well-lived, the world silent and peaceful but in a rushing, alive way.

Surfing is better than skunk. Better than those silver whippets of nitrous oxide that Dodo gave him, saying, 'Take this, it will blow your very consciousness off the sofa, my friend. All the great thinkers did the same.' Although by the sounds of it, drugs bit that French fellow Jean-Paul Sartre right on the arse, gripped as he was by giant invisible lobsters and crabs pursuing him forevermore after tripping and falling on mescaline, the dickhead.

Any rate, writing about surfing is no good because words are not enough. It is a thing felt in the pit of your stomach. Individuals who have only known land might think that a ratio of a second's ride across the face of a sweet barrel or straight broad-reach plunge through thick frothing foaming white water to the shore, when measured against the effort spent getting out, is not worth the bother.

Dav has done the calculations for him, the ratio being 1:900 – that is, one single second of joy to every fifteen punishing minutes paddling out, hit again and again by each new breaker, and taken under by a fair few.

Those who think this ratio constitutes a massive waste of time are wrong. It is the effort that matters, that makes it what it is, the thing it becomes. There is no joy without struggle, no scrambled eggs without first breaking their perfect shells, nothing to be gained for staying safe in bed, not a single fish caught without the hours mending nets.

The art of surf is one that must be made without fear or thought for the reckoning of reef and rock beneath. Or so thinks Rhys on the bus to Exeter.

'Okay, then,' says Dav to Owen at the flat. It's getting late and his revision is calling. Tomorrow will bring the second part of his test in the hall where Rhys once sat his detentions. 'Just a quick trip to get Binty and the board. No hot tub, mind.'

'I put a hot tub in my writing task. Mrs Hill said to write about Home. I wrote a lot of words, Dav. Miss is going to mark it tonight and then we're going to write it up in best for the wall.'

'Hot tub in Jubilee.' Dav laughs. 'You'll get top marks for imagination, mate. Hope you wrote about your palace as well.'

Dav's phone screen being as indistinct as the sight of harbour from an iced-up trawler in heavy freezing fog, he leaves a note for Rhys in case the bus is cancelled and he comes back while they are gone and starts fretting.

> **Rhys, mate,**

says the note.

> **Me & Owen are going to Long View Farm by the tor. Lady there has the Gerry Lopez you can borrow for Croyde.**

And while Dav gets Rhys's forbidden racer, Owen draws one of his dotty coloured pictures for Rhys: a hot tub with Dav and Owen in it and a big bed with Dav and Owen watching telly atop tasselled cushions. He leaves a note with it:

> **Hope you can do a sleepover here too.**

Then, hearing Dav's voice – 'Owen, get out here!' – he obeys.

The journey up the hill is not so hard as before; at Long View Farm there are no cars on the drive, all the lights are off and the keys are where they should be, in the key safe. The garage door padlock falls open. It's going well; could not be better.

'Here's the board,' says Dav, stroking its curves. Even Dav cannot help but run his hand along a womanly Lopez and sigh, for this surfboard is a thing that stuns you with its beauty – more like a work of evolution or mathematics than something made by man. 'Rhys will like it, eh? We'll put it back after Croyde, soon as he gets out the water. Let's clean it up for him first. Gritty, isn't it? Rub of wax, then it'll be gorgeous!'

He borrows two bungee straps from the garage and ties the precious board flat on Rhys's bike, nose on the handlebars, fins astern the saddle. Owen shimmies up and lies on the waxy sandy bobbles and driveway grit and plans to land-paddle it all the way home like that.

So excited is Owen that he forgets about Binty and scrambles to his knees on the board, saying, 'Can I stand up on the board, Dav? Can I surf all the way home?'

'Go ahead,' says Dav, thinking this will be quicker than Owen's slow walking. 'I've got you.'

Still kneeling, Owen takes three long strokes with his hands, employing the smooth technique Rhys had taught him. He looks back up the lane to see if the wave is yet shouldering. It is surely cresting foamy white in his imagination because he takes one last stroke then pops to his feet. Magic.

Rhys would have been proud to see this. He has always known that Owen is a natural; arms steady, hips pivoted, loose in the shoulders, knees soft. Owen moves *with* the wave, not *against*. Dav tries to steady the wobbling bike by the handlebars, making a good performance of sea swell and winning the battle against gradient and gravity.

On the other side of the hedge, cows scratch their tufty heads to see a bike and board and boy surf by. *What wild things humans are*, they must think, not trusting the testimony of their eyes, it being a dimpsey kind of light – that is, towards dusk.

'The film men are back,' says Owen, who can see further than Dav and whose keen ears hear a new commotion. 'They're burning down the Picture House! They've got fire engines, Dav! Can we go and watch?'

'No, Owen. We cannot.'

At the steepest bit of the lane, Dav walks behind Rhys's bike, backwards-leaning, gripping each side of the tail, a labour he swears he will not repeat, though with Owen, once you start a new game, it's hard to stop.

On corners, Dav leans him into the turn and the handlebars, fixed in one direction, obey.

Only once does Owen wipe out on a grassy bank but, if this lane is sea and Dav the wave, it is no harder than surfing in shallows. In fact, Owen thinks, it may be a far safer place to fall – no jellyfish, weevers, moray eels. *But maybe dogfish poo*. He gets up, laughing.

'Again!'

Dav helps his brother up and so runs the longest wave in history. Dav turns as pink and red as a sunset, but it gets easier as the slope bottoms out into Lythcombe. Safe on the high street, Dav no longer fears that if he accidentally let go of the rail, Owen will surf on without him.

A siren wails. Lights flash and flicker at the road into the Jubilee estate in a rematch of last night.

This is bad, thinks Dav. *What shit will we fall into next?*

'Wrong way,' says Owen as he bends for home.

Having a sixth sense that Children's Services will be waiting outside their flat, Dav has pulled in the opposite direction. 'I know,' he says, 'but let's surf a bit more, first. Land-surfing. It'll catch on, you'll see. Everyone'll be doing it soon.'

They surf the length of town and duck in again, outrunning the crackling, breaking glass on the high street to the prom. Owen's shadow, projected by the streetlights, races ahead and wins, disappearing until the next lamppost. Dav's arms ache with effort.

The sea is inky-flat. Far out, torches on a fishing boat and marker buoys wink at them. Owen waves back. 'Ahoy! Ahoy! Ahoy!' No answer. Dav stops outside Mr Barker's surf shop. The onshore wind has ripped off the binbags that are taped to the shop window and is now helping itself through a hole in the glass, making the wetsuits dance on their rails.

What if the police see this broken window and then see us with this board? thinks Dav, because the law won't stop to examine the grit, the tell-tale tarry smudges and scrapes, evidence of its age. The boys will be called looters and burglars and be arrested as criminals guilty of crime. To avoid the risk, he pushes Owen down the alleyway cut, a different way to get to the same place.

More shouts and sirens.

'Lights, camera, action!' says Owen, having fun.

On the other side of the Jubilee estate, three police vans and a mini fire brigade car are sitting outside the Fisher family flat. Dav and Owen are too far off to hear the officers banging on their door for Rhys, and even if they were closer, their senses would be encumbered by all the other noises ringing in their ears.

Owen must have a quieter place to sleep. 'Let's get out of here, squirt,' Dav says, dreaming up a dry place to kindle his future. 'Fancy a ride on a zip wire?'

The tide is on the turn. Even in Exeter, Rhys can feel it draw upon his back like a change of key. *I don't know about God*, he thinks. *We are more like puppets of the moon. Muppets, if you like.*

He rings the gold-plated doorbell. Who would have thought the struggle would be led from a period townhouse, its six bedrooms now fragranced by skunk and redecorated with revolutionary art?

'Property is theft,' says Dodo, shaking Rhys's hand at the wide front door. On the corridor wall behind Dodo, Milly has newly painted these exact same words in scary burning shapes, full of pin-striped monsters and flames, like something out of Owen's nightmares.

Poor Owen, thinks Rhys, and poor Dav for the work of Owen. But Rhys will not be here long. Once Dodo has explained their new aims, Rhys expects Owen's hand to be in his by home-time tomorrow, the little squirt's batshit ramblings hammering his ear. That is, after a small detour to take back what is rightfully theirs, in the manner of his great-great-grandaddy Owain Glyndŵr from history.

No Progress Without Revolution, as the poster says in the bog.

Milly is asleep. Her artwork accomplished, she is resting her eyes in advance of the next sweet wave of inspiration, much like sitting out a couple of sets when your arms are sore from paddling.

So, property is theft, now, is it? thinks Rhys when Dodo goes into the kitchen and leaves him on the sofa, less than the breadth of a breeze block from Milly's batik sarong.

With he and the wall agreeing that property is a kind of robbery, Rhys also thinks, *Hang on, which is worse? To steal a mate's girl who cannot belong to you? Or to keep her trapped inside like this when she would do better outside?*

The surf poem left unwritten, except in his head, Rhys considers just asking Milly out straight. It is a free country, after all. He has a vision of himself opening a shiny car door, Milly stepping into a polished red hatchback, a new air freshener dangling from the rear-view mirror, or riding pillion on the back of his Kawasaki, her arms around his middle, fingers tucked below his belt for warmth – *Bless me*, thinks Rhys – her hair flowing in the wind, or else not, if he could stretch to a spare helmet.

These things are nice to think about, but a want

of winter employment is not the only reason Rhys is doomed in love. There is also the matter of his brothers, because with greater age comes great responsibility and while Phil Fisher is away, his eldest son is charged with their care and general protection.

Dav might be the one who plates up the evening meal with a left-over cucumber garnish brought home from the pub, because he has seen the things chefs de partie do. But it is Rhys who peels and boils the spuds, since, unlike rabbits, man cannot live on salad alone. And it is Rhys who instructs Owen to take a bath and sees that his teeth have been brushed and sand emptied from his shoes. Moreover, he is the one who dries their school uniforms on the pallet palace to catch the sun at ten o'clock, and feeds the meter every week – money he'll get back off his dad – and maintains the bikes when cash allows, and tops up Dav's phone with call-time for emergencies, and lets Owen crawl into his bed, kicking Rhys all night in the shin and balls.

How many boys do you know, a fish-fart shy of eighteen, who will say, 'I'm on it' when their little brother needs a tin of baked beans for the non-uniform day in aid of the Lythcombe foodbank?

Remembering this, Rhys realises there is no way he can pick Milly up. It's not only for want of a job or a car, nor because of Dodo, whose girl she is. Nor is it because he has Dav, scowling at girls like they are no good for him.

It is because of Owen, who will wipe his snotty nose on Milly's lovely untouchable boobs, the exact height of his hug. Truth told, there is nothing Rhys would not do for the little squirt. Rhys knows he is a better person for having the boy as his brother. And Owen looks more like their mum than any of them, as if she finished the best child last – third time lucky, the first two being practice, blueprint, sketch.

Owen is why Rhys built the pallet palace, a tower commissioned and designed by the batshit mind of a small child that the council would surely confiscate if they knew about it. Its top level is particularly dangerous, requiring the correct measure of care when Phil Fisher pulls into the yard to park his Iveco, in case the structure topples to the concrete, a ruin of all their hopes.

There. That's it. That's why he can't invite Milly home.

What might she think of it, looming as high as Mrs Morris's kitchen window, just one more pallet to go and their dad home soon to finish the job?

Perhaps she would not be surprised, though Rhys speaks few words in her company. After all, she herself drew *There Lies A Sleeping Giant. For When He Wakes, He Will Shake The World* in the bedroom where she sleeps, shampoo-smelling, in Dodo's arms. Rhys sticks his head in on his way to the bog. It is a sorry room with curtains drawn and ashtrays full. No stars above or breaching whales or breaking waves in Exeter, only rumbling buses and pissed clubbers, clever students on their way to better things, like Dav.

Well, thinks Rhys. *I too can Shake The World as well as he.*

*

Contrary to the claims made on Airbnb, 'Fisherman's Cottages (sleeps 4)' is not a tranquil spot. Squadrons of seabirds screech and squabble over their perches all day, while black water smashes to foam at night, hammering the cliffs for all eternity. Waves rake pebbles in the little cove below, pummelling them beyond resistance into smooth balls.

There are many child safeguarding hazards at the former Fisherman's Cottages. Respect is due to Dav; it is not easy looking after an eight-year-old on your own. The zip wire in the garden goes almost to the edge of the grassy cliff, which sounds dangerous, but is so much worse in trainers, the slick path a-zigzagging down to the beach. The button seat of the zipwire is too stiff for Owen, and he too dinky to drag it, but nor will he get off and help. Instead, he stays put, holding the rope with both hands, and at the end of each ride says, 'Go on, again, Dav! Please!'

Dav's arms are sore from dragging him up, his legs from running him down. The onshore wind, straight off the sea, is biting. 'Last one, squirt,' he says, but Owen leans back with one hand and shrieks, 'Again!'

'No,' says Dav, meaning it this time. 'I must revise.' And he turns his back on Owen to fetch the key to the place, knowing if you leave Owen he will find you, having an aversion to being alone.

There is the key box, in the porch; 8462 is the code. The numbers light up blue, there follows a mechanical click and it opens like a safe in a heist film to reveal the treasure: a Chubb key, free for the taking.

Backalong in history, this had been three cottages before its walls were knocked through to make rooms the size of the brothers' whole flat. The kitchen is as cold as the *Maria*'s ice room, and decorated in the trawler-style, too: lobster pots hanging on the walls, seine nets above the stove, crab creels, shiny aluminium buoys and cork floats. The sitting room is a beach of bleached driftwood skeletons, seashells stuck to clay pots. A stuffed Alaskan sockeye salmon sits on the window-ledge, glass eyes looking out at the sea that was once his home.

Dav turns up the thermostat to thirty degrees and flagstones toast their feet. He is setting-to with a hot drink when a noise outside makes him smash the lighthouse-motif mug in the sink.

'Only a fox,' he tells Owen on the porch, but then he hears engines a way off on the main road, and thinks, *Our luck can't last*. Dav knows they are not meant for this world of hot tubs and hot floors and zip wires and private coves and the little pots of shampoo in Welsh-slated wet-rooms, square beds and long pillows and monstrous-cold fridges.

Be patient, he thinks, because he also knows this time will soon be consigned to the past. In the morning, Phil Fisher will dock at Plymouth and when his loads have been cleared, the paperwork stamped, he will turn for home. Once Dav's test is done and the uprising, as Rhys terms it, has burned itself out, its agitators arrested,

Dav resolves to never be the guest of an Airbnb again.

The likes of the Fishers are not made for such places, he concludes. Their pockets are too shallow. They are like a landed bream seeing, side-eyed, the upper world, the dry world, and how sore it makes their lungs!

The phone rings. Dav tells Owen to ignore what's none of their business and they zip wire some more and collect shells in the moonlight to add to the ones the grockle sprogs find. Then they go inside, choosing the biggest bedroom, and unburden the bed of its assortment of vermillion cushions.

'Now, get yourself comfy-like.' Dav puts on the widescreen. 'Porridge in the morning, mate,' he tells him, having spotted oats in the kitchen.

'Don't leave me on my own if you wake up before me,' says Owen, not knowing his brothers would never leave him, unless forced to do so by revolutionary necessity.

Dav makes up for the scant tea and near-child abandonment with cheese and onion crisps to eat in bed. At seven, Owen falls asleep under Dav's arm, snivelling and hiccoughing a bit because of Binty left behind. Soon he is quiet, a little furnace of hot sleep so Dav turns off the telly and ploughs into Test Paper 2.

The phone rings again. It gives Dav a bad feeling. He sees lights coming up the lane. He shakes Owen and drags him and their stuff out of bed and down the stairs and into the undergrowth in the nick of time, no less, because a Mercedes A-Class drives up so fast it nearly dinks the board-bike Dav propped against the hedge. A man gets out, examines the open front door and empty key safe.

'I don't know!' he shouts into his phone in Received Pronunciation. 'There's no sign of arson. I know. I *know*. I saw the news.' He looks out to sea, picking his nose. 'Anyway, get onto Airbnb. I don't care if they were flipping elderly! Put in a formal complaint. The heating's blaring! And they've taken the key!'

The moon is full and very bright, drawing triangles of light lines over the water. Moored yachts in the bay rock like white cabbage butterflies. A pod of silver dolphins comes by, not far from the beach, and the man takes photos. Will he ever go?

'Dolphins have boobies, you know,' whispers Owen and for this information gets an elbow in his ribs.

'Shut it,' Dav hisses, but takes the bait. 'They're mammals, all right,' he says, a sotto voce scientist all of a sudden. 'Same basic skeletal structure as us; as bats and elephants.'

Bird-shape silhouettes fly over the brothers' heads, shouting at each other in fish-breath language, and not a biologist in the world can tell what they are saying.

'There's the ISS!' whispers Owen, not knowing enough about the world to be scared.

'Shh,' says Dav, knowing exactly enough.

From their great vantage at the end of the zip wire on the edge of the earth, they can see a heavenly panorama all about them. Tanker lights flash by the refinery, and the coast path dips and rises along the cliffs, disappearing in the distance down to Plymouth.

South-southwest is Lythcombe town, where the closure will soon bite; the half-moon bay and dunes, the white mast of the Coastguard office like a ship headed nowhere, and the lighthouse where Siân Fisher loved to eat her sandwiches.

To the north, before the moon sticks her shy head in a cloud, they can see a shoelace-lane strung from the tor. A small fire is burning somewhere on the moor, like the ones that keep the bracken down, or like a stack of straw bales sent up in flames, which farmers light themselves when the straw goes sour; you can't always point the finger of blame at angry boys.

The flames light the hillside, a halo of smoke.

Dav thinks, *Such beauty, especially at night. What a place to live and be alive! Who knows what goes on in the sky and in the sea and under the surfaces of this world when we're sleeping?* And, in the grockle accent he intends to use at university, he adds, in his head, *Jolly good show for Airbnb. If we'd been in our beds, we'd have missed this.*

The man locks up the cottage and pisses in the hedge, so close that Dav and Owen nearly see his wrinkly todger. The moon and ISS duck under cloud. Darkness is on the brothers' side; they do not see his todger and the man leaves before spying their double-borrowed board-bike by the zip wire.

Of course, they could creep back in now the man's gone but Dav is spooked. 'How about a night surf on the bike?' he says when the Mercedes is gone. 'Can't stay here, any rate.'

Dav has a big push ahead, two miles across

Lythcombe Bay, but where they're headed will be worth it for a bed and no fancy thermostat to dob them in. What's more, there'll be no police knocking on their door, saying, 'Where's your father? Where's your mother? Right, then, chummy. What's this? A Gerry Lopez Hawaiian Pipeliner? Six foot eight? Found it in the charity shop, did we? Bought it with our pocket money?'

'Sure,' says Owen. 'Let's build a fire and sleep in the dunes. Rhys is not here to stop us.'

'A fire on the beach won't keep us warm all night,' says Dav. 'I need to study.'

So Owen lies atop the bike-board, firm in Dav's hand. Two short strokes and he pops to his feet again, little champ that he is.

'Waikiki!' he says, as jubilant as you can be when you are eight years old on a board-bike with no test tomorrow nor girl to break your heart.

'Honolulu,' says Dav, less elated.

'Uluwatu!' says Owen. 'Fistral!'

'Fistral's hardly exotic,' says Dav, 'try Big Sur.' And he steadies the board-bike while they name other places in Rhys's surf movies and the twenty-year-old magazines he finds on eBay. 'Never a wave out of date,' as Rhys says – a veritable truth.

Dav runs out of places first and starts, in his mind, making new plans on the hop that don't involve police knocking on their door or teachers chatting in the staffroom or Children's Services taking them into care, and Phil Fisher coming home to an empty flat.

Part of Dav is also worrying that Rhys will be arrested for his part in this nonsense and taken to Princetown in North Dartmoor, a fair drive from Lythcombe, where he'll be made to share a cell with hardened criminals. For all that the thought of men pumping iron in the prison gym stirs Dav's boxers, he won't let that happen to Rhys. He has the antidote to his brother's troubles and Owen is riding it.

What Dav needs now is the Shepherd's Nook cabin, a posh wooden hut on wheels that is rented out in the summer to artists and writers seeking the kind of solitude that is not too far from a pub. In days gone by, huts like that provided shelter for a shepherd to hunker down during the lambing season. Tonight it will provide a place to slide the board between mock-ancient wheels, where Owen can sleep and Dav revise, the sheep all around cropping the grass and bleating their night-conversations.

'This is fun!' says Owen, getting a second wind powered by cheese and onion crisps, and they sing 'EVERYBODY GOES SURFIN', SURFIN' USA!' at the top of their lungs, alarming any seabirds not yet in their clifftop beds.

'WHAT SHALL WE DO WITH THE DRUNKEN SAILOR?' is Owen's next selection on the board-bike jukebox.

'THE BIG SHIP SAILS ON THE ALLY-ALLY-OH' is started by Dav.

'ALLY-ALLY-OH, ALLY-ALLY-OH,' they sing together. 'ON THE LAST DAY OF SEPTEMBER.'

And the cattle in the fields and the rooks in the trees and the gulls on the rocks and the fish in the sea all sing back, 'PUT A BLOODY SOCK IN IT!'

Dav is feeling much better, now. His thoughts run like this: Dad will be home soon and Owen will be happy. Rhys will have a tidy championship board and triumph once again. His picture will appear in the *Express & Echo* and *Carve* magazine.

And in a few years, Dav thinks, *I will take my place at Nottingham where boys are kind and give sweet-tasting kisses.*

No more glass and fire and running away for the Fishers. Enough.

FOURTEEN

In Exeter, Rhys and Dodo are occupied with their own great thoughts and conversation. In the time it takes to agree new tactics, two packets of incense have burned to the wood, twenty tealights to a waxy pool and nigh on an eighth of resin, softened by flame, crumbled and drawn through the watery bong for a mellow draw.

Rhys and Dodo have also downed five stubby Belgian lagers apiece. For her part, Dodo's girlfriend swallowed a benzo the colour of a blackbird egg, and fell back to sleeping prettily.

'It is time to lay off the serfs,' says Dodo as the lava lamp roils up and down. 'We must hit the landlords. Our natural rights must no longer be ignored. Look up the Levellers on your phone, my friend… Ah, sweet. But no, not your father's favourite band. The rural rebels of the 1600s.'

Nor do Rhys and Dodo eat so much as a pot of instant noodles as they face the truth that they alone are to blame. None of their demands had been broadcast across the news because most of the boys legged it before the media arrived and those that stayed were arrested; their Snaps have condensed into the Cloud. All that remains are handheld clips from frightened neighbours and next-day headlines calling the rioters thugs, vandals, out-of-control NEETs – that is, persons Not in Education, Employment or Training – running on the roofs of good people's cars, pulling road signs out of their foundations like onions.

To be fair, some of the lads were a bit beery. But it's not only that – they don't have the words. They can't spin fine phrases like the oil protestors in London to explain why the closure would hurt everyone. Their only tools are broken glass and fire, and those tools have proved worse than useless. They've been fighting the wrong war. Hurting the wrong people.

Dodo goes on to say they must make a similar statement, something to make politicians sit up and capitalist investors shake in their bespoke shoes.

Rhys wonders what 'bespoke' might mean. But the general direction was clear enough – namely, the plan must be tailored. They must strike or be stricken. There must be fires from Lythcombe to Kingsbridge and Salcombe. Dartmouth, too. 'It will be like the Spanish Armada,' says Dodo. 'A necklace of fire along our coast to warn of colonial corporate invasion. Anywhere with an unconscionable number of unoccupied investment properties will burn.'

What was 'unconscionable'? Again, Rhys could not rightly say, the gist of it being that they must also torch surf-adjacent garment shops unaffordable to any but grockles, such as White Stuff, Seasalt, Finisterre or Crew, and likewise fancy-pants restaurants where celebrity chefs will plate up a mackerel sarnie for twenty-five quid – a miracle of increase not seen since the Bible.

Airbnb lets that exist only to make a profit for their owners must have their windows smashed. The empty cottages of the wretched rich must be torched. Businesses must be turned to ashes, although Rhys hopes they will make an exception for the Co-ops and SPARs and the pubs where good fishermen go.

The government, seeing everything alight, will 'curse the day' (Dodo's words, not Rhys's) that they cut youth services, social services, housing services, family services, dental services, Sure Start—'

'And maternity services?' says Rhys.

Dodo nods. 'And the hope.'

According to Dodo, Westminster politicians claim they are *levelling up*, but he holds that there is another meaning of *levelling* that was more true of what had been done to the West Country. Namely, that its people have been *flattened* and *crushed* and *buried* like trash until no more of them can be seen.

Rhys sees then that Dodo has dedicated his life to setting everything right. He is more than a good man. He is the very best of men.

'But what if we're caught?'

'Ha!' says Dodo, smiling. 'How opportune that they have also levelled policing.' Rhys might never be apprehended, he says, and if he was, cuts to Crown Court services meant that he would be dribbling in an old folk's home before his case was heard.

Rhys does not like the sound of Crown Court, but his contribution is thus, trying for a phrase in Dodo's style: 'Let them keep the peace whose futures do not involve safety goggles and steel caps deducted out of the first payslip and home to a cold flat at the end of it. Let *them* obey the law!'

'Hear, hear!' Dodo says. 'They will rue the day they stole our future and made working men angry.' At this, Rhys looks at Dodo's soft poet's hands and wonders if words can ever count as work. He strikes that from his mind; someone must be tasked with writing history.

'Must it all burn?' says Rhys, thinking of the climbing ship, now ashes, and Owen with nowhere to play.

'Indubitably.'

This being decided, the warriors select four holiday homes to set in a fiery necklace, each a half-hour walk from Lythcombe and Rhys's bed. One is a 'non-working' farmhouse, a fine place with 'a luxury hot tub at the disposal of guests, wide-reaching views over the coast and the moor behind. A panorama for relaxation'.

Rhys is mindful throughout of people's health and safety: he is careful to check the bookings calendar, ensuring that no guests will be in occupation, before moving on to the slideshow of the bedrooms, kitchen and bathrooms, and the garden. *Nice tassel cushions*, thinks Rhys. *When I have a wife, we will stick some of them on our bed.*

Next, he scrutinises the floorplans, as he had been taught at college, noting symbols for ingress and egress, inferring where the supporting stone walls might be and which will only constitute thin MDF, at what points the roof joists will intersect and where they will likely be suspended or cantilevered. Despite not completing his NVQ Level 2, Rhys finds that knowing how a building is made is much the same as knowing how to knock it down.

The coast is a lonely place at night. At the end of Lythcombe Bay the cliff hangs its head over the sea, maybe saddened to see two boys on their own in the dark. Owen asks Dav for a story to keep him warm, about when he was a baby and went to Guernsey. This is mostly a true story, based on the first of Phil Fisher's screw-ups when he started being a lone parent. However, the yarn has been somewhat embellished over time.

'The one when you floated away?' asks Dav.

'Yes,' says Owen. 'The one where I snuck into someone's blow-up dinghy in an offshore wind.'

'It was a hot day—' Dav starts the tale, soon interrupted, as per usual.

'—and it took years to find me,' says Owen. 'I came back nearly grown and talking pure gibberish I'd learned from a fish. Dad cried and cried. So did you and Rhys. A whale came, remember? Don't forget the whale.'

'The one that took you in its jaws to El Dorado?' says Dav.

'Not that whale.'

'The one like a mountain that rolled and the wave of it sent you home?'

'No, the other one. But don't miss out the bit before that when I taught myself to fish with flotsam and navigate by the stars and I discovered a new island off Guernsey that no man had ever before seen.'

Now Dav is clear what yarn Owen means, he begins.

'So, it was hot…'

Dav steers him down towards the sand. The Shepherd's Nook, where they are headed, is located on the other side of the bay, behind a gale-bent hedge, where farmers used to bring pigs down to eat the bladderwrack and sea lettuce and other salty plants now consumed by well-off grockles in restaurants.

Of course, Dav turns down the slipway onto the sand where the driftwood washes up at high tide, to navigate a more direct route across the arc of the bay. He tells Owen to hop off for now; a board-bike with a rider is too hard to push on sand but it makes a good cart for the sticks they will need – the least useful of which is a long branch Owen insists on dragging.

'… and Dad was taking a nap. Rhys and me were supposed to keep an eye on you but you had other ideas. Our kelp-man sand sculpture and seaweed sandwiches made of real sand couldn't hold your interest for long. You wanted adventure.'

'A life on the ocean wave is better than being at sea!'

'Exactly. Only one year old – not even one – you crawled to some grockle's blue blow-up dinghy.'

'Orange,' says Owen.

'Ay. My mistake. With three chambers in case of puncture and a plastic oar.'

'And a big sticker on the side.' Owen's face is a picture of glee. '*NEVER leave little kiddies unattended near water.*'

'Right. You got inside. It was in a lagoon. At least at the start, it was.'

'Low tide?' says Owen.

'Right. Dead safe, shallow-like, a sand bank between you and the sea.'

'But the tide came in!'

'Yes, Owen! Fast. Too fast.'

'It came in and a wind grew!'

'Yes, a mighty wind.'

'And I floated away to the Channel Islands, Dav!'

'Not yet. You met the whale first.'

'It rose like a mighty mountain in the bay!'

'Bigger than a mountain...'

'... and it reared!'

'Ay, like a rearing pony and twisted on its side. The wave nearly swept Lythcombe away. Which is why,' says Dav, 'we couldn't find you.'

'All the boats were sunk?'

'Exactly!'

'And the telephone lines went down! What's a "telephone line" again?'

'It's a wire coming out the wall that phones used to have in olden days. All Dad could do was watch you, a speck on the horizon.'

'Soon I became hungry!'

'Starving.'

'So I paddled to some marine flotsam – baler twine, fish hooks, crab pots...' Owen stops.

Dav waits. 'Don't you want to finish the list?'

'You say it, Dav. I'm tired now.'

It takes the whole long of the bay to tell it – in fact, they run out of beach long before they run out of yarn, leaving squiggly lines of swept sand behind them from Owen's branch.

Ahead, a thin shiny pencil line on the far beach grows long and fat and resolves itself into something solid, shaded with shadows and sharp crevasses. It is the breakwater. And the dot on the end of it resolves itself into Mrs Morris.

In Exeter, Dodo says, 'The only thing necessary for the triumph of evil is for good men to do nothing.'

He's a clever one to be sure, like Dav, slick with words and seldom wrong. Next thing he tells Rhys is, 'The hour has come. Will you go?'

'Me?' says Rhys. 'What – right now?' And Milly, rousing from her attractive slumber, smiles his way as if to say, 'Who else could be that strong?' and drops her eyes, shy-like, to the creamy wine-stained rug.

Dodo writes down a poem for Rhys in his curly

handwriting, pretty letters following each other like bead-strings of bladderwrack that snag your fins and upend you off the shoulder, as if an underwater hand just grabbed hold of your leash.

Close up, it turns out to be more of a shopping list and it goes like this:

Gin or vodka.

Absorbent cloth.

Glass bottles.

A knife or scissors.

A flame.

A map.

A holiday home – empty, but all the same a warning, adds Rhys in his head. *A window made of the breaking kind of glass.*

And since such things breed like mice on the web, Dodo makes a note for Rhys to tell the Lythcombe boys to use tags like #MebyonDewnans #SonsOfDevon and #TakeBackWhatsOurs to advertise their fight.

'We will leave those egregious landlords in a cold sweat,' says Dodo, pressing the list into Rhys's hand. 'Once the fires have started, they'll be calling their estate agents within an hour.'

What he means is this: if their lardy London arses warm at the pyre of a climbing frame, then one or two burned cottages later, their nerves will give out and there will be a forest of For Sale signs sprouting in the lanes and streets. Property values will drop faster than anchors.

'And you?' says Rhys. 'Will you come too?'

At this, Dodo passes Rhys his joint – he is never one to hold on too long – and says, 'My place is here, for strategic oversight and operational coordination.'

Rhys sees no problem with this. It is likewise aboard fishing trawlers. If, like Dodo, you have reached your late twenties or early thirties, you can expect younger men to do the heavier lifting.

Rhys wants to leave and do it that night, but skunk and stubbies have mashed up his head. Then, Dodo passes Rhys his spliff and goes for a slash, leaving Rhys alone on the sofa with Milly. When she opens her eyes and blinks, Rhys puts the following question he has no right to ask.

'Will you watch me surf?'

It is plain Rhys does not mean *now* but *one day* because there will be no buses running for a fair few hours, and though he would love to show her the ocean at night, it is too soon for such closeness.

Seeing Milly gather her cardigan against the cold, Rhys's hopes rise, thinking she is ready to leave with him right then, but those hopes fall as her eyes flick to the Indian elephant shawl covering the toilet door, then swell like a spring tide when she touches his knee and takes the spliff from him. She licks her finger and dampens the Rizla to give it an even burn. Rhys wishes he was that spliff.

'One day,' she says. 'After the revolution.' Which in Rhys's mind is the exact same thing as saying 'Yes'.

✳

Seeing Mrs Morris out in the dark at the end of the breakwater, Dav and Owen abandon the board-bike at the dry end, jamming a pedal in a concrete crack and leaving the pile of polished sticks like white antlers on the sand. Dav climbs over the boulders, Owen follows, slower, sleepy, still dragging his branch. It is not right, Owen being out at this hour – he needs his sleep – but Dav cannot go past Mrs Morris without saying hello.

'How are you, then, Mrs Morris?' says Dav, finding her barefoot on the end of the breakwater, dipping her swollen toes in the piddly waves, nails yellow in the moonlight, skin puffy and cracked around the joints. She is a stranger to shampoo and brush, her hair like the wild shock of white feathers you find on the moor after a sparrowhawk has been at work on a pigeon.

'I don't like to, no,' she says.

'Good place to paddle,' says Owen, grinning. He shows off his branch. 'We're going to burn it. Tonight. I've been land-surfing. Would you like to see how it is done?'

'Not today, thanks,' she says. 'No.'

'What are you going to do at high tide?' says Dav, because the water won't stay tickling her ankles for long; winter tides run high. She is in peril of drowning, with no lifeguard on duty, no one strong like Rhys at this late hour to pull her out.

'I'd rather not,' she says. 'I'm going away now. I'm not coming back.'

Owen puts his little hand in hers, his head on her arm, even though she smells putrid.

'Not today, thanks,' she tells him and dips her shoulder to shake him off, but he keeps it there and curls his fingers round hers and looks at Dav.

'I did that, too, didn't I?' he says to his brother. 'I went away and nearly never came home. Tell it to Mrs Morris, how I went away and didn't come back for—'

'Months,' Dav says.

'Years.'

Mrs Morris chews her lip. 'Oh no, did you? Liar.'

'No, really. There was a dinghy, see,' says Owen, looping back.

It's okay because the boy tells it quick: the lagoon pool, safe and shallow; the incoming tide, wind; the whale's breaching engulfing the town; no boats, no telephone, no rescue; drifting for days; gnawing hunger; flotsam, a hook!, a fish; an island never before seen by the eyes of man.

'And you remember all this, do you?' says Mrs Morris in her lumpy gravy voice.

'No,' says Owen. 'I was only a baby at the time. I used to think babies could remember but now I'm not so sure. Mrs Morris, do you think Thing will be hungry?'

'Thing?'

'Your cat.'

'Cat,' says Mrs Morris. Her face turns angry, a new storm on the water. 'Cat,' she says again, her tone menacing. Mrs Morris's mind often falls into troubled waters. It's best if you catch her on a Monday when she has been to Mr Vadic for her bottles. The further on from then, she gets more mardy and her hands start to shake. Best leave well alone.

'C'mon, Owen,' says Dav. 'Let's go. See you, Mrs Morris. See you soon.'

'Cat,' she hisses. 'You're lying, I can tell by your face.'

Owen puts his hand on hers again and says, 'I didn't mean to scare you. Thing'll be out hunting right now. He'll have a bellyful of mice. All he wants will be a scratch behind the ears when you get in.'

Owen smiles and Mrs Morris draws her cracked lips back from her missing teeth in something very close to a smile. Maybe she can't decide if he is grown up or little.

Maybe, inside, he is bigger now than anyone thought. But will his words do the trick? Will she be off home, as the water rises? Owen seems to think so by his grin, but by her countenance, Dav thinks not.

Turning, he sees fires down the coast. They look like burning oil on water, like a tanker-spill lit up, and he feels jellyfish stingers shoot electrics through his body.

Board and bike and driftwood set, the brothers move on. Owen folds about Dav's back like chimp babies do with their mums, riding to the Shepherd's Nook, the sheep and his sleep.

'Get down and walk,' says Dav when they are nearly there. 'I can't carry you no more.' But Owen's breath is now a piglet snuffle in his ear. He is what Phil Fisher calls 'gone', from the time when Owen was very little and went to bed before his brothers, who stayed up longer for a film, taking their rightful place on the sofa, one each side of their dad. But Owen would toddle out and they would take turns to put him back, and out he would toddle again. In the end, their dad would say, 'He's gone.' Which was when they could bring out the biscuits.

Dav leans the bike against the Shepherd's Nook. Lythcombe is just on the other side of the dunes, out of sight. He and Owen have found a safe haven. A sliver of moon sparkles over the sea to lie at the brothers' feet and they do not concern themselves with the smoke that rises over their town.

The Shepherd's Nook padlock combination is in the code book; six clicks and the internal clockwork turns, pinions retract and release their feeble grip on property law. The burner has been left ready to go: sticks on newspaper and logs in a basket. A note says: *More dry wood under the wheels* but Dav knows this already from when he slipped the board out of sight. He strikes a match, uses the sticks he and Owen gleaned and the hut soon becomes so toasty that an artist or writer shipwrecked in a storm might pay three hundred quid a night to kip here in the warm, when fog rolls in or horizontal rain pelts upwards under their rain mac from below.

The sheep bleat. The fire crackles.

Owen makes a ball in the narrow bed, knees to chin, and Dav takes the rocking chair, to keep the fire going against winter.

Last time for this lark, he tells himself. *Dad'll be home soon, so there's no point getting sad.* He misses Phil Fisher, as he sits there in the chair with the fire and the sheep and the waves, and for once he misses Rhys, who he rates a dickhead most of the time.

Dav thinks Rhys might like a shot at this chair, with a net to mend and a pipe to smoke, like the men in the black and white photos at Fisherman's Cottages.

My brother has simple needs, he thinks. *When I am earning big dollars, I will wire him money so that he can buy a scallop boat. We will be partners, of a sort, and as long as he doesn't bad-mouth my boyfriends, I will accept the girls he chooses, though they will probably break his heart.*

Then he gets out his maths book and dreams of what is to come – one more test in the morning and a place on the mentoring scheme, something he now feels somewhat less sure about. Between sums, life flashes towards him, both the good and bad of it, like bands of weather coming in from the sea: sweet love, but in a lonely city, land-locked and far from home. Like sets of waves, you cannot stop your future coming; it is always one thing, and another, then another, and again.

FIFTEEN

Rhys does not sleep well this night, or thereafter, not because Dodo's sofa is a foreign and insanitary place, nor because of the heart-scorching things that follow, but because he loves Milly more than he wants Dodo to be his mate. He loves her more than waves and sea. And, in the space of that room and moment alone, though he will learn the wrong of it by morning, he loves her more than his own brothers.

Bad dreams stir him. Heavy barrels roar over his head – not ones from these parts but places he has seen the webcams thereof, like Uluwatu, Big Sur, Fistral – and wildfires make these breaks a steaming, hissing mess. The seas evaporate and he walks barefoot from here to Brazil over the bodies of still-pulsating jellyfish, gaping mouths of dogfish and spider crabs too lanky to lift their weight in air. What Rhys needs is someone to help him know what to do, a God or prophet to show him how to put the water back where it is supposed to be and smooth the ocean over.

At 4 a.m. he gives up the sofa for a bad job and leaves, taking Dodo's Zippo (later labelled *Exhibit 56-*

W: Monographed Gold Cigarette Lighter belonging to Rupert Cavendish) for courage in his pocket and a reminder of his rebellious duty. Soon, he is walking past singing students, nicking their empty bottles as he goes and stuffing them in his bag. A fight breaks out outside a club. Rhys puts up his hood and crosses the road.

Nearer the bus station, he sees an estate agent's window and it puts him in mind of when Phil Fisher said they should find a bigger flat. His dad does not mind kipping on the sofa, it being nicer than his lorry cab, but by rights his growing boys could do with having three bedrooms between them, not one.

'Now, what if they go ahead with the Lythcombe Regeneration Zone?' his dad had said. 'They won't need wrecking balls to knock Jubilee down, all they will need to do is blow on it. We'll be out on our ears, then. Relocated. And once we've been relocated, they won't ask us back. No, son. I've got to work hard and get the money together. So we've got choices, like. A rental deposit ready to go.'

Rental deposits in Lythcombe being sky high, Phil Fisher will need to put a few more hours on the tachometer, counting up the miles. But as soon as he has a deposit, they can start looking. Rhys said he did not want to leave Lythcombe but if that was the case, he would find a paying job and chip in.

His dad said, 'No, son. It's my responsibility, as your father.'

Rhys did not say, 'It is also your responsibility to be with your sons and not on some motorway in Europe,' though he sorely wanted to. Instead, he gave him some other lip to which Phil Fisher replied that Rhys must finish his NVQ and learn a trade.

'You'll have the rest of your life for bills. Right now, you're a boy.'

'I am not,' Rhys said at the time. 'I'm sixteen.' But Phil Fisher cared no more for how old Rhys was than what he had to say.

Now, in front of the estate agent in Exeter, Rhys sees what his dad had meant by sky-high rental deposits. The houses in the window come furnished, suitable for immediate letting, and their owners do not even have to come down to Devon if they don't fancy it, for the agents offer a full management, no-tenant-headache guarantee.

There is a tidy little place in Lythcombe, near the harbour, with two bedrooms. The sign in the window says to expect 'High Season rental yields in excess of £1800 per week'.

Rhys thinks, *Do they not know that we live here all year, winter included? And who can lay their hands on £1800 a week, short of winning the lottery or robbing a bloody bank?*

Even if he got a job tomorrow, he and his dad together could not make that kind of cash.

It's only 4.15 a.m., but as luck would have it, next door to those high-yield rental portfolio opportunities in the estate agent's window is the open-lit door of a Nisa 24/7 that sells spirits and tea towels and other items for the purposes of premeditated arson. These bought, Rhys proceeds to the bus station where he will use up all his remaining data on the business of their New Tactic, the precise *where* of it, now that he has the *how*. He smiles at the thought of its impact, which will kill two birds with one stone.

The first bird being the feathery heart of capital greed in the vacation lettings market.

The second being the love and admiration of Milly, who will soon no longer think of him as *Rhys, the apprentice hod-boy*, or *Rhys of the parking ticket shed*, but *Rhys, the revolutionary*, and *Entrepreneur-Rhys, the small mammal millionaire*.

And in the coming weekend swell or soon thereafter, if he can speak to Jakey about the loan of his fibreglass stick for Sunday's heavy-thumping forecast at Croyde, he will become *Rhys, the champion surfer* again, coming in from the sea with his fat winnings while she, Milly, in the midst of selling her pretty painted seascapes in a fluttering cotton smock like the artist she is, will look up with a flip of desire in her belly. And as for Dav and Owen, he'll give them a fiver each to make themselves scarce.

Thus, as Rhys stands waiting for the first number 7 bus of the day that will take him home from Exeter, the jigsaw pieces of his reckless heart, his soul, his rage and his love, fall into place, fitted and complete.

At 5 a.m., the bus pulls up, hisses. Up on the top deck, front seat over the driver, Rhys daydreams a future in which Milly, with her blonde hair, burning eyes and talent for art, will use that talent to customise a board for him. He pictures a time when independent shapers will ring him up and say, 'Rhys, mate, what length do you need for the swell midweek? There's a belter coming in,' and he will tell them, 'Six-four swallow tail,' then add: 'Can you leave it blank, mate? No epoxy, because Milly will finish the job.' And they will say, 'Is that the same Milly who works for Pyzel now?' And Rhys will reply, 'No, mate. BIC poached her for their team in Hossegor, but what can you do?'

Rhys can see the look of those surfboards in his head on the bus home, exactly as they will be: *There Lies A Sleeping Giant. For When He Wakes, He Will Shake The World* written along the stringer, like no art ever before seen on a surfboard, and her purple sea monsters from the deep insides of her imagination winding down the deck, from rim to rim and nose to tail. It will scare the mackerel out of the water to see it coming.

His mood sinks when he sees the bodies of deer and pigeons and badgers on the road as the bus hurtles on from Exeter to Lythcombe. They were young once and trotted behind their mums. Now, they are a pile of bones and guts. Foxes will come to tug them off the road, and while they are doing that, they will get hit, too.

Life, he knows, is full of things waiting for their turn to be broken.

One day, you are getting a new brother and you are colouring in bubble-writing on the backs of five envelopes taped together, saying *I Love You Mummy* and *Hello Baby*. And next, you only have one of those things and not the better one, not the one you wanted all along.

Not the one you loved.

Some things cannot be mended.

And then he remembers what it is he must do, which is not to mend but to break, and in breaking make something new.

Dozing, Rhys falls back into the waves where he belongs. When fins move through water, the water moves too. It parts and goes away and joins back up again, and you can never tell where it had ever been apart, not one millimetre. How can you explain the ins and outs of fin configuration, the best angles for sweep and splay, the trickiness of telling when to use a quad, when a tri or twin, and when to paddle out with one lonely skeg – a single cut, a slice?

These things are not easy to know and harder to explain. It is not something that can be taught. You will have to learn by yourself and sometimes it is nothing more than a feeling.

But what Rhys can say is that only dolphins and porpoises can surf without a stick, nature having given them a nice tri fin with a swallow tail for manoeuvrability and speed, a twitch of muscle working like a thruster – every fibre, even the skin, designed to make water its kingdom and dominion.

The fact is, a surfer needs a board, and being without one, Rhys will not give a monkey's arse if that board is old and battered or even cracked. Any pile of crap would be a bloody sight better than the nothing

Rhys has in his possession because, like they say, bad workmen blame their tools and a little bit of elbow grease goes a long way to making something better.

He remembers when Owen was four: he would give the squirt a scraper and they would work for hours getting the sandy brown wax off, down to the resin, mint-condition, and then rub on the new.

'Here and here, mate. Keep scraping, good boy, proper job. Now for the wax, just where you need to grab the rails and where your soggy feet will go, right there.'

Owen is good at all that.

In a better future, when Mr Barker at the surf school begs Rhys to wear a rash vest with Sunrise Surf School on the back, Rhys will say, 'No, not unless you give my littlest brother a job in the workshop and pay him minimum wage for over-eighteens even though he is ten years short, because you will not find a finer board restorer in the South West.'

And neither will Rhys agree terms about taking his old job back teaching grommets because he will have no further need of the cash. What with the accumulation of his surf competition winnings in Phil Fisher's bank account and the lovely problem of a farm to purchase and whether to get a pocket trawler or shoot for a vessel that can plumb deeper, he will be extremely bloody occupied.

Rhys will say, polite-like, though forgive him if there is a little smile on his face while he signs grockles' T-shirts, 'Sorry, Mr Barker, but my answer remains, so do not ask me again in case refusal gives offence,' or some such wording like the sign on the till in the SPAR, though Mr Vadic has never yet refused the credit the signage claims he will – not if some poor sod needs milk or bread.

On the bus from Exeter to Lythcombe, the countryside goes by so fast it makes Rhys think of lying on his belly on the *Maria*'s bow, up by the stack of creels they chuck over with their red flags and bring up later; blue lobsters and brown edibles trapped in their netted bellies, bait gone, clawing for the exit. He remembers what Mitch says about the way pots trap curious crustacea with a simple one-way hole: 'Easy for a lob to get in; it's finding his way out that's an arse.'

And Rhys thinks about how, when the pots are up and the *Maria* gets to five or six knots, they can dip their heads in the bow wave spray and bend to kiss a dolphin on the nose.

These thoughts are good.

Around 6 a.m., the bus stops and a big lady gets on with a sprog the size Owen was once, back when he was proper small. They sit on the other front seat, next to where the bus smashes low branches and looks about to crash into the hedge but misses it at the last second. This is fun when you are a squirt, but not for Rhys on this particular morning. He wants to be on his own, away from the camera they have recording and members of the general public who might see him and later say, when called upon as witnesses, 'I saw Rhys

Fisher on the bus, the surf champ that was in the paper, handsome fellow he was, red hair, twenty miles from Exeter.'

Rhys pulls his hoodie over his ears, though it is steaming on the bus, picks up his rucksack from the floor and puts it next to him, claiming the seat. Not taking the hint, the little squirt fits himself in next to the rucksack, he is that small. It makes Rhys sad to look at him because teaching Owen the way of the waves and the proper upkeep of a board feels like such a long time ago, before the board he borrowed broke and with it his hopes, in the days before his construction apprenticeship took him places so far inland, he could no longer imagine what salt in sea tastes like or which road he would need to run down to get home.

On building sites, it is very noisy with shouting and machines and shouting over machines like heavy thumping surf on a big day. On building sites, dust gets in your ears. You might shower for so long your dad says you are burning money, but nothing gets you clean; there's powdery cement up your nose and under your nails and eyelids, and your balls are itching too. Only a dip in the sea can fix you, inside and out, teeth and skin and nails and heart and hair. The sea will flush out your lungs if you let it; let it take you under and keep you there and hold and hold and hold *and hold*, and only when you give up will it release you – *pop!* – a bubble to the surface.

There it goes again, the bad and the good together, taking turns: pond-flat sea one day, choppy mess of wind-over-wave the next – and then, when you have given it up as a bugger of a bad job, comes a glassy-smooth break, silky, clean; a sweet sky mirror the likes of which you can brush your teeth in on the drop.

Rhys moves his rucksack off the seat, the better for the boy to balance the bends and sudden braking and not fall. When Rhys was sixteen, on his way to college, he used to surf this bus by standing in the aisle as it kidnapped him north to dry land, till the driver told him, 'Sit down or I will stop this bus and proceed no further.'

In those dark days, it was the only surfing he got.

The little 'un's mum smiles at him. 'Number seven drivers got a death wish,' she says.

'Yes,' says Rhys.

He smiles back at her, then wishes he hadn't. He should be looking out of the window, a hard man with a cold shoulder, and he also wishes that his Molotov bottles were not clinking so, informing her of his dire purpose or, at the very least, indicating a drinking party for which he is underaged.

'Work?' she says.

Rhys cannot explain to her why he told the foreman to stick his job up his hairy arse, nor can he say, 'Arson with intent to damage property belonging to a third party' either, so he nods.

Revolution *is* a species of job when you come to think of it.

True enough, Rhys ought to have looked away from the lady on the bus but he smiles again. His rucksack is open a crack at the top, the matches and tea towels a tell-tale sign.

She knows my face now, he thinks. *She will point at my photo in a line-up and say, 'It was him!'*

The bus rounds a bend and he feels a queasy-sick lump rising to his throat, something that never happens on Jakey's boat – not even past Sidcombe Point where the rollers start. He swallows, hoping it is not the thought of his fatal mission giving him the heaves but the driver doing his best to keep to his timetable. Then he thinks of what he drank and smoked and swallowed in Exeter, and wonders if he is in a state of toxic shock.

My mission is pure and righteous, he reminds himself. *It will make Milly think as good thoughts of me as I do of her.*

He pictures her lips and hair. Will she watch him surf one day? Will he introduce her to Phil Fisher? Will he get to say, 'Here's my baby brother, Owen, still in primary,' and, 'Here's my middle brother, Dav, who is a gay but very smart,' and study her reaction. Although he has no particular concerns about Milly's attitudes, owing to her being at art college where gays are sure to be, it is still a concern. Try calling Dav a homo in front of Rhys, and he will break your teeth clean out of your head.

Rhys will admit he has not always been tolerant himself, but he learned the error of his ways back in May after they met that grockle Anthony on the beach with his boyfriend. Dav claims he would have turned out gay anyway, because he was born like that, but to tell the truth, Rhys was more worried about Dav banging on about Maths at Nottingham, and saying things like, 'It's called *reading* when you do a degree.'

It happened like this. Rhys had been going round Lythcombe on the hunt for those boys, fists balled. When he found Anthony alone at last, without his nice mum there to spoil his dark purpose, Rhys had said, 'Bloody go near my brother again and—'

He never finished what he was going to say, partly because he had not yet composed what it was going to be but mostly because at that moment, an old white man and Anthony's mum got out of a long shiny black Mercedes like they were on their way to a funeral, though there was no crying and she was alive. The fellow turned out to be Anthony's dad – Phil Fisher's age and a bit like Phil Fisher, except he wore a suit and tie and spoke like this: 'Gentlemen, do we have some kind of misunderstanding here?'

Anthony's mum said to Rhys, 'Are you okay?' and when he did not speak, she frowned and said softly, 'Do you have a problem with my son?' and Rhys wanted to say, 'Yes, and so should you,' but nothing came out.

'Right,' the man said, and looked at his watch; sparkly gold it was, a genuine Rolex. 'Listen, today's my birthday and we're running late for our reservation. If there's a problem, can we sort this out quickly?'

Then he smiled and Rhys got angry. He told him straight, 'Your son kissed that boy on the beach,' and the man and his wife looked at Rhys as if he was the one in sore need of help.

'Ah, is this about a kiss?' The lady smiled and

touched Rhys's arm, a soft, pretty mum she was, and said, 'My dear boy, there are plenty of kisses to go round. You'll get yours soon.'

After that, Rhys came to thinking it might not be an unmitigated catastrophe if Dav turned out gay because there would be more girls left for him. Also, she was right about kisses.

Though Rhys has not had all the kisses he has ever asked for, he has had a fair few.

Since Exeter, Rhys knows there is only one girl that will make him happy. Milly, who is Dodo's girl and therefore forbidden. Then again, if Rhys's contribution to the revolution is a bloody brave and almighty burning, Dodo might say, 'Mate, you are twice the man I am. Her heart is yours, rightfully. She loves you better than me, therefore no hard feelings, *et cetera*.'

The number 7 bus window whacks into a branch, adding fear to the mix of beer and skunk and Xanax coursing, noxious, through his blood – a combination he swears to quit.

'Are you okay, my lover?' says the lady on the bus. She does not wait for him to answer but presses the emergency button. The bus stops. Rhys's heart stops too but carries on all the same and he stumbles down the steps and out of the doors and just makes it to the grass verge before his stomach empties in stinking pretty colours.

The driver gets out and rubs his back, saying, 'There, there, lad.' People on the bus look at him, holding sick in themselves or else looking sympathetic.

'Somebody call an ambulance!' says a lady.

'Ah, he'll be fine,' says the driver. 'Had a skinful, have you, son?'

'Get him some water,' says another lady.

Rhys is given a bottle. He drinks, spills it, wipes his mouth, drinks some more. Someone gives him a tissue. He has made a nuisance of himself, the last thing he needs, in case it will stop him doing the thing he is ordained to do as a Welsh warrior.

Come on, Rhys lad, he thinks. *You can't bottle it now.*

Twenty-nine miles from Exeter, Rhys stands at the side of the road and takes some deep breaths. At the same time, he works out how he might say sorry to Dodo for screwing their plans, and thanks the heavens Milly did not come with him directly to watch him surf and instead watch him spill his guts on the A38 southbound.

The lady gives Rhys more tissues. He thanks her, takes a swig from the bottle of water, tells her he's feeling better now and can go on with the journey. Inside, he is less sure. To feel better, he wants a dip in the sea, the comforting squeak of his blow-up bed and sleep. Lots of sleep. He cannot have these things yet, of course. He has a fire to start.

Panic weighs him down, like a twisted leash caught on a reef, tied fast to his ankle.

Snagged leashes are not something you see in Devonian waters, but such horrors happen in places like Australia where coral reefs can catch a leash and the surfer drowns, or so the internet claims. Rhys has nightmares where he swims down to find his mum on a reef. Having no choice, he surfaces for air, then dives down again to find her disappeared. Rhys wipes his face and runs up the stairs, where he takes his seat at the front again.

I must be stronger than my nightmares, he thinks. *I must be the nightmare.*

'What's your stop, my lover?' says the lady.

'The last,' he says, sweating but no coward. 'The final one. The end.'

Since Rhys's stomach emptied he no longer feels queasy, though he wishes the driver was as good a driver as his dad. Stagecoach South West does not much care for corners or the comfort of its passengers. They would have been better off in the back of Phil Fisher's trailer with the lettuce.

Calm again, Rhys turns to his phone to look over the pretty holiday cottages in their tranquil spots, henceforth to be called *targets*.

The mum and her little sprog gather their things and get off at the next stop. She pats Rhys's shoulder as she goes and says, 'You'll be all right, now. Good lad.'

The bus is near-empty. Rhys presses the button in anticipation of an obscure and lonely stop two miles from Lythcombe. He thanks the driver, then regrets thanking him, glances at the security camera, then wishes he had not. He is new to stealth. No matter; he is on his way, a true Son of Glyndŵr, not a broadsword in his hand but spirit and fire.

And if he succeeds, there will be a forest of For Sale

signs, just like Dodo foretold, rents plummeting like gannets in the deep.

This will be it for Phil Fisher. No more lorries parked up on a Tarmac sea, long-tall ships leaving in the night. No more stacked metal, un-held men – no wives nor mothers, nor babies, nor children, except crumpled in wallets. No more canteen beers and sick-stained decks. No more telly in a strange language.

He will never have to leave his sons again.

SIXTEEN

If you asked Owen, he would probably say the Shepherd's Nook is his top Airbnb so far, because when he wakes at first light it is high tide and the waves sound like they are breaking onto his pillow. The air has a special fresh-caught quality, as if anything can happen and all futures are possible.

Now that he has seen how the rich of this world live – with their feathery beds and too-many pillows, and how they boil their balls in luxury hot tubs and watch telly in bed and put their mouths to fridge doors and press buttons that spill slush down their throats, and how much that stings, though it seems a good idea at the time – he has reached the conclusion that being rich is not everything it is cracked up to be. But it's okay for a holiday.

Rhys had also come to the Shepherd's Nook, back in the summer, to find Caroline again and see if she might change her mind. At his soft knock, she flung open the top half of the stable door – stupid, if you think about it, because what kind of shepherd would share his hut with a pony? – and smiled at Rhys. She was wearing voluminous purple yoga pants and a very strappy kind of bra top that made him blush.

'I'm not going to have sex with you, Kevin,' she said.

'I know,' said Rhys. 'You can call me Rhys if you like. Kevin's, like, the name of my first rabbit. I just used it on Tinder because…'

'Walk with me?'

So they walked along these very sands looking for sea glass and shells, and Caroline snorted a laugh through her nose when Rhys dropped to one knee and covered the band of white skin where her wedding ring had been with a pebble-ring.

'You're sweet,' she said, messing his hair. 'You'll find a lovely girl one day.'

Now, in the Shepherd's Nook, Owen picks up Dav's fallen maths books and puts them on the stove out of the way. Then he sneaks out, leaving his brother sleeping, to see what the sea has brought him. He is hoping for perhaps a dead whale, like the one he once saw on the beach, or a drowned fisherman. He has not seen that yet, but expects to, because, while the waters off Devon do not see many deadly hurricanes, Phil Fisher often lectures Rhys about the dangers to life and limb that come from joining the fishing fleet too young.

According to Phil Fisher, Plymouth, Sole and FitzRoy are the only bits of the radio shipping forecast that anyone in these parts needs to hear: Plymouth for the weather that's happening now, and Sole and FitzRoy for what's blowing in soon. There are also ten levels on the Douglas Sea Scale, from 'Calm' to

'Phenomenal', so when some grockle on Lythcombe prom says, 'Get in! The waves are phenomenal!' you can tell him they are not, because 'phenomenal' means the kind that knocks a ship sideways and upside down and are taller than two schools, one atop the other.

The night the whale came to Lythcombe, the sea had only been a number 5 on the Douglas Sea Scale. Rough. Not even Very Rough, but sometimes young whales lose themselves and can't find their families. Jet skis and storms confuse them and they run the wrong way to where it is shallow when they should be in the deep.

The whale was still breathing when the first anglers went out with their beach rods. They dropped their lines and knocked up the town, the Fisher brothers included. People started crying. Mr Vadic came with buckets, soaked blankets and Vaseline to rub on the whale's skin.

Lythcombe Natural Healing & Souvenirs brought lavender water, a Buddhist bell and their biggest piece of titanium aura quartz, a blue crystal they said spoke a spiritual language the whale would understand.

The brothers found it strange looking in the whale's prodigious eye. He didn't look scared. He didn't look like he was feeling anything much. He studied the humans digging a channel and sang none of the ghostly whale songs Rhys would later hear playing on Milly's phone in Dodo's flat.

People ran up and down the beach and shouted for the sea to come back, but it was no good. Then he died.

Dav told Owen it was because his insides couldn't work outside of water, though not in the same way as fishes drown in air. Whales breathe air like the rest of us, but the weight of his body crushed him when he was not held up by sea.

The whale lay on the beach for a fair bit after that. The first day, Owen ran up his tail and stood on his back, and sat on him like a pony, *giddy up*.

The second day the whale was on the beach, Rhys went on his own and kicked it in the ribs till his foot stung and shouted words at an unholy volume. Words like, 'you bloody bastard', 'bloody bitch' and worse ones, too.

The fifth day, grockles started complaining about the smell. The council sent a tractor and a flatbed and you could hear chainsaws whining as far as the school.

On the seventh day, the three brothers stood on clean sand where the whale had once lain.

Rhys threw Owen atop his shoulders. 'Look, mate!' he said, pointing at the sea. 'A blow, mate! A blow! Our big fellow got away!'

Dav said nothing to Rhys, and Owen might have been seven at the time, but he was not stupid. Both could see it was a number 4 or 5 – 'Slight to Moderate' – wind-blown spray off the crests, not a spout from the nose of a whale.

But Dav and Owen smiled all the same, because it is good to be loved by your family. You only get the one.

✱

Long View Farm would have been a tidy place in its day: the cattle barns warm in winter; brick kennels for the dogs; three fireplaces, judging by the chimney stacks – and a big one for the kitchen. Walking up the drive at 6.35 a.m., Rhys can just about smell the bread the farmer would have smelled on his way home for breakfast, his wife frying bacon from their own pigs on the fire, three fat hams swinging in the smoke. He can picture that same farmer come to this porch from a blizzard, knocking the snow off his boots and saying to his collies, 'Okay, boys, just this once,' and letting them flop by the stove, the black of their shaggy coats restored as the ice melted, and for his wife to shake her head at the puddle on the flagstones but love her husband all the more for his compassion and good character.

But he *must not must not must not* think of it as a living farm where babies had been born and men had worked and died of old age in their beds, surrounded by their family, taking in the long view of the coast and their lives and these dry stone walls whose un-mortared jigsaw pieces they had cut and set themselves. If he thinks of these things, he will not do it. He must think only of the future for him and his brothers, the farm being a pretty egg that needs cracking.

Rhys locates the places he will start: the corners, underneath the wooden eaves, the log-stack and the thatched roof, likely made with reeds from Slapton down the coast. The hot tub looks tidy, but he is not here for fun so he pulls back the plastic cover and pisses into the steam. He opens the vodka and takes a drink because he is thirsty. It settles his stomach, and then it does not. He throws up his guts again. His hands shake and he finds himself too weak to rip tea towels into wicks, so he goes to the garage-barn to find a Stanley knife to do the job. He knocks off the padlock with a rock. Inside, he spies a surfboard sock on the floor, like a giant adder has lost its skin. There are some lifejackets and wetsuits in there too. It's a shame for good kit to burn so he puts these items by the gate, shares the rest of the vodka between the bottles and sets the wicks.

It is time. He wishes it was not, but it is, and he is settled on a path. He wishes it was darker, afraid he will be seen, but he has no choice but to do it now. His brothers will be waking in an hour. There are breakfasts to be made, school bags to pack. He promised he would always be home for them.

He thumps on the windows and doors, front and back, and rings the bell on a rope.

No one answers, so he turns his mind to the fragile creatures of the attic. Swallows have stuck their muddy nests under the eaves. *They will surely be holidaying in Africa*, thinks Rhys, *but what about bats and mice?*

Rhys borrows a ladder from the garage to survey the gables, rakes and behind the soffits with his phone torch. He listens for the scratch of tiny-hearted fearful things sleeping their winter sleep beyond the fascia. He does this because he is a revolutionary and not a murderer, not reckless as to the life of another.

All is silent, and when he is satisfied that not a living soul is home, he strikes a match, kindles the wicks and circles the farm, dibbing and dabbing, a fiery round.

The thatch ignites and away he runs.

*

'You've got young eyes,' the fisherman says, on the beach near the Shepherd's Nook. 'Can you undo this knot for me?'

'Probalob,' says Owen. 'But if I can't, my brother will. He is sleeping in the sheep place. I'm not allowed to wake him up.'

Owen has been watching the man throwing out his line from the shore, like Rhys does, waiting for Dav to wake up. A haze-glow illuminates the north, Dartmoor shining dark purple. He wonders what his biggest brother is up to now, knowing from Rhys's yarns that while some adventures happen when you leave home, worse ones get in your way when you are trying to return.

The fisherman brings in a bass and puts it in his bucket. It flits round one way, then turns to try a better direction. Owen counts fulmars, shearwaters, five kinds of terns, six of gulls, petrels, guillemots, gannets, skuas arguing and kittiwakes shouting their name: *kittee-wa-aaake, kittee-wa-aaake.* On the horizon, a rust-red mountain of a super-trawler, in contravention of the closure no doubt, sits far out in the roadstead, so big as to be near-seeming, like it was the size of the *Maria*. Soon, there will pass yachts from Plymouth and

Kingsbridge, flapping their sails like sheets hanging out to dry.

Owen does a good job of untangling the tangle in the fisherman's tackle, little fingers being better for the job. The man asks why he is not getting ready for school. 'It's still open, despite the fire.'

'It's the weekend,' says Owen, not knowing his arse from his elbow. To which the man says, 'No, it ain't. It's Friday.'

A stone's throw away, Dav wakes to the smell of melted plastic and finds his textbooks stacked on the stove. Inside the fiery chamber, embers collapse, turn orange then grey. He peels the bottom book's cover off the stove top, leaving *Higher Level Maths Revision Guide* in back-to-front mirror writing on the cast-iron top. As he scrapes it off with the coal shovel, he hopes its contents are as glued to his brain, so that this test, university, leaving home, will one day be memories – irrefutable evidence that he has become himself.

He recalls the time when he had gone to Phil Fisher about some unkind words of Rhys and a messy fracas during which he gave his big brother a nose bleed. His dad had listened and then said, 'One day, boys, it'll all be gone. Like me and you and now. This moment…' and he nodded to the sun melting into the sea 'today and tomorrow. You know, life. Gone. All of it. In a flash.'

At that, Dav and Rhys's eyes met and they started grinning.

'You're a bundle of laughs today, Dad,' Rhys said,

stuffing bog roll up his nostrils, a bit impressed that his middle brother had such manly retaliation in him, if he was honest.

'Button it, Rhys,' said Phil Fisher. 'Rag Dav again and you'll see my fist as well. This is important. Listen to me: Dav, you do you. Rhys, you do you. Boys, girls – at the end of the day, who gives a flying crap?' And hearing their big hairy dad talking like he is on *Strictly*, Rhys and Dav blushed and stared at their sandy toes.

'It's time to shine!' Rhys says, kicking open his bedroom door at 7.15 a.m. The Fishers' flat is sweet to his eyes. He feels like a rabbit returned to the warren, welcomed by the smell of mud and roots and Dav's Lynx. But it is also sad, because there is no sight of his brothers. This not something he was expecting at just after seven in the morning.

'Hi, Thing,' he says, back in the kitchen, starting to open the package he ordered – a new inner tube for Dav's bike so that he does not keep nicking his racer. 'What are they up to, eh?'

Thing rubs his legs, not helping much, more getting in his way. Rhys gets the cat treats and scatters some biscuits on the floor.

'When Dav gets home,' Rhys tells the cat, 'he'll be in for a surprise. His bike will be working, except for the brakes – but who needs brakes when you have feet? Better to fix a tyre first. Without it, you don't have a bike at all. Can't let the neighbours think we're too skint even for bikes and their proper maintenance.'

In the kitchen, there are crumbs to wipe and his brothers' dishes in the sink to do, lazy gits. He rinses them in cold water to save gas and stacks them on the drainer. Better make the place look respectable. He sets Dav's duvet straight, pulls Owen's sheet tight where it always comes loose, and tops up the air in his airbed. He would put the vacuum round if it was working, but for now he picks up the most obvious signs of life – wrappers and fluff and the like.

Up on the hill, Long View Farm is burning fast. There can be no undoing what has been done. Even from Jubilee, he can hear fire engines crying on the tor. He looks out of the window. A great oily coil of smoke rises up the hill and he feels a sadness he has to swallow down in case it knocks him off-kilter. He is supposed to be happy in victory, but it does not feel that way. He misses his brothers. The flat is too quiet without them.

He moves back to the kitchen, which is also the Fishers' sitting room, and straightens the sofa cushions. The Santander ferry will be docking in Plymouth around now. Phil Fisher will need his bed tonight. Rhys gets a clean sheet and puts it on the back of the sofa, ready. Then he fetches the post from the wire cage on the back of the front door and takes the sundry letters and promises of free pizza delivery and puts them on the table. Dav's phone is there, on top of a drawing by Owen in his inimitable dots, like the one he did of the *Maria*. Rhys had a photo of that masterpiece on his phone, which he later showed Milly in Exeter, saying, 'This artwork is by my little brother. Can you believe he's only eight?'

The drawing on the table is a cartoon of Dav and Owen in a hot tub and the two again in bed. The caption talks of having a sleepover. Rhys smiles and puts it to one side, taking up a leaflet from the church offering a warm bank with coffee and fellowship.

'They can piss off.'

And a payslip for £1187 net from Freight Logistics Ltd, minus £314 damages to paintwork.

'They can piss off, and all.'

Next, he draws his finger under the glued flap of a letter from the council addressed to Phil Fisher, his dad liking all post read so there are no surprises when he gets home.

It reads thus:

Dear Mr Fisher,

Following the recent public consultation, recommendations from our estates management contractors, Knightsbridge Property Management Ltd, and in light of the Healthy Homes Initiative report which highlighted the unacceptable conditions within the Jubilee estate housing stock (Survey Phase: P1) it has been decided to move forward with our exciting plans for the Lythcombe Regeneration Zone.

Council-owned housing units that fall below a standard fit for human habitation will be demolished, making way for a stunning rebuild with 15% affordable and low-income units for those with a local connection, including five units of social housing. The Regeneration Zone Build Phase (P3) will, of course, boost employment opportunities in the long-term and improve the appearance of Lythcombe, making it a competitive alternative to Salcombe for visitors.

Your block has been identified as falling below the government's new Warmer Happier Homes standard. You will be offered medium- to long-term alternative accommodation and priority school places in Exeter, and be invited to apply for re-accommodation in Lythcombe at a later date.

As you are aware, the Community Stakeholder Relocation Phase (P2) was scheduled for late next year, but after the recent spike in crime and vandalism, rise in unemployment owing to the fishing closure and absence of safe play facilities for children following the Jubilee estate arson attacks, we have taken the decision to bring forward P2 to mid-December, with the demolition scheduled for late January.

```
We are sure you will be delighted to hear this
news and sincerely hope you enjoy the wealth of
employment, travel, healthcare, educational,
leisure and sporting opportunities Exeter
has to offer, including NHS dentistry, now
open for applications with fast-track care
for former Lythcombe residents under 18.

Moving forward, our specialists in crisis
accommodation will be in touch.
```

'Piss off, this is our home,' says Rhys, screwing up the letter. 'Mum's home. Was. If those surveyor-rats come here again, I will—'

The balled letter lands on Owen's drawing. Sharing the back of the envelope with the dotted steam of a hot tub is a message for Rhys in Dav's handwriting. Three words stand out above and beyond all others:

Long View Farm

Rhys blinks at the sink drainer, terror nicking and gutting and crushing his lungs. No cereal bowls. No breakfast things. Only ketchup plates and a brown apple core. Their school uniforms are still on the backs of the chairs. They did not sleep here last night.

Where the hell did they sleep?

He goes back to the envelope. Dav's hand:

> Me & Owen are going to Long View Farm by the tor. Lady there has the Gerry Lopez you can borrow for Croyde.

Owen's hand:

> Hope you can do a sleepover here too.

Rhys kneels, collapses, his spiked thoughts run like guts, spilling, looping, winding out the evisceration line grinder all about him on the floor.

I knocked, he thinks. *I rang the bell. I went up a ladder.*

Were they hiding when they heard me knock? Were they scared? I should've broken the door. I should've checked under the beds. Did flames burn them or smoke choke them? Did they pass out soft-like, falling asleep? Did they call for Mum? When did they take their last breath?

SEVENTEEN

Everything is gone when Rhys gets to the farm at 8.05, the whole place levelled except for the kitchen chimney, built for eternity in good granite. The roof has collapsed – thatch gone, doors gone, beams gone, partitions gone, staircases gone, ceilings gone.

'You are not allowed here,' says a fireman, guarding the crime scene. 'Go home.'

Rhys sees a scrap of blanket on the porch and picks it up. Binty. It smells of guilt.

'Give it back,' the fireman says. 'The police want nothing touched.'

Rhys shakes his head and says, 'There was no one here. No one was here when it burned.'

'We don't know that,' says the fireman, 'and we can't check because the first floor caved in. Neighbours say two boys were staying here with their family. Are you the caretaker?'

'Yes,' says Rhys, trying not to cry and almost succeeding, trying to breathe and failing.

'I'm sorry,' says the fireman. 'It was a lovely place.'

Rhys retches. Nothing comes; he is empty.

'The blanket thing?' says the fireman, and puts out his hand ready to reclaim what's left of Binty. 'It's been a night of this bloody nonsense all down the coast.'

Rhys's throat shrinks and his eyes burn.

Then he stuffs Binty down his top and turns and runs and does not stop till he is home. And all the while he is running, he counts the ways he could end his sorry life.

I have murdered my brothers.

If he had been even a little bit braver, he would have killed himself right then. But he is not.

Back at the flat, Rhys thinks about writing a sorry note to his brothers but how can you say sorry to them that are dead? How can he know if he will see them in heaven or if there will be sea there or at least other good things?

I should have told them what Mum was like, he thinks. His mum would have loved Owen if she had got the chance, and he expects she did love him for the small minutes she had, though Rhys was sent up to Mrs Morris and could not see anything except the lights flashing and medics coming in with their green bags.

He did not know there would be a worse day to come.

Now Owen is gone, how can Rhys tell his brother he loves him, though he tried his best not to? The truth is, when Owen was little, that was the worst. His baby crying and jealous fuss took them all away. But when Owen got to walking, he was all right and Rhys started to love him.

I think of Mum as mine, he thinks, *but she's theirs as well and I am sorry for keeping her inside.*

Rhys had always denied his brothers and now it is too late. He kept their mum for himself alone, and had not shared her in case sharing made her less. He wants to tell them now how she was so much smarter than their dad, and how her lips were Vaseline-shiny against the wind, and how her hugs half crushed your ribs.

He wishes it had been him in the fire. He prays his brothers' leaving had been quick, a drowning kind of smoke that made them fall asleep. He has never known a pain so sharp as these thoughts.

His pain should have killed him already, but hearts do not give out that easy. They keep going like solar-powered clocks, your lungs too, in and out and in and out and in and out. You cannot think yourself dead, only by deed is it done.

After writing a sorry note to his dad, Rhys turns to how he will revenge his brothers against himself.

I must not be afraid, he thinks. *People have been dying for millions of years. I can die too, if I set my mind to it.*

He tries not to fear the going: the pill, the cut, the fall, the sea – all at once to be certain. Not that he deserves the quickest way.

Dad is better off without me, he thinks. *If I was Dad, I would snap my neck and club me with a stick, like a mixy bunny or a fox in a trap.*

He sees himself as a fox now, leg mangled beyond repair, feathers and pullet blood proof of guilt in his mouth. The taking of his life, he supposes, would be as much mercy as vengeance. These thoughts make him cry until he is on his knees.

I am already dead, he thinks. *A dead man walking, already gone, only waiting for the means.*

He gets a spud knife from the cupboard and three paracetamol from the first aid kit. He does not know how many are needed to switch off a life as strong as his. He will stop by Mr Vadic's on his way out for more.

✳

Dav opens the top half of the shepherd's hut door and breathes in salt air and a whiff of diesel. The sea goes from navy stripes to grey to a brilliant gold that needs sunglasses to look on it. He sees Owen chatting to the fisherman and jogs over, thinking he'll ask him the time.

'Where's your parents?' the man is saying.

'Dad's coming home soon,' Owen says, trying to think if Children's Services would fish on their day off. The man glances down the beach as if Phil Fisher is coming in from an early one with his rod, six medium macks, a nice five-pound bass and some leftover bait lugs in his bucket.

'It's okay, I'm with him,' says Dav, joining them. 'We fish here too sometimes. You might know our dad.'

'And you'll know our Rhys,' says Owen. 'He lights fires here.'

The man's eyes cast out to the red of their hair. 'Not Rhys Fisher, I hope.' He nods to the tor; black smoke billows above Long View Farm like a hurricane column spiralling up from hell. 'I've had enough of it. That one's been going since dawn.'

'What time is it now, please?' asks Dav.

The man looks at his watch. 'Ten past eight, though you would think it was midday in town. I came here to get some peace. Two boys are missing, presumed dead...'

'How can they know?' says Dav. 'It's not even registration yet.'

'My wife's a teacher up at the school. One of her kids wrote about staying up at the farm in his homework and he's not come home. She's saying that Rhys murdered him. They've got evidence. CCTV. The boy's pure evil.'

'No,' says Dav, quick as you like, a whooshing pulse of blood in his neck. 'Not Rhys.'

And his fear-befuddled brain asks, *Since my brother has not murdered us, who has he murdered*?

'Did they catch him, the bad Rhys?' says Owen. 'Is he in prison?'

'Soon will be,' says the man. Dav feels strung on an eel hook, his skin flayed in strips. 'Along with the other troublemakers from Exeter.' The man holds Dav's gaze hard in the teeth of his eyes. 'Those that betray them do no treachery, if you get my meaning. We've had it with fires. They're bad for business.'

Dav turns and pulls Owen away with him, a look on his face so mean Owen says, 'Did I say wrong? What if Rhys never comes home? What if, Dav?'

'I'm not playing,' says Dav, thinking Owen wants their stupid question game, like, what if lobsters grew as big as dogs? Or, what if seagulls were pets?

Locking up the Shepherd's Nook, smoke curling on the tor, Dav feels he is drowning in currents moving faster than he can swim, and, *Where the bloody hell is Rhys?*

'Please, Dav.' Owen tugs his sleeve. 'Tell me what if?'

'Shut up a minute. I need to think.'

That Rhys might be a murderer smacks Dav deep in his chest. At times, Rhys can be a homophobic dickhead and an annoying shit, but Dav knows his brother would not hurt a fly.

And yet. The farm is burning. They might have been inside. Someone else might have been inside.

'I need a poo,' says Owen.

Dav is truly glad to hear it. Granted, eco bog roll is rough and it is hard to hold Owen's legs to stop him falling down the shitty sawdust pit, but the reek of a composting bog is very comforting. It is not a smell you would be able to smell if you were murdered and dead.

Rhys has enough spirit left to light the pallet palace in the yard. Before the neighbours can call 999, all is lost: melted metal struts, twisted nails, the hours of labour gone. Thing's paws will track ash through the flat. But Rhys cannot let himself feel sad. This is what an eye for an eye means: fire in exchange for fire.

Next, he burns his vacant half-built hutches.

He would have loved his rabbits better than any. They would have known their names and come to call, no matter what people say. And if Rhys had been a farmer, he would have shorn his sheep better than any; they would not have rolled their eyes and panted, not in his kind hands. And if he had been a trawlerman, he would have killed fish better than any. Their goodbyes would have been quick as a flash from God – no pain, no sorrow, no feeling. Only nothing, the darkness of their first egg.

Rhys has seen many marvels in his life and unexplained phenomena.

The weight of a ten-foot wave atop his head, yet no harm done.

A shearwater, hunting so close to the waves you could not fit a Rizla between wing and water.

Sunset with Lianne and her pretty boobs in the dune, soft as jelly and as sweet.

Jakey jumping bare-arsed off the dock, the knob.

A Lionhead rabbit at Longleat, very fluffy. An English Angora, fluffier still.

A rich lady asking would he say nice things and kiss her; she would pay for his trouble.

Concrete pouring in a pit, the soil-life under it never to see light nor air again.

The mum of him powdered and laid to rest.

That'll do.

Enough for one life.

*

Rhys cannot rightly tell the story of his feet on their last walk. But walk he does, till there is no more land to stand on, nor air to breathe, and then what comes? Death is an unknown foreign place, like Spain, but without the acres of salad and sweet citrus growing by the motorway for anyone to nick.

Now turning down the high street towards the prom, Rhys feels very much like a seal on Lythcombe Point ready to slip away into a dark shadow beneath the green. He considers how, on a calm day, fish scratch their backs on the barnacles there, to get rid of the bugs that live on them. Do they gaze up at the cliffs and feel giddy? How can they imagine the vastness of fields, the windiness of moor, the greenness of woods? All that air and gravity. All that heavy slow thickness, like wading through wet concrete.

And then he thinks, *What do I know about anything*?

He had left his trainers at home. Phil Fisher will get the use of them, being a size nine, and so he walks on the naked soles his mum gave him. It does not hurt. Rhys was never a wincer on stones when others totter and lose their balance and ding their board getting in at low tide. But on the high street, window glass stings his feet; he picks up a shard and puts it in the litter bin in case it cuts some poor creature's paws or the beak of a juvenile gull, and in the process leaves his own blood samples on Lythcombe prom.

There's dog shit smeared on the estate agent's

window. *The boys did well,* Rhys tries to think. *The authorities will be sorry they started the closure. When I am gone, the others will fight for better.* Though to be honest, he does not know quite what *better* might be made out of this mess of bricks and burned garden fences and broken glass.

He sets right an upturned recycling bin and a lady smiles at him. 'You young 'uns,' she says. 'You're not bad as all that.'

You are mistaken, thinks Rhys in his head. *I am the worst.* But he cannot tell her that because she gives him a kind nod and he goes.

On the prom, the Coastguard information board has been updated to Red, though there are no stirrings in the water, no clouds on the horizon bringing the necessary changes for a thumping swell. In normal times, Rhys would have known this in his belly, long before online forecasts or local signs made it official – but he cannot think of surf, only of his brothers and how they are gone.

At the end of the breakwater a lady is going in, like one of those Later in Life Swim Club ladies who go in all year like a bob of wrinkly grey seals, giggling and chatting. But it is not their day today. Also, she is naked. Rhys stops to ask himself why a lady would be going in for a dip with no wetsuit on. Being winter, she should not be there by rights, so he proceeds for closer inspection and sees that it is Mrs Morris.

She is no swimmer, Mrs Morris. Some call her a mad lady, but even the mad can swim, given lessons.

Rhys watches and sees that she does not thrash when the icy water spikes her skin. On the contrary, she persists, going in calm till her shoulders and neck are covered. She lets a slight push from the swell unseat her feet and under she goes.

Hang on a minute, says Rhys to himself when her arms and legs perform none of the actions necessary for buoyancy and forward motion. He strips off his hoodie on the prom, vaults the railing, runs to the sea, dives in and front crawls to Mrs Morris like a streak of human lightning through the water. Upon reaching her, he stands in chest-deep sea and gathers her to the surface.

Not having wrapped his arms around a naked old lady during his time as volunteer in the Lythcombe lifeguards, Rhys notes her skin is as cold and blue as a dolphin's nose when they come up to your boat to say hello. On a normal day, he would blush to see her scant white wisps of pubic hair but nothing about his life is normal any more.

'Now, Mrs Morris,' he says, scooping her up and out of the next soft wave and trying his best not to look at her shrivelled boobs. 'What's up with you today?'

'Going,' she says.

'No, you're bloody not,' says Rhys, and he shoulders her through the shallows, easy-like, her having no more weight than Owen for all her years.

'You bugger, I want to go.'

'No, you don't,' says Rhys, and carries her up the beach and over the stones and sharp dry bladderwrack

and bottle tops and samples of severed nylon net.
'You'll catch your death in this water.'

'You little shit, put me down.'

He does, but only to alter his grip, gathering her next in the manner of a husband carrying his new lady wife over the threshold of their new-built semi in a desirable redevelopment location. He imagines this more preserving of her dignity, her arse no longer on general display, and carries her direct to Mr Vadic, who is sweeping up his window for the second day in a row. Seeing the SPAR's broken glass and a pile of singed copies of the *Echo* on the kerb, Rhys is sorry he was not there to say to the boys, 'Not Mr Vadic, lads. Move on to Costa.'

'Can you help her?' says Rhys.

Long ago, Mrs Morris had helped him, though it did not feel like help when the ambulance came and Phil Fisher told Rhys and Dav to go up the steps to her flat 'for only a little while' that grew into a night and a day and another night when their mum...

Enough of that. It doesn't matter any more.

The Fishers' flat was a midden, but they had nothing on Mrs Morris. Who could tell what colour her floor was for all the clothes, boxes, tins, bags and cat crap decorating the surfaces; a noxious surprise for unsuspecting social workers? It was not entirely her fault because the building has always been sick. Its leaking roof still tends blooms of black mould over wall and ceiling, lending moisture to the Fishers' below; the exact level of humidity needed to nurture the unidentified mushrooms by their front door.

But what Mrs Morris lacked in cleanliness she made up for in godliness at their time of most need, nearly nine years ago, calling Rhys and Dav 'little mice' and making them boiled eggs and soldier toast and letting Dav give his to Thing from his fingers, for they were not in a hungry mood, more worried for their mum. When Phil Fisher did not fetch them as promised, she gave them her bed, and in the morning took them to Jubilee Park to watch them play on the swings. And all the while she was *in loco parentis* – though her hands shook and she muttered nonsense – not a drop of vodka passed her lips.

Children's Services called Phil Fisher 'reckless' to leave his boys in her care. They used it against him when his boys were sent away, but Mrs Morris was good to them. Rhys would have said as much, had anyone asked.

Outside the shop, Rhys checks her pulse and breathing, and collects her clothes, scattered on the stones the way grockle-sprogs leave theirs. Mr Vadic says he'll take her home now and call her next of kin.

'You'll be okay,' Rhys tells Mrs Morris, pulling his hoodie over her head against the cold. 'Owen'll feed Thing if you need.'

And then he remembers Owen cannot feed Thing, nor Dav, for they are dead and he has killed them.

His eye catches the cindered newspapers outside the shop and he remembers that photo of himself from back when he was famous. He thinks of his lost promise, the gold medal between his teeth.

Next time, the caption will be different: *Local hero Rhys Fisher, 17, is wanted on suspicion of arson and murder.*

Shit me, thinks Rhys. *So now I will be wanted. Whoever wanted me before?*

He sets off to the cliffs, Mr Vadic calling him back with promises that all can be mended.

Rhys never got the paracetamol but there are other ways. He is, at this moment, the saddest and sorriest thing ever seen weighted on earth, flying in air or gliding through sea.

EIGHTEEN

Allegedly dead, Dav and Owen pass broken windows, burned-out cars and road signs bent like metal trees uprooted in a storm, untouched since the riot. No one stops to say, 'That's a fine board you've got' or, 'Hang on a minute, aren't you…?' Lythcombe is far too busy.

As it is nearly 9 a.m., they are late for school. Dav pushes the board-bike and Owen trots behind as far as the port lockup where Jakey's dad keeps his crab creels and lobster pots. Council dustmen with rotating brushes sweep the pavements. It is very like a holiday, what with the smell of bonfire in the air.

'Is it Saturday?' asks Owen.

'No, mate,' says Dav. 'It's Friday, the same day you woke up in this morning. I'll drop you at school but we need to go home for our uniforms first. Wish me luck with my test today.'

'It looks like Saturday.' Owen makes things true in his head, so it is no good arguing. At any rate, half his little friends are playing outside like soot-faced warriors ready for battle. He asks for Binty next.

'I don't have her,' says Dav.

Owen's eyes widen. A tear. 'I remember now! I forgot it at the nice lady's house.'

'Come,' says Dav. 'We'll get her another time. Dad will be back soon and all will be well. Let's go home and see what new muck Rhys has stepped in, and cheer him up with this lovely board.'

On the Jubilee estate, Dav and Owen are two boys among many. Seeing the crowd of nosy parkers that have gathered outside their flat, Dav thinks, *I hope Mrs Morris is okay, not drowned or missing.* Then he remembers what the fisherman had said. Are these people here on account of a murder? Was this why no one was saying hello?

They head round the back to the yard where it is quiet.

'Who did that?' says Owen, seeing the prototype hutches and pallet palace a-smouldering, a soggy black pile of cinders and steam, Rhys's dreams of rabbits turned to flecks of ash in the sky. The firefighters have doused their kitchen window in foam. A bit of wall is singed but the rest of the building is okay.

'Poor Thing.' Owen is thinking how little Thing liked to sit on the topmost pallet where the sun reaches in the yard and warm his coat, but there is nothing there for him now. The boy wipes charcoal fingers across his snotty nose and his face crumples. 'Oh, Thing!'

Back out at the front of the building, standing on the grass, a reporter lady from BBC Devon is telling the camera that a local teacher raised the alarm first thing in the morning after reading a composition in which

Owen Fisher wrote about staying at Long View Farm. The police are now searching for bodies in the ashes.

When the reporter stops speaking, the vicar pipes up and tells her that the Fishers are in his thoughts and prayers.

'It's a tragedy,' says a weeping lady the boys have never met. 'Those poor scamps!'

Someone else says the family is 'known to social services and the police. Sprogs running out all hours'.

The camera drops, the reporter turns. Faces tilt to Mrs Morris's front balcony and there she is, in Rhys's best hoodie, hair bedraggled, knobbly feet bare, horn nails yellow, and smiling a terrible smile, like a seaweed-angel come in from the sea. And there is Thing, in her arms, his purr rumbling over the voices and engines, as loud as any cat whose owner has come home.

'Piss off, the lot of you,' she says.

'Did you know the brothers?' calls the reporter lady. 'When did you see them last?'

'The little one was out surfing last night,' she says. 'I saw them.'

'Where was that?'

'On the high street, along the prom and the sand to the breakwater and up the lane. He's a good little surfer.'

'On dry land?'

'Yes, on dry land, where else? The sea was piddly and small. Now piss off!'

A lady tells the reporter to take no notice because

Mrs Morris is a known alcoholic and how would she know anything, seeing as the murders were committed at dawn, not last night?

Dav takes Owen by his coat and wheels the board-bike to his front door, making tracks through the foam. He leans the magnificent Gerry Lopez Hawaiian Pipeliner against the wall for all to marvel at its sleek lines.

'Hi, Mrs Morris,' says Owen, waving up.

'Hi, lads,' she says.

Dav pulls Owen's hood and sends him inside the flat. The door shut, Dav turns to the crowd and, like a class of well-raised children, they cease their chatter and stare at him like cows.

What will the murdered boy say?

'It's all right,' says Dav. 'We're not dead. Like Mrs Morris says, we were playing out, that's all. Rhys is not a murderer – not even a half one. But he is a bloody good surfer and if you come up to Croyde this Sunday, you'll see him winning a gold medal on this here board.'

Dav pats the Gerry Lopez, the way you would pat a fine pony, then feels stupid.

The flat is tidier than they left it but smells like bonfire and also burned toast because Owen is going at it with the toaster.

'Switch it off before you use that knife,' Dav tells him. 'You'll electrocute us all.'

'You know the film set?' says Owen. 'Did they put it in the film that me and you died? Are we going to be on Netflix?'

Dav considers whether their lives are shitty enough to be turned into a film. 'No.'

Owens spreads jam on his toast. Dav sits on the sofa, his back aching from a night in a chair and pushing a boy on a board on a bike here, there and everywhere, along with his other, more mathematical burdens and responsibilities.

'Hurry up and brush your teeth,' he says, not feeling hungry, 'it's time for school.'

To which Owen says, 'Hello, Binty!' finding his scrap on the table, more in need of a wash than ever, on top of Dav's note.

'Thank goodness for that,' Dav says. 'Now you've got her back, keep her close.'

Dav sees his note. Beneath his words are some more from Rhys, the most Dav has seen him write in a lifetime of being his brother. The note says:

> Dear Dad. Im sorry for killing my brothers. Im going to mum now. Im not afraid of high places or rocks or water. Im sorry Im bad. I wasnt always bad. I never meant to hurt them. Love from your son Rhys

Dav's revision notes are packed and ready, the

sum of six hours' night work. This is when he sees that university will always be too far away for him – a stupid lovely dream, like when you buy a lottery ticket and let yourself think for a minute about the foreign holidays you would have, the buffets you would eat and the surfboards you would buy your brothers.

When all is said and done, Dav is a Lythcombe lad, meant for box washing and table-waiting and sitting out the winter with the telly. *Nottingham is not for the likes of me*, thinks Dav, with the sorry note in his hand. *I cannot reach it and if I do, it will only turn to shit like everything else.*

But he can reach his brother, knowing exactly where Rhys will be.

School can go to hell, thinks Dav, and puts his books in the bin.

'Told you I left Binty at home,' Owen says, expecting Dav to rag him for his carelessness but Dav looks at him with glassy eyes.

'Come on,' Dav says, no punch or tickle. He gets Owen's coat and opens the door, his forehead wrinkled like sand after the cockle rakers have been out. 'Don't dig in your heels. Not this time. Please?'

The uncommon note in Dav's voice makes Owen understand he must shift himself. He is up and out before Dav adds, 'Rhys needs us.'

'Why,' says Owen, 'what's he doing? Where is he?'

'The lighthouse, mate.'

Owen knows it well. It is the place where they go and his dad cries and then they sing *happy birthday, dear*

Mummy and eat sandwiches and crisps and talk about her. He remembers Phil telling him how, backalong when lighthouses were manned, they had clever cats living in them and wives cooking stargazy pies. They were light, happy places. According to Phil, when a ship came too close to the rocks in poor seas, the Lythcombe lighthouse used to say, *It's not too late!* in sound and light. This gave sailors time to turn the tiller and change course. *Ready-about now and you'll be safe. Lee-ho!*

Phil Fisher was right – they have become *scattered boys* and Dav and Owen must be the good collies and find Rhys on the cliffs. And as soon as they have found their lost sheep, they must stick him on that Gerry Lopez and let him paddle about till his mojo is restored.

'We're taking your bike,' says Dav. 'You've got to ride yourself this time, on your own.'

Thing gets in Dav's way but he works fast to pump the tyres, and soon they are full of air. 'You must be brave,' he warns. 'I can't leave you behind.'

'I am brave,' says Owen, knowing that mostly he is not.

And so the squirt mounts his little bike, pretending it is a Dartmoor pony that he has drifted himself and raised by hand, that loves him and will look after him and keep him safe from harm.

Rhys is on the coast path, now. He is headed onwards and upwards to the lighthouse, where the cliffs are highest and terns sit on the edge having their quarrels. Skylarks hiding in the grass fly up to sing him away. He would not hurt them, no more than he would hurt the rabbits that flee from him not knowing that he would care for them, if they let him. He would remember dandelions and fresh grass and a bowl of water with their meal.

It's not hard to make a rabbit happy.

One bunny looks at him bold in the eye before bolting to its burrow. Rhys wishes Mrs Kevin and Ginger had been set free here, after his mum died. Would they remember him as he passes and astonish their little friends by hopping over for a scratch behind the ear?

Rhys stops between the lighthouse and the Coastguard lookout, where the footpath and its information board have been moved inland, for safety – because grockles do not understand what waves and weather do to cliffs.

He follows the grassed-over rut of the old path to another sign:

DANGER
DO NOT GO BEYOND THIS POINT
DANGEROUS CLIFF EDGE

He is on the edge, the ocean at his feet. To the east, an aeroplane pulls a banner of words over the Torbay sky; Rhys cannot read them because his eyes are wet.

He roars at himself, 'Coward!'

Before the slice of cliff slid off here, locals and grockles – hikers and wanderers, bird-fanciers and scientists – walked the old path, safe as houses. It is dizzying to think that he and his mum had sat with her birthday picnic, right out there in thin air, where none but birds can now go.

Rhys reaches the drop, a sunken fissure where a stubborn bit of rock has held on. One day, it too will shave off, as by an unseen knife in a cake to neaten it up. Here, he lowers himself over, where a careless influencer might lose his grip, and climbs down the gully-crack.

It is cold. Water drips out of the rock like a tap with a perished washer. He licks and tastes iron and salt. His foot knocks a nest of moss and lichen. It falls and he cannot put it back.

He kisses the oyster shell Owen gave him that hangs around his neck. Now is his moment to let go.

Rhys tells himself, 'Let go.'

He screams, 'You bloody bastard coward! Can you not even do this, after everything?'

He does not know why he holds and holds and holds.

Waves hit the rocks below in thumping sets and he thinks of the competition when his borrowed board broke, the coming swell and Croyde, and Milly watching him and not seeing who he is.

Letting go would be an easier thing by far if there was a storm, or fog rolling off the moor to hide the space between him and the sharp rocks so that he could not see the end they would bring.

He holds and holds.

The rock cuts his fingers but he cannot let go.

In the end, he takes the spud knife from his pocket and scratches about the veins of his wrists. And though the knife is blunt and the cuts shallow, he bleeds. He thinks of his mum with this very knife, peeling an apple for him the way he does for Owen – or used to. No more.

His fingers are cold. He hears Siân Fisher say, *'Now put that down, Rhys, I'm your mum.'*

The knife slips like Jakey's did off the *Maria*, clinking against the rocks, sparkling as it falls. Rhys gives out a howl like an animal in pain, which is what he is – paws bleeding, trapped in the snare of his own error.

A red and white Coastguard helicopter flies overhead, the winchman's legs swinging, and turns out to sea; they must be training today. Winkle pickers in the pools below look up, not knowing if they are seeing a bird or boy nesting. A pocket trawler motors by, as close to shore as it dares. Its skipper waves. A dog barks.

Unseeing, Rhys thinks of gulls singing winter shanties and kelp-leaf, and now bladderwrack, dead man's fingers, and sea-lettuce growing on nylon creels. Smells that rise when the nets are unknotted; untaken bait, rust, open-scallop brack, black silt clay. Engine smoke too, fumes deep in the bilges' slump, bodies of iced fish, the bloody knife turning all to fillets.

'Fear no more,' he tells himself, at peace now. *Go.*

*

Mrs Hill pulls up in her car at the Fishers' front door. When she sees Dav and Owen coming round the back on their bikes, she gets in a tangle with her seatbelt, which locks itself, thinking her violent tugging is a terrible crash.

'Hi, Mrs Hill,' says Owen. He takes a hand off to wave, clips the bins, lists a bit and rights himself like a catamaran rounding a buoy, now slowing where uprooted traffic signs block the road.

'Mind the glass, mate,' says Dav behind him, worrying their tyres will spring a leak and sink them. 'Go on the pavement!' he says, and Owen does as he is told.

Mrs Hill takes a different way, to cut them off at the church. When Dav and Owen pedal by, she calls out, 'Owen, stop! Talk to me! You said in your homework you were *living* at Long View Farm!' She's crying now. 'You said it was your new home, a bedroom each! I went to your flat... Oh, Jesus... I thought you were dead!'

'I'm not dead, miss,' he says. 'Honest.'

The brothers are on a mission, no time to explain. *She'll have to work it out for herself*, thinks Dav.

The beach is cold and long, the tide in, paint peeling on the prom railings. Dav beats Owen to the cliff road where he waits for the squirt to catch up. He curses his brother's peculiar style: short, wobbly sprints standing up, then sitting down for the glide. Reunited, they ride up the bank to avoid the cars queuing like summer for a parking spot.

A police car comes down the road, lights flashing. Owen skids and stops. Not having the best brakes himself, Dav spins sideways where the road is slippery, oil on water, and does not stop till he reaches the bollard put there to stop cars going over.

Shit me, thinks Dav. *I'm falling.*

Here, Dav and his bike part company. He sits up, groaning, with a split chin, and picks grit from his palms. The cloth at his knees and elbows bloom red. A lady gets out of her car and leans Dav's bike against the Coastguard sign warning of rip tides and danger of death – category Red: no swimming, no surfing. Owen can't wait to tell Rhys this prediction of great waves to come.

Dav tries to get the chain back on the bike.

Come on, he thinks. *Come on!*

He now has blood and black chain grease on his fingers.

'You should get your head checked out,' the lady says. 'Shall I call your mum?'

'No, thanks.'

Owen opens his mouth but Dav shakes his head. 'Don't,' he tells Owen. 'Not now. Just hold up the pulley, will you?'

The brothers work together to fix the chain while more people crowd round Dav as if he is wounded in a deadly sort of way. 'I'm fine,' Dav tells them and proves it, beyond reasonable doubt, by getting on his bike and pedalling uphill like he is in the Tour de France. The idea of Rhys not being there is a kind of sorrow that Dav has not felt before. His legs pump faster as he resolves to find Rhys and catch him in a blanket of words, and if not that, then a blanket of arms.

'Is Rhys in mortal danger?' says Owen, as they near the lighthouse car park.

'I think so.'

'Will he be scared?'

'Probably.'

Owen remembers last Sunday on the *Maria* when they lost a good knife at sea but were saved all the same, no hands lost. 'Is Rhys being a colossal twit again?'

Dav pauses for breath and says, 'When did he ever stop?'

NINETEEN

Rhys hears a voice and opens his eyes. He looks up at the sweaty face of his dad peering over the edge of the cliff. Phil Fisher is lying on his fat belly, arms out as far as arms can go without losing himself.

Rhys hears his dad's voice call down. 'My love, my love, it's me. I got home quick, I did. First on, first off and there's your old dad, right at the front in customs! Reach up, now. Give me your hand. I saw your note. I knew right enough where you'd be going…'

His next words pour out like sand in an hourglass.

'I'm sorry, son, for everything that is hurting you. I wish I could take it away. I haven't forgotten what I promised Mum when you were little – that I would take care of you and keep you safe, even when you have a beard on your face, even when you grow older than I am now,' Phil Fisher tells him. 'She's with me all the time. Whatever I do, it's with her. When I say, "Put your coat on" or, "Brush your teeth" it's with her. When I yell at you for trashing your room, she's by my side, yelling at you too. She's with us now, son. Always will be. We can't do without her and we don't have to either. We've been too much together to ever be apart.' His voice becomes gentle. 'She's proud of her boys. You know that, Rhys. I promised I'd take care of you and that's what I will do. Now, hold my hand, hold it firm, and come back up.'

And when his son does not reach up and take his hand, he says gruffly, 'Do you not think I didn't want to die? After she passed? I felt worthless.'

A moment ticks by.

'Give me a chance, son.' Up on the cliff top, Phil Fisher is praying to a god he does not believe in. 'I can make it better for us.'

Rhys shifts his position, looks up again.

'Son,' says Phil Fisher. 'Hold my hand.'

'I burned down Long View Farm,' says Rhys. 'I have killed my brothers.'

Says Phil Fisher, 'No. No. No. That is not so. Mrs Morris, the BBC, everyone saw them this morning. Come back up. I love you.'

'How can you love me?'

'How can I not love you, son?' says Rhys's dad, his big arm coming down to Rhys, sausage fingers flexing. 'That is the better question. Now, give me your hand.'

Then he, Phil Fisher, father of boys, takes his son by the wrists that are dripping with blood and Rhys feels himself pulled bodily, the all of him, his weights and sorrows, up from out of the darkness as if he weighed no more than a rabbit.

He never knew his dad was so strong.

He hears the sea and his heart and his dad's

breathing, all three pounding in sets.

This is the magic of things: that lost and broken pieces may be found and mended so well, it can come to seem as if they were never broken in the first place.

✳

'Get a wiggle on, will you, mate – for me? If we don't get there soon, it'll be too late.'

Dav pedals fast despite his grazes and one eye not working too well after his crash, and he does not stop on the long slog up the lane.

It is no day for a picnic, yet the car park is full. Police, an ambulance lady and a couple of firemen are having their Greggs breakfast slices after another night of nonsense in Lythcombe. Their radios are still crackling.

Dav and Owen skid in the gravel and throw their bikes against the squat lighthouse wall that stops sheep crapping in the porch in a gale. Next, Dav proceeds to circumnavigate the lighthouse proper, muttering the way he does before leaving for school in the morning, except instead of, 'Where's my blazer? Where's my pen?' he says, 'You freaking door knob, Rhys, where the flip are you?'

Abandoning the bikes, Dav and Owen hike up to the cliff edge – a terrible place, the sea being so far below.

'RHYS!' roars Dav, so loud he sends up gulls in a white snow flurry. 'RHYS, YOU SHITHEAD! YOU TOTAL BLOODY CORNISH WANKER! WE'RE ALIVE!'

Dav and Owen run up the coast path, scattering sheep and rabbits. The next car park along is the one by the Coastguard lookout, where Dav sees Phil Fisher's Iveco jack-knifed in the hedge.

Owen's eyes fill with light and he cries out, 'Daddy!' and soon after, 'Rhys!', for there he is, swaddled in a silver blanket, his head on Phil Fisher's chest, looking younger than Owen and very small. A police officer stands by while a medic is bandaging Rhys's wrists.

Owen wonders if he has a master criminal for a brother, but throws caution to the wind and his arms around Rhys. Tears and snot smear his brother's neck, but Rhys does not say, 'Get off me, prick.'

Dav comes in for the hug and Phil Fisher kisses the tops of all their heads, the police officer and doctor excepting, and says, 'See, son? What did I say? Here's your reason to live.'

'Dav just called you a Cornish wanker,' says Owen.

Rhys does not lift his head. 'I slipped up,' he says.

'Ay, you have,' says Phil Fisher, 'and so have we all.'

'Is Rhys good or bad now?' says Owen.

'He is himself,' says Phil Fisher. 'And we love him.'

'Phenomenal, gents,' says the policeman through gritted teeth, his radio crackling on his chest. 'Rhys Fisher, shall we go? This is an arrest, not a picnic.' And to the gathering onlookers he says, 'Thank you! No video recording, please, let's give the family some space.'

On the way to his car, Owen tells the policeman that today is in no way 'Phenomenal' because the waves are not big enough to knock a ship sideways or throw anyone overboard. No need to harness-up and use the cables. No point battening any hatches.

'It's only a 2 or 3 on the Douglas Scale,' Owen says, once again happy to know more than an adult. 'No one'll get hurt today. We're all safe and sound.'

'Is that right?' says the officer.

Phil Fisher is crying; he has only just got home from Spain and was going to take his boys to Croyde. He was not expecting a tragedy.

'You hold on when the sea gets rough, don't you?' Phil says as Rhys is put in the police car. 'This is no different. Hold on, my love.'

✷

The police interviewer says to each brother in turn, 'I do not want any yarning from you, just "yes" or "no", dates and times, the whole truth and nothing but the truth.' Each time, Phil Fisher, sitting in, smiles.

She asks them all, separately, 'Have you heard talk of a Rupert Cavendish?' and 'What were your movements on Wednesday the first of November at twenty hundred hours?' and, 'Was your brother aware of your whereabouts?' and, 'Are you an agent of or work in any capacity for Knightsbridge Property Management Ltd which allegedly stands to benefit from the fires?'

Fire, it seems, is good for business.

Rhys will not talk in his interviews but Owen has an answer for every question.

'We don't have a Rupert in Lythcombe, unless you're meaning a grockle... Me and Dav played on a zip wire... We slept like writer and artist people do... I remember the bog stank, but the hot tub was tidy-like... That's right, Miss. He does! My brother Rhys always lights the biggest fires. He's the best fire-starter in Lythcombe!'

Owen has some questions for her too, like, 'Mrs Hill says there are twenty-four hours in a day so where did you find *twenty hundred* of them?'

He also tells her Rhys would never hurt him and should not be in prison because he is not a baddie but a goodie in the wrong story. She did not look like she believed him, but no matter.

Trespassing charges were dropped against Dav after the laundry lady from GUEST-READY 24/7 changed her witness statement. Having heard about the Fishers from a hot-tub technician in Salcombe and a lawn-maintenance man from Paignton, she swore blind she'd got her dates mixed up about seeing two boys at Long View Farm.

In court, Rhys's barrister helped set the scene of his life to made him look more human – that is, less like an ill-trained dog shitting on the beach. Unlike the cocky prosecutor, Rhys's barrister used his real name; not 'the defendant' but plain 'young Rhys'.

The job of the jury in a court of law, you see, is to hear the tales of two protagonists – in this case, one Rupert Cavendish, Oxford graduate, and Rhys Fisher, a Lythcombe NEET – and decide which is a tragic fallen hero and which a nasty piece of work.

The jury deliberated, which is much the same as deciding which of the defendants they would sooner have a pint with down the pub.

Dodo was given some stern words. Rhys was given six months.

On his first visit to see Rhys in the Young Offenders, Owen told him he would fly him a pet seagull with the keys. And if that did not work, he would send an armour-plated lobster to snip through the bars. Then he would set a board on the back of a remote-controlled wave so he could surf his way home. Rhys will know who it was from.

These things never came, but Rhys never stopped looking out for gulls in the exercise yard.

On his visits to see Rhys, Phil Fisher writes down search engine keywords for Kawasaki parts, jigsaws, nail guns and screws to his son's dictation, noting the quantity of pallets required to build a new palace and hutches.

Phil is especially noisy when Dav gets his place on the university mentoring scheme.

'Your brother's a bloody genius,' says their dad, reading the letter to Rhys that explains how, though Dav bunked off the test to find Rhys, he had proved himself enough. 'When you get home, my boy, we will have a Chinese. We will throw a bloody party in the street.'

And that's not all: 'When you get home,' says Phil Fisher, 'we will build a palace fit for princes. We will saw and cut and bang and nail it together in the yard till it is done.'

'What about the move to Exeter?'

'They can't move me. I'm Lythcombe. That's all I am.'

In his cell, with the other boys there for being poor, Rhys likes to think about Thing purring like a road drill on the top of that new palace, a little hop from Mrs Morris's balcony, and her dropping cigarette ash down like the first flakes of snow on the moor, except grey.

Prison is not so bad as he imagined. None of his cellmates are surfers but some have fished on the canal in freer days. Trout, mainly. But they're nice enough boys. They call him 'Match', on account of his red hair, and have few yarns to tell about the fires they've lit in their time.

Rhys gets on with Abdi the best, who laughs when Rhys tells him about the carpet crab. Abdi's granddaddy had been a fisherman in the Gulf of Oman, and his nan had looked after their family's thirteen sheep, till war put a stop to that. Coming from Camden, Abdi has never dipped his toes in the ocean, but the boys have other things in common – both dream of proper cooked fish, not the breaded cardboard they serve in prison, and they miss their lost mums something rotten.

Abdi knows Plymouth and Exeter from his trips

down to the West Country from London. At sixteen, he is an expert on the national rail network; he has been taking trains since he was eleven years old. From Glasgow to St Ives, there is not a city or town he has not visited while working county lines – such is the demand of smackheads, thrill-seekers, sufferers of pain, the hopeless and the disheartened everywhere.

Rhys tells Abdi to look him up when he gets out. 'Take the number 7 bus from Exeter,' he says, 'and don't get off till you see the sea. That'll be me in the water, roundhousing a glassy break. Mate, I will teach you to surf, if you like, and we'll cook mackerel sarnies on the beach.'

In May, when his case is reviewed, a judge decides Rhys is not a menace to society. Phil Fisher had said as much to the officer on the cliff, who could have saved the Crown Court a lot of bother if he'd passed on the message. Rhys is given a release date, which is not the same as being let off because he will have to do unpaid work they call 'community payback'.

'Dad, when Rhys gets home, will Angie still do our tea and have sleepovers when you're in Spain?' Owen asks on their last visit to Rhys, because that will be the end of Angie's haddock pies.

'No, son,' says Phil, turning pink at the sound of her name. 'Rhys will be back.'

'You can stop here a bit longer, then,' says Owen, dead serious-like. Then he laughs and hugs his brother till a prison officer comes over and tells him to stop. 'Only joking, Rhys. I want you home.'

'Proper job,' says Phil Fisher, still looking dreamy. 'But we like Angie, don't we, boys? Would it be okay if she comes around, like, for dinner?'

'I know what kind of sleepover you're after,' says Rhys into his hands.

'Enough of that. Angie is a special lady. She's missed you, Rhys. No, stop laughing. Everyone's been asking, "When's the big fellow home?" and I now can tell them—'

'Tomorrow!' says Owen. 'Fair to Moderate westerly, three-foot swell – Jakey's giving you his board, says it's yours to keep.'

Dav punches Owen's arm to shush him.

'That's right,' says Phil. 'Tomorrow. And we'll be ready for you.'

*

Young offender institutions are said to teach viciousness and criminality, but Rhys can't have been paying attention because when the doors open, he comes out as soft as he went in, a bracelet on his ankle, not knowing what to say, not even hello. Phil Fisher runs to him, then wraps his boys up in his arms like birthday presents, and says all the words that need saying.

'Come here, my darling sons, my waterboys,' Phil says, kissing their heads. 'You're safe now and that's us. It was reckless of me to ever leave you. We shall make

Mum proud. We shall go fishing. We shall fly kites. We shall keep rabbits. We shall go camping. We shall grow flowers in pots. We shall go surfing and swimming. We shall live wild and eat like kings. Tell me, who is like us?'

*

Rhys's first day of freedom is a sunny day. Owen and Dav ride up front in the Iveco to the lighthouse car park and Rhys follows on his Kawasaki, radiator mostly fixed, only smoking on the steepest bits.

'Locals Only Day today, boys,' says Phil Fisher, after parking his lorry cab over the remaining six spaces.

He might drive for a living, but the lane is single-carriageway – no passing places and not a lot of room to turn at the top if you are not in an average size of car – so Rhys says, 'What the hell, Dad? How're you going to back it out of there?'

'I'm not,' says Phil Fisher. 'They can come and get it. I quit. As of now.'

They walk up to the windy top where he brings out three kites. Owen picks first but they are all the same.

'Glory, glory, there's the sea,' says Phil Fisher by the Trig Point, a clear view of everything. 'Can you hear it, boys? Here's the place!'

The tide is out. Anglers look like beetles on the rocks. Seals bob about in the waves like kiddies' lost balls. Kittiwakes and terns come and go from their stations on the cliff. The Fishers watch them shit a streak of fishy white and see it fall, dizzy-down.

Fingers crossed it hits some poor sod below.

'Strike!'

They find a spot to fly the kites and chuck tangerine peel off the edge till Phil Fisher says for them to take it home, it being the wrong colour for the coast. While his boys are flying, he slides his nail under the metal ring of his photo keyring, to take it off his cab keys, and kisses Siân Fisher's sweet face and puts her safe in his pocket. Then, when he thinks no one is watching, he sucks in his belly, clenches his jaw and chucks the lot – ignition, fuel cap, unit doors and toolbox keys – out over the cliff. He would have made a good cricketer; you could not hear them fall.

Who knows where they landed? What will the winkles think? And how will the Fishers get back, three miles from Lythcombe with one Kawasaki and one helmet between four?

Granted, it would be a long walk home so Rhys runs down the gorse path to the cove and finds the keys, shining like fairy gold in a rock pool.

Coming back, Rhys throws Phil Fisher the bunch because a good son knows when his dad's romantic gestures will be later regretted. 'Don't be a muppet,' Rhys tells him. 'We're going to need your job. When we're ready to go, wind down the window and I'll direct you out.'

The kites are moving nicely. Phil Fisher lies in the sun like a fat starfish on a bed of sea pinks, the photo keyring now back in his sausage fingers. 'Can you hear the sea?' he says at last. 'We have something rich about us, boys, that will repair all sadness.'

The kites fly with the birds and the boys with them, and now and then Phil Fisher opens his eyes a crack to see his sons and say, 'How very good it is to live and be alive, eh, boys? To live and be alive!'

And just when Rhys thinks his old dad is snoring, Phil Fisher gets to his feet and tackles his eldest son by the ankles and pins him down while Owen and Dav get in quick with the tickles.

That's when Rhys gives in. He has no choice but to laugh. And then, it seems, he has no choice but to cry; Owen holds his kite while their dad holds Rhys, then Dav joins in too, their arms a net and Rhys a fish, so Owen has to man all three kites that tangle but keep on flying all the same.

Because Rhys is a kite that the Fishers will not let go of, the fish they will land, the sailboat they will bring round, a tent pegged to the ground by all four corners, guy-lines driven deep against the storm.

He's the pride of Lythcombe, champion surfer, duck-diving the worst of the break and through to the calm beyond.

And the next wave.

And the one after that.

And all the waves to come.

Where to get help

FOR DRUGS A GP is a good place to start. They can discuss your problems with you and may offer you treatment at the practice or refer you to your local drug service. If you're not comfortable talking to a GP, you can approach your local drug treatment service yourself. If you're having trouble finding the right sort of help, you can call the **Frank drugs helpline** on **0300 123 6600** or text them at **82111**. They can talk you through all your options. **www.talktofrank.com**

FOR SUICIDAL FEELINGS If you're feeling like you want to end your life, it's important to tell someone. Help and support is available right now if you need it. You do not have to struggle with difficult feelings alone. These free helplines are there to help when you're feeling down or desperate. You can also call these helplines for advice if you're worried about someone else:

- **Samaritans**: Call **116 123** or email jo@samaritans.org (it may take several days to get a response by email)
- **Papyrus Prevention of Young Suicides**: Text **88247**, call **0800 068 4141** or email: pat@papyrus-uk.org
- **Childline** (for children and young people under 19): Call **0800 1111** (the number will not show up on your phone bill)

WITH BEREAVEMENT AND GRIEF You can find someone to speak to at the following organisations:

- **Barnardos**: Call **02890 668 333** or email cbsreferrals@barnardos.org.uk
- **Grief Encounter**: Call **0808 802 0111** or visit www.griefencounter.org.uk
- **Cruse Bereavement Support**: Call **0808 808 1677** or visit www.hopeagain.org.uk

For schools and book groups

EMPATHY

1. The narrator describes Rhys as *'half-hero, half-villain, half-good, half-bad, half-this, half-that and half-of-the-other'*. How does Rhys show he is these things in the story?
2. What do you think of Phil? Is he a good parent, or irresponsible?
3. *On the Edge* explores grief. How have each of the Fisher brothers dealt with the loss of their mother?
4. Think about the title *On the Edge*. How many literal and metaphoric *'edges'* can you think of in the story?
5. Which stereotypes of working-class boys and men are challenged in the novel?
6. When Jakey bullies Dav, Mitch says, *'Cut it out, son... I'll have none of them phobias on my boat.'* In what ways is homophobia challenged in the novel?
7. What do you think of Rhys and Jakey's behaviour on the dating app and when talking about girls. Is it serious or a bit of fun? Why do some people behave differently online? What does Rhys learn when he meets Caroline?

SOCIAL ISSUES

1. What do you think of Lythcombe? Would you like to live there? What are the positive and negative things about living in a beautiful place where tourists go?
2. The UK government's 2024 report into coastal poverty found double the national average rate of drug use in coastal

communities, higher rates of hospitalisation for drugs and alcohol, and a higher death rate for drug poisoning. Rhys and his friends take dangerous illegal drugs in the novel. Why do you think they take these risks?

3. What is the effect of second-home ownership on communities in tourist areas like Lythcombe?

4. In court, *'Dodo was given some stern words. Rhys was given six months.'* Why do you think they were treated differently?

EXPLORING THE NOVEL FURTHER

1. Who do you think the narrator of On the Edge could be?
2. In what ways is the narrator unreliable?
3. Early drafts of the novel were written as poetry. How many poetic techniques (such as alliteration, personification and simile) can you find in the prose?
4. Rhys admires Dodo's mastery of language, but in what ways are Rhys and Phil the real poets?
5. The working title of **On the Edge** was **Reckless**. How many types of recklessness can you identify in the novel?

SHAKESPEARE TREASURE HUNT

There are fifteen quotations from Shakespeare's plays hidden through On the Edge in dialogue and description, and many more half-quotations. How many can you spot?

Find the solution at **www.nicola-garrard.com**

Resistance Movements in On the Edge

Read on for more about the Welsh and West Country rebels and resistance movements mentioned in *On the Edge*:

Owain Glyndŵr (1400–1409)

Owain Glyndŵr led the Welsh Revolt against King Henry IV of England. He retook large areas of Wales, but, with a small army and no warships, he was defeated by the English in 1409. Despite huge financial rewards offered by the English, Glyndŵr was never given up by the Welsh people.

Michael An Gof and the Cornish Rebellion of 1497

Michael 'the blacksmith' was a Cornish rebel from St Keverne who lived at the end of the 15th century. He marched on London to present a petition to Henry VII against new war taxes to pay for the English to invade Scotland. By the time Michael An Gof reached Devon, over 15,000 people had joined the march. They got as far as Greenwich, London before being brutally suppressed. Michael An Gof was captured, and on the way to his execution it is claimed he said his name would be 'perpetual' and his fame 'permanent and immortal'.

Meibion Glyndŵr (1979-1993)

Meibion Glyndŵr (Sons of Glyndŵr) wanted to stop rich English people buying second homes in Wales because this was driving up house prices and causing schools, shops and pubs to close. When areas have a lot of holiday homes, small village schools are forced to close because there are not enough pupils to warrant the employment of teachers and maintenance of buildings, and businesses fail when there are insufficient customers living locally. Meibion Glyndŵr burned over two hundred Welsh cottages and attacked government offices and estate agents. Like their namesake, Owain Glyndŵr, not a single member of Meibion Glyndŵr was betrayed by the Welsh people, despite a £50,000 reward (more than enough to buy a farm in 1980) and appeals on television. Only one man was found in possession of materials linked to arson and was sentenced to twelve years in prison.

Acknowledgements

I owe enormous thanks to the following wonderful people: my literary agent, Abi Fellows; publisher, Ruth Huddleston; editor, Emma Roberts; cover designer, Michelle Brackenborough; publicist, Nicky Potter; and everyone at Bounce Sales and Marketing.

I am extremely grateful to Theresa Gooda, Juliet West, and editors, Arzu Tahsin and Joan Deitch for their help with early drafts.

My thanks to John Sharp and his South Dartmoor Community School's Ten Tors team for their list of Devonian swear words and insults. I promise never to call you Cornish.

I want to thank my family and friends: my mum and dad, Sue and Dave, for giving me a perfect Devon childhood, full of waves and wild places; my brother, Simon, for your expertise as a surfer of huge waves and driver of huge lorries; Dick and Jane for the bluebells (as always); my beautiful children, Elsie, Ben and Sophie (thanks for playing the ukulele whilst I was editing); Nadia, for your friendship and being a team; Sadia, my social justice inspiration, for putting young people first; Georgie, for our therapy runs and understanding grief; Jane and Paul for your love and encouragement; and Little Bear, for reminding me to get some fresh air.

The biggest thanks of all goes to my wife, Miriam; without you, I couldn't write a word.

Nicola Garrard's debut YA novel, *29 Locks* (HopeRoad), was shortlisted for the Lucy Cavendish Fiction Prize, the *Mslexia* Children's Novel Competition and longlisted for the Berkshire Book Award and the Branford Boase Award. It was picked by the *Financial Times* as one of their 'Best Books of 2021'. Her second YA novel, *21 Miles* (HopeRoad) was described as 'One of the very best pieces of fiction to come out of the refugee crisis' by Anthony McGowan, Carnegie Medal-winning author. Her poetry is published in the *Frogmore Papers* magazine, IRON Press Publishing, Mslexia magazine and the Poetry Book Society.

Nicola grew up in South Devon in the 1970s and 1980s. Her family grew their own fruit and vegetables, and kept rabbits and poultry for meat and eggs. Her mum worked in a nursing home, at Torbay hospital and in a fish processing factory. Her dad spearfished bass and dived for spider crabs, which he cooked for his family on the beach. They ate like kings.

For more books and updates:
www.nicola-garrard.co.uk

On social media:
- x.com **nmgarrard**
- instagram.com **nicolagarrard7**